I0748736

WHAT THE TIDE TOOK

BLAKE GUNNELS

Cover design and interior layout by the author.

Printed in the United States of America.

First edition.

ISBN: 979-8-9989578-6-4

For those raised where water remembers everything,
where the river runs dark and patient,
keeping what it's given.

For the ones who learned early that silence can be an inheritance,
that some truths are carried like stones in a pocket.

For those who have stood at the edge of a dock at night,
listening to lines creak and hulls knock softly,
knowing what never came back.

For the ones who know the weight of low tide,
the smell of pluff mud and rain,
the way storms arrive without asking permission.

For every soul shaped by salt and consequence,
by names spoken carefully,
and stories altered to survive.

For those who stay, who keep watch,
who live with what the water took.

This is for you.

For Tammy, who believes in me,
and in the future we're building together.

For my mother, who is always there when I call.

For Mary Grace and Jack,
my reasons for everything,
and the pride I feel watching you build lives of your own.

This is for you.

PROLOGUE

Fifteen Years Before Present Day

The river ran black under a quarter moon.

He stood on the dock at Delacroix, watching the water move. The Cape Fear River was running fast tonight, swollen with three days of rain, carrying branches and debris down toward the ocean. Out there, five miles downriver, maybe six, a boat was sinking. Three people were dying, or already dead.

He checked his watch. Eleven forty-two.

The phone would ring soon.

Behind him, the lodge was dark except for a single lamp in the study. He'd sent the staff home hours ago. Privacy, he'd said. Important business. They knew not to ask questions.

The dock creaked under his weight as he walked to the end. Cypress planks, original to the property, replaced only where rot made it necessary. He'd bought Delacroix in 1987, back when the lodge was falling apart and the land was worth more than the buildings. Twenty-three years now. He knew where to step and where not to. He knew the sound the river made against the pilings when a storm was coming, and this was that sound—low, insistent, the water talking to itself.

A mullet jumped in the darkness, the splash loud in the quiet. The air smelled of rain coming, heavy and electric, another front pushing in from the Gulf.

He lit a cigarette. The flame from his lighter threw orange light across his hands—old hands now, spotted and veined. Seventy-two years old. He'd built something in those years. An organization that ran through this county and half the coast. It had taken patience. Discipline. A willingness to do what others would not. And a talent for recognizing when a situation had changed, when the plan you'd made was no longer the plan you needed.

Tonight, it had taken three lives.

The cigarette smoke mixed with the smells of the river: brackish, heavy, carrying the faint petroleum tang of boat fuel from upstream. He exhaled and watched the smoke disappear into the dark.

The *Miss Carolina* was insured for twice her value. The captain had been paid. The crew knew to be ashore when the time came. A fire in the engine compartment, a distress call placed too late, and by morning there would be nothing left but an insurance claim and a few headlines about a tragic accident.

But operations went wrong. You planned for contingencies and you accepted that some nights the river took more than you offered.

The phone in his pocket vibrated.

He let it ring twice before answering.

"Sir." The voice was Hatch—former Navy, current problem-solver, the kind of man who called him sir without irony. "We have a situation."

"Tell me."

"The fire spread faster than projected. Banks got the distress call out, but the engine compartment blew before the crew could reach the tender." A pause. "Three of them didn't make it. Pruitt, the Galloway woman, and Rodriguez."

"I was told the crew would be clear."

"They were supposed to be. Someone changed the schedule without telling them. I'm still working out who."

He drew on the cigarette. The ember flared bright, then faded.

"And the survivors?"

"Three. Banks, Petersen, and Marks. Coast Guard picked them up twenty minutes ago. They're being taken to Dosher for observation."

"Banks." The name sat heavy in his mouth. "How much does he know?"

"He knows he was paid to scuttle his own boat. He knows three people died because the plan went wrong. He knows enough to bring us all down if he talks."

The dock swayed slightly as a wave from a passing boat reached the pilings. The old man watched the water settle back to black.

"Where are Petersen and Marks?"

"Same place. Dosher. Petersen's in shock, won't stop shaking. Marks is talking about moving to Jacksonville, getting out of town before anyone asks questions."

"They'll need to be managed. All three of them."

"Understood. But Banks is the problem. He's the captain. He's the one who'll face the investigators. And he's not the kind of man who lies well."

The old man flicked the cigarette into the river. The ember hissed and went dark.

Russell Banks was a good man. That was the problem. The kind who would crack under questioning, who would tell investigators everything because his conscience wouldn't let him stay quiet. He would not understand why lying might be necessary. He would not understand that the truth would destroy his family faster than any lie.

"I need options."

"He can be managed. He's got debts: the boat, the mortgage, a wife and daughters to protect. We can make those debts go away, or we can make them worse. Either way, he'll understand the cost of talking."

"And if he doesn't?"

Silence on the line. Then: "Understood. But the call is yours, sir."

The old man stood at the end of the dock, looking out at the water. The quarter moon had risen higher now, casting a pale light across the current.

And now Russell Banks was in a hospital bed, a man with a family of his own, carrying a secret that could bring everything down.

"Whatever's required. Banks keeps quiet. Petersen and Marks keep quiet. The investigation finds nothing but a tragic accident. The insurance pays out. By this time next month, the *Miss Carolina* is a footnote."

"And if they won't stay quiet?"

The old man looked at the water.

"Then Russell Banks will learn what happens to people who can't keep their mouths shut." He paused. "Same as anyone else."

He ended the call.

The dock was quiet. Somewhere downriver, wreckage was washing ashore—charred wood, melted fiberglass, whatever was left of a boat and three people who'd been alive six hours ago. The tide would scatter it. By morning, beachcombers would find pieces and wonder what they'd come from.

He walked back toward the lodge. The lamp in the study window threw a yellow square of light onto the grass. Inside, there was whiskey and paperwork and the slow business of making tonight disappear.

He paused at the door. Looked back at the river one more time.

Three dead. Three survivors who knew the truth.

Then he went inside.

Ten Days Before Present Day

The lunch crowd at Fishy Fishy had the line out the door and halfway down the side of the building by the time Nora found a spot on Moore Street. She could smell the kitchen from half a block away—fryer oil and Old Bay and the hot vinegar bite of coleslaw. A family from somewhere inland stood blocking the entrance, the father studying the specials board like it might solve something, two kids yanking at his shorts while the mother fanned herself with a takeout menu. The noon sun sat on everything. Nora could feel it through her shirt, through the soles of her sandals on the concrete. A dog was panting in the shade beneath a raised planter outside the restaurant. Smart dog.

She almost didn't see Mary.

Her cousin was standing in the dirt gap between Fishy Fishy and Potter's Seafood Market, half in the shade where the building blocked the noon sun. Three cars could fit in that gap, and past them Nora could see the dock pilings and the water. Mary wasn't waiting in line. Wasn't looking at the specials board. Just standing there with her purse strap crossed over her chest and her eyes on the street, watching, making sure she wasn't followed.

"Nora." Mary's voice was low. She stepped forward and took Nora's arm above the elbow. Her grip was harder than it needed to be. "Walk with me."

"I was going to grab shrimp and grits—"

"Walk with me."

Mary pulled her deeper into the gap, away from the lunch crowd, the dirt loose under their sandals. She'd lost weight. Nora noticed it in her collarbones. Her sundress hung loose at the shoulders. But her eyes were sharp. Alert. Whatever was happening to her body, her mind was running ahead of it.

Mary stopped where the dock pilings were visible past the parked cars. She reached into her purse and pulled out a key. Small. Brass. The kind that opened a padlock, not a door.

She pressed it into Nora's palm. Her fingers were cold—startlingly cold for August, for a noon that had already hit ninety and wasn't finished climbing. Nora closed her hand around the key and around Mary's fingers both, holding on.

"Unit 47," Mary said. "Fish Factory Road. The climate-controlled building in back."

"Mary, what is this?"

"If I'm not back in a week, you know what to do."

"I don't know what to do. That's what I'm asking you."

Mary's mouth opened, the beginning of an answer, maybe, or a warning—and then she shut it down. Swallowed it. Her lips pressed together and she looked away, down Moore Street, like she was calculating distance.

She pulled her hand free. She looked past Nora toward the waterfront, where the shrimp boats were tied up at the fish house dock and the gulls were working the pilings. Her eyes had become moist. She blinked twice, fast, like she was trying to clear them before Nora noticed.

"You'll know," Mary said. "When you see what's in there. You'll know."

"At least tell me where you're going."

Mary shook her head once. Then she squeezed Nora's arm—quick, hard, a touch that meant *behave* and *I love you* in the same gesture—and walked away up Moore Street. Her sandals on the concrete. The sundress catching the breeze off the water. She didn't look back.

Nora stood in the dirt gap with the key cutting into her fist. The brass was already warming from her grip, but she could still feel where Mary's cold fingers had been. A truck rumbled past on Yacht Basin Drive. The lunch noise from Fishy Fishy carried over, forks and laughter and a cook calling an order through the window.

She opened her hand and looked at the key. Small. Brass. Ordinary. It told her nothing.

She put it in her pocket and walked back toward her truck, and she did not get lunch.

CHAPTER 1

The Boat

Present Day

The Cape Fear was black glass and Nora Banks was running out of time.

She cut the throttle on the Boston Whaler and let the ebb take her, drifting toward the channel marker at the mouth of Dutchman Creek. Red flasher. Four-second interval. She'd been counting without meaning to. Behind her, past the dark hump of Battery Island where the brown pelicans roosted, the lights of Southport bled orange against low clouds. The old pilot tower on the waterfront. The sodium glow from Provision Company, where the dockworkers would be drinking until last call. Home. If she could still call it that after tonight.

The tide was wrong. She'd planned for slack water, that forty-minute window when the river rested between flood and ebb, but the northeast wind had pushed everything off schedule. The Cape Fear ran faster than the charts promised when the wind backed the current, and now the chop was building where the river met the Intracoastal, slapping the hull hard enough to throw spray across the gunwale. Salt on her lips. Salt in her eyes. She wiped her face with the back of her hand and tasted it—that mineral bite that had been part of her since before she could remember.

She checked her watch. 11:47. The harbormaster running her own water at nearly midnight, navigation lights off, and if anyone from Station Oak Island happened to be watching their Furuno, she'd have some explaining to do. The station was three miles south, past the rock jetty at the river mouth, and the petty officer on duty tonight was Kenny Burroughs. Kenny had taken the overnight rotation because it let him sleep through his shift. Nora had made it her business to know the duty roster. She made it her business to know most things in this town.

A mullet broke the surface twenty feet off the port quarter, running ahead of the storm. Silver flash, then gone. The river was thick with them this time of year, August schools stacked so dense the commercial guys could fill a net in a single set. Nora had grown up on these waters. She'd learned to swim off the municipal pier at Waterfront Park—barnacle pilings, water that tasted like diesel and shrimp boats—before most kids her age had finished swim lessons. Could handle a Carolina skiff before she could see over the steering console. Read a tide chart before she could read chapter books. The Cape Fear was in her blood, as it was in the blood of everyone whose people had worked this coast—watermen and pilots, shrimpers and oystermen, going back to before the war that had nothing to do with them and everything to do with the cargo that moved through this harbor.

The Whaler rocked in its own wake and she steadied herself against the center console, one hand on the throttle, the other gripping the rail where the gel coat had gone chalky from years of sun and salt. Her father's boat. The *Sarah*. He'd bought it off a dentist from Raleigh in '98—sixteen-foot Montauk, Merc 90 on the transom, the hull still solid despite the cosmetic neglect. Russell Banks had used it for dawn patrols when the Spanish mackerel were running off Bald Head, for sunset fishing when he needed to think, for the occasional midnight run when the shrimp were mating at the river mouth and you could fill a cooler with a cast net if you knew where to look.

Now it was hers. One of the few things he'd left her that wasn't complicated.

The package was under the center console, wedged behind the fire extinguisher where she'd shoved it three days ago. Black plastic and duct tape, about the size of a boot box. She hadn't opened it. Didn't want to know exactly what Mary had been collecting all these months—what documents, what photographs, what kind of proof got people killed in towns like this one. She could guess. That was bad enough.

She'd found it in the storage unit on Fish Factory Road, the one Mary had rented under a name that wasn't hers. Unit 47, climate-controlled, tucked at the back of the facility where the security camera had a blind spot. Nora had stood in the doorway for a long time, looking at Mary's things. The careful organization. The labeled boxes: GRANDMOTHER, BOAT RECORDS, NEWSPAPER CLIPS. The small shrine she'd built to a woman she'd never known: Iris Galloway's work gloves, cracked and stiff with age. A faded photograph of Iris on the deck of a shrimp trawler, squinting into the sun, her dark hair pulled back the same way Mary wore hers. A newspaper clipping from the Southport Times, May 2010: THREE DEAD IN FISHING BOAT TRAGEDY.

The unit had smelled like mothballs and mildew, that funk of spaces left closed too long.

She'd grabbed the package and left. Locked the door behind her. She hadn't opened it—didn't want to, couldn't let herself—because she'd understood in the doorway, looking at Iris Galloway's work gloves and the newspaper clipping and the careful boxes, exactly what Mary had been building. And if she knew the specifics, she couldn't unknow them. She told herself she'd figure out what to do with it later.

Later was now.

The current pushed the Whaler sideways and Nora corrected, muscle memory doing the work while her mind spun elsewhere. Twelve years as harbormaster, she knew every sandbar in this stretch of river, every oyster rack where the bottom shoaled up to grab a propeller. She'd pulled enough drunk fishermen off the flats at Striking Island to map the whole channel in her sleep. Knew where the loggerheads fed in the seagrass beds. Knew where the dolphins ran mullet against the marsh banks, working them into the shallows where tourists paid money to watch from the deck of the *Adventure*.

* * *

The spot was a hundred yards off the old fish house, where Dutchman Creek bent hard to the east and the bottom dropped away into a dredge hole that hadn't been touched since Nixon. Thirty-two feet at mean low water, according to the charts, though Nora had sounded it herself last spring and gotten thirty-four. Soft silt bottom. Strong tidal flush. Anything that went down there would stay down until someone came looking with side-scan, and nobody was going to do that. Not for a package that didn't officially exist.

The fish house had been shuttered for fifteen years, same year as the sinking, now that she thought about it. Jansen Brothers Seafood, three generations of buying catch and shipping it north, killed by a combination of declining stocks and a contamination lawsuit that had dragged on for a decade. The county had tried to redevelop the property twice, but the environmental studies kept coming back wrong. Mercury in the soil from the old processing chemicals. Arsenic in the groundwater from God knew what. The oyster shells they'd used for fill had leached something that made the test wells glow.

Now it was a hulk of rusted corrugated steel, the loading dock rotted through in places, the windows dark or broken. During the day, you could see it against the tree line—loblolly pines and a few scrub oaks that had taken root in the shell pile. At night, you couldn't see it at all, which was part of why Nora had chosen this spot.

She killed the engine and let the boat coast. The slap of water against the hull was loud in the sudden quiet. A tug was pushing a barge up toward Wilmington, running lights red and green against the dark. She watched it pass the tip of Battery Island, where the old quarantine station had been, where yellow fever victims had died in the summers before anyone understood mosquitoes.

To the south, past the river mouth, the Oak Island light was working. Four white flashes, then darkness, then four again—the same count she'd memorized when she was young enough to think the light was something alive, something keeping watch over the water. Her father had navigated by it before GPS made landmarks optional. She still did, by habit, by something older than habit. She could feel the Atlantic beyond the jetties in a pressure change, a different quality to the wind. The river carrying everything it was given toward the sea, and the lighthouse standing at the mouth counting the seconds, and her sitting out here in the dark with a dead woman's evidence in her lap trying to decide whether to bury it or use it.

She pulled the package from under the console and held it in her lap. Maybe two pounds. Maybe less. Mary's whole case against this town, reduced to something Nora could throw overboard with one arm.

She'd seen a therapist in Wilmington for six months after her father died. Drove nearly an hour each way on 17, past the Harris Teeter and the boat dealers and the billboard for the aquarium, so nobody in Southport would see her car in a parking lot that might require explanation. The therapist had wanted to talk about feelings. About grief. About the night fourteen-year-old Nora had woken to her mother sobbing in the kitchen, her father's voice low and wrecked, saying words Nora had spent fifteen years trying to unhear.

I didn't have a choice. They said they'd hurt you. They said they'd hurt the girls.

Nora had stopped seeing the therapist after six sessions. Talking didn't fix anything.

Throw it. Right now. End this.

Her arm wouldn't move. She stood there in the rocking boat, package in hand, arm cocked back, and nothing happened. The wind pushed spray across the gunwale. The channel marker flashed red. The current pulled her east. And still she stood there, frozen, while some part of her brain screamed at the rest to let go.

A brown pelican glided past, low over the water, so close she could hear the whisper of its wings. It banked toward Battery Island and was gone.

She lowered her arm.

She thought about what was in the package. The weight of it. Fifteen years of silence, wrapped in black plastic. Her father's confession. Her mother's complicity. Her own, for keeping quiet this long.

If she threw it, the secret stayed buried. Mary's work disappeared. The men who'd forced her father into that corner, whoever they were, whatever they'd threatened, would never face what they'd done.

If she kept it, everything could come apart.

Her fingers wouldn't open.

She thought about Mary, about how she'd looked that day outside Fishy Fishy, the lunch crowd spilling out onto the sidewalk, the smell of fryer oil and Old Bay thick in the August humidity. Mary had pressed the storage unit key into Nora's palm. Her fingers had been cold—Nora remembered that. Cold and damp despite the heat.

"If I'm not back in a week," Mary had said, "you know what to do."

Nora hadn't known. Had asked and gotten nothing. Had stood there with the key in her fist while Mary walked away, cutting through the crowd on Yacht Basin Dr., disappearing around the corner onto Moore. Heading toward the bus station, maybe. Or the ferry terminal. Or some other place Nora couldn't follow.

Mary hadn't said to wait. Hadn't said anything about contact. But Nora told herself it was safer that way. No calls, no texts, no trail. Mary would make contact when she was ready.

Nine days now. No contact. No trail.

Throw it.

The current pulled her east toward the shipping channel. A container ship was making the turn at Bald Head, running lights stacked high, probably headed for Wilmington with Chinese goods or German cars or whatever else moved through this port these days. Nora watched it slide past the island. All that tonnage, all that momentum, and here she was in a sixteen-foot boat with a package she couldn't bring herself to dump.

The wind was building out of the northeast, bringing the ozone smell of rain from past Frying Pan Shoals. Storm coming. The weather service had been tracking it for three days—tropical depression, maybe a named storm by morning. The shrimp fleet had come in early, the trawlers rafted up three-deep at the commercial dock. The marina was locked down tight.

Good cover for a midnight run.

* * *

She'd told Mary not to come back.

Eight months ago, when Mary Galloway walked into the harbormaster's office with her mother's maiden name and her grandmother's eyes, Nora had known exactly who she was. The shape of the jaw, squared off at the corners, standing with her weight on her heels, ready to move. Galloway women all stood like that. Nora's own mother had stood like that, back before she'd married Russell Banks and taken his name and his silence. Sarah Galloway Banks, Iris's niece, which made Mary and Nora second cousins. The last of the Galloway line.

The office had been chaotic that afternoon. July, the harbor stuffed with transients, a dispute between two charter captains over the finger pier assignments, three messages from the mayor's office about parking for the Fourth of July parade. Nora had been buried in slip contracts and fuel receipts when the screen door banged open and a young woman walked in. Dark hair pulled back in a ponytail. Jeans and a flannel shirt with the sleeves rolled up despite the heat. Work boots that had actually seen work.

"I'm looking for a job," Mary had said. "Heard Jansen's fish house might be hiring."

Nora had looked up from her desk.

"What's your name?"

"Mary Galloway."

The name sat in the air between them. Galloway. A common enough name on this coast, old Brunswick County stock, but Nora knew exactly which Galloway this was. Could see it in the shape of her face, the stubborn set of her mouth, the eyes that were brown shot through with gold, the same gold that had caught the light in every photograph of Iris Galloway that Nora had ever seen.

"You from around here?"

"My grandmother was. Long time ago."

Nora had made herself breathe. Made herself look down at the paperwork on her desk, then back up at this woman who should not be standing in this office, not when her grandmother was forty feet down in the cold Atlantic with a boat hull for a coffin.

"Jansen's closed down," Nora said. "Fifteen years ago."

"I know. Thought maybe someone else was running it now."

"Nobody's running it. Place is condemned."

"Then maybe you know somewhere else that's hiring. I'm not picky. I can work a deck, clean fish, run a register. Whatever."

Nora should have sent her away. Should have said there's nothing for you here, this town will eat you alive, your grandmother is dead and so is the man who killed her. Should have done anything except what she did, which was write down an address on a Post-it note and slide it across the counter.

"Provision Company, down on Yacht Basin Drive. They need counter help. Tell them I sent you."

Mary had taken the note. Read it. Looked back up at Nora with those gold-flecked eyes.

"Thank you," she'd said. "Ms. Banks."

She'd known. Even then, she'd known who Nora was.

Nora had watched her walk down Yacht Basin Dr. toward the water. Watched her stop at the corner by the ship's chandlery and look back at the harbormaster's office. Watched her turn and keep walking, disappearing into the crowd of tourists and fishermen that clogged the waterfront on summer afternoons.

That had been eight months ago. Since then, Mary had become a fixture—at the office, on the docks, twice at Nora's kitchen table. They never talked about Iris directly. Never talked about the *Miss Carolina* or the night it went down. But they circled it, every conversation, the way you circle something you can't look at straight. Until Fishy Fishy.

Two weeks before that, a man Nora didn't recognize had been parked on Howe Street for three days running, watching the harbormaster's office. Not a tourist. Not a fisherman. Just a man in a rental car with a clear line of sight to her door.

She'd called Mary that night.

"You need to stop coming around," she'd said. "Whatever you're building, you're being watched. And if they're watching you, they're watching me."

"I'm close," Mary had said. "Two more weeks."

"I don't care. Stay away."

Mary had gone quiet on the line. Then: "Okay."

She hadn't argued. Hadn't pushed back. Just okay, and then nothing for ten days.

And then Fishy Fishy.

Cousin. The last blood she had on her mother's side.

* * *

The package was still in her lap.

Nora looked down at it—black plastic, duct tape—and thought about her father.

Russell Banks, who'd run the *Miss Carolina* for twenty-three years, who'd fished every inch of water from Cape Fear to Cape Lookout, who'd survived three hurricanes and a nor'easter that sank boats on either side of him, and who'd finally gone down on a clear May night with six souls aboard, three of whom never came home.

One of them was Iris Galloway. Mary's grandmother. Forty-one years old, a deckhand because nobody else would hire women on a fishing boat and Russell Banks didn't care about that kind of thing as long as you could work. She'd been good, by all accounts. Strong for her size. Knew the water. Kept her head in rough weather.

She'd also been standing in the wrong part of the boat when the fuel line blew.

The official story: engine fire, fuel leak, catastrophic and fast. The *Miss Carolina* had gone down in less than four minutes, too quick to launch a life raft, too quick to do anything but jump and pray. Three people made it out of the water that night—Russell Banks, Dutch Petersen, and Leo Marks. The other three didn't. The town called Russell a hero. Put up a plaque at the marina. Held a ceremony every May for the first five years, then every five years after that. The whole town came out, even people who hadn't known any of the dead, because that was what you did in Southport. You honored the lost. You remembered the drowned. You pretended the past was exactly what the plaque said it was.

The plaque was still bolted to the wall outside Nora's office. She walked past it every morning.

In Memory of the Crew of the Miss Carolina. *May 17, 2010. Gone But Not Forgotten.*

Three names underneath: Thomas Pruitt, First Mate. Iris Galloway, Deckhand. Elena Rodriguez, Deckhand.

Three dead. Three survivors. And a story that had never added up.

The real story was in this package. Whatever Mary had pulled from courthouse records and insurance filings and the banks that had handled the payout. The story of a boat that didn't catch fire by accident. The story of men who knew exactly when to get off.

Russell Banks had survived that night. He hadn't lived long enough to enjoy it. Five years of guilt or cancer—take your pick, both had been eating him by the time Nora sat beside his hospice bed in Wilmington, holding a hand that had gone thin and yellow. He'd tried to tell her something at the end. She hadn't listened.

Protect this family, Nora. Whatever it takes. Whatever you have to do.

* * *

The wind shifted and the Whaler swung broadside, rocking hard enough that Nora grabbed the gunwale to keep from going over. The package slipped off her lap and thudded against the deck sole—a black rectangle on black fiberglass. Her hands shook, like they did the night she'd found her father's confession letter in his desk drawer, six months after the funeral, hidden under a stack of old charts.

She had to do this.

Mary was gone—nine days now, no address, no note, nothing but a storage unit key and a sentence that could have meant anything. *You know what to do.* Nora didn't know. She didn't know if Mary was hiding or dead. She didn't know if destroying this package was protecting her family or betraying the only cousin she had left. She didn't know anything except that the tide was running and the storm was coming and a man named Grady Pruitt had shown up in town two days ago, asking questions nobody wanted to answer.

Grady Pruitt.

Thomas Pruitt's son. First mate on the *Miss Carolina.* One of the three who'd gone down and stayed down.

Mary had never mentioned him. Eight months of careful conversations—in the office, on the docks, twice at Nora's house when she'd needed a place to stay that wasn't her rental—and Mary had never once said she was working with anyone else. She'd said she was alone in this. She'd said the research was hers, the risk was hers, the choice to come to Southport was hers and hers only.

Nora had believed her. Wanted to believe her. A woman working alone was easier to protect. No allies meant no witnesses. No witnesses meant the secret stayed buried with everyone else who'd gone down on the *Miss Carolina.*

* * *

She picked up the package and stood in the rocking boat, feet spread, weight low. The channel marker pulsed red off the port bow.

Her phone buzzed.

Nora froze. The package hung in her hand, arm cocked, while the phone buzzed again in her jacket pocket. Then a third time.

She lowered her arm. Fished out the phone with her free hand.

Three texts from Marla Hutchins, who ran the dispatch desk at the town marina:

Someone at the office looking for you Won't leave Says he'll wait all night if he has to

Marla was sixty-three, had worked the marina desk since before Nora was born, knew everyone in Southport and most of their business. If Marla was texting at midnight, something was wrong. Marla went to bed at nine and church at seven and didn't appreciate anything that disrupted the routine.

She should text back, ask who it was. Her stomach already knew. Had known since the moment she'd heard Grady Pruitt's name two days ago, standing in the checkout line at Lowe's Foods while Kathy Burroughs gossiped about the stranger who'd been asking around about the *Miss Carolina.*

Some relation to one of the dead, I heard. Here to dig it all up again. You'd think people would just let the past alone.

The wind was picking up. Whitecaps on the chop now, spray coming over the bow. The Whaler drifted faster toward the shipping channel, toward the deep water where the big ships ran, where a sixteen-foot boat with no lights would be hard to see until it was too late.

She shoved the package into the waterproof hatch under the bow.

Started the engine.

* * *

The run back took less than twenty minutes. She kept to the Intracoastal, hugging the marsh side where the spartina grew thick and the fiddler crabs had riddled the mud with their burrows. No lights until she cleared the no-wake zone at the yacht basin, then she throttled down and flipped on her spots. Routine night check. Channel markers. Dock lines. The things a harbormaster checked when she couldn't sleep.

The marina was quiet. Most of the slips dark, the commercial boats gone before dawn, the pleasure craft buttoned up against the coming weather. A security light buzzed at the fuel dock, drawing palmetto bugs that spiraled in the yellow glare. A loose halyard clanked against an aluminum mast in a rhythm that would drive the owner crazy if he'd been aboard to hear it.

He was standing at the end of the dock, under the light outside her office. Tall. Rawboned. A canvas jacket that had seen weather. He watched her tie off the Whaler and step up onto the pier, and he didn't move, didn't speak, stood there with his hands in his pockets and his weight on his heels.

The dock creaked under her boots. Thirty-year-old boards, salt-swollen and splitting in places, the kind of wood that remembered every storm. She could smell the pilings from here—creosote and barnacles and the low-tide funk of whatever had died underneath and gotten wedged in the rocks. A mullet jumped in the dark behind her.

Waiting.

Nora walked toward him. Her marina, her town, her family's wreckage. Whoever this man was, he was standing on her ground.

She stopped ten feet away. The security light threw his face into hard relief—deep-set eyes, a jaw that hadn't seen a razor in a few days, a scar that hooked around his left eyebrow like a question mark. Mid-forties, maybe. The kind of man who'd spent his life working with his hands and hadn't let it break him yet. He shifted his weight when she got close. Not backing down. Settling in.

"Office is closed," she said. "Come back in the morning."

"You're Nora Banks." Not a question.

"Sign on the door says so."

"Harbormaster."

"Twelve years now."

He took a step toward her and she held her ground. She'd dealt with drunk captains, belligerent fishermen, Coast Guard inspectors with something to prove. She'd dealt with her father at the end, when the morphine had worn off and he'd thought she was her mother and had grabbed her wrist hard enough to bruise.

One man on her own dock at midnight wasn't going to make her flinch.

"My name is Grady Pruitt," he said. "I'm looking for a woman named Mary Galloway."

She kept her face still.

"Mary worked at Provision Company for a while. Quit about three weeks back. Then she left town, nine, ten days ago. Didn't leave a forwarding address."

"That's not what I've heard."

"Then your sources need better sources."

"My sources say you and Mary were close. Say you were seen together the day she disappeared. Down at that place on Yacht Basin Dr."

"Fishy Fishy. Best shrimp and grits on the coast. You should try them before you leave. You are leaving, right?"

Grady Pruitt didn't blink. The wind off the Cape Fear cut through the gap between the buildings, carrying the scent of the marsh—pluff mud and salt and the faintly sulfurous rot of spartina at low tide. He didn't notice. Or didn't care.

"Mary found something. About the *Miss Carolina.* About what really happened that night."

"A boat sank. Three people died. It was fifteen years ago."

"My father was one of the three."

The words hung there. Thomas Pruitt. First mate. The man whose name was second on the plaque she walked past every morning.

"I'm sorry for your loss," Nora said. "But I don't know what that has to do with me."

"Your father was the captain."

"My father's dead too."

"The difference is, my father's death wasn't an accident." Grady took another step. Close enough now that she could see the grain of his stubble, the red threads in the whites of his eyes. Something came off him—desperation, maybe. Or grief gone sour. "Mary spent six months proving it. Then she disappeared. And you were the last person seen with her."

His hands were out of his pockets now. Not threatening, not yet, but ready. The hands of a man who'd worked construction or fishing or hard labor that left calluses and scars. She noticed a wedding ring, pale skin where it used to be.

The words landed. She made herself breathe. Made herself stay still. The evidence was twenty feet behind her, stuffed in the bow hatch of her father's boat, and if this man had any idea what was in that package, he wouldn't be standing here asking questions. He'd be calling the sheriff. Or the FBI. Or whoever handled maritime insurance fraud and negligent homicide and whatever else the truth would add up to.

"I don't know where Mary is," she said. "That's the truth."

"I don't believe you."

"That's your problem, not mine."

They stood there, neither moving, while the security light hummed and the loose halyards clanked against a mast in the darkness.

Grady Pruitt's eyes were gray. She noticed that now. Gray like the river before a storm.

"I'm not leaving," he said. "Not until I find out what happened to her. This town has secrets, Ms. Banks. And I'm very good at digging up secrets."

"Then I hope you brought a shovel. Ground's hard this time of year."

She walked past him toward her office. He didn't move. Didn't try to stop her. She could feel his eyes on her back as she climbed the three steps to the door, keyed the lock, and stepped inside.

Through the salt-streaked window, she watched him stand on the dock for another full minute. Then he turned and walked back toward town, his boots heavy on the boards, and disappeared into the dark beyond the streetlights.

Gone. For now.

* * *

Nora sat at her desk without turning on the light.

The office was the same as it had always been—one room, steel desk, wall of filing cabinets, VHF radio setup with the volume turned low. The chair creaked when she shifted her weight, the same creak it had made for twenty years under three different harbormasters. The walls were covered with charts and tide tables and photographs: the marina in 1962, when the docks were still wood and the shrimp fleet numbered forty boats instead of twelve. Her father shaking hands with the governor at a groundbreaking ceremony, both men squinting into the sun. The *Miss Carolina* at anchor in calm water.

She reached for the phone. Put it down. Reached for it again.

Who would she even call? The police? Chief Purvis would ask questions she couldn't answer. Ward Cranston? Judge Cranston, who'd signed the official report, who'd ruled it an accident, who'd been running this town from behind the bench for thirty years. He'd know what to do. He always knew what to do. That was what made him dangerous.

Her sister in St. Simons Island in Georgia wouldn't answer. Hadn't answered in five years, not since she'd changed her last name and built a life that didn't include Southport or Russell Banks or any of the rest of it.

She thought about calling anyway. About what she'd say if Anna actually picked up—Anna Banks who was Anna Miller now, had been for six years, married to a man who designed golf courses on Sea Island and didn't know the first thing about the Cape Fear or any of it. Two kids she posted pictures of at Christmas and Easter. Nora had a nephew she'd met once, at the funeral. Blond like his father. He'd looked at her the way children look at strangers.

After the funeral, Anna had stood in the church hall with her husband's hand on her back and said she wasn't coming back. Not for the estate, not for the paperwork, not for anything. It's done, she'd said. I was done the night I left. You always knew that.

Nora had been the one to stay. When Russell got sick, she'd handled the medical decisions. When he died, she'd handled the estate. When their mother moved to the smaller house on Charlotte Street, Nora had helped her pack and haul furniture and repaint the kitchen. She'd done all of it because Anna was gone and their mother was sixty-two and somebody had to.

She'd never resented Anna for leaving. Had tried not to. The town their father had given his life to protecting was the same town that had crushed him under it, and if Anna couldn't live with that, Nora understood. They'd just made different choices.

Maybe that was what staying did to you. Every morning, she walked past the plaque with her father's name on it, past the boats he'd known, past the people who'd thanked him for his service, and she knew what was underneath. Staying meant knowing. Leaving meant you could still tell yourself a story.

Anna had made the smarter choice.

Nora had made hers.

Nora didn't call anyone. She sat in the dark and listened to the wind rattle the windows, the water slap against the pilings, the creak of the dock lines on the boats outside.

Where is she?

Mary was hiding. Mary was safe. Mary had a plan, and Nora was part of that plan, and all she had to do was hold the line a little longer.

That was what she told herself. That was what she had to believe.

Where is she?

She opened her desk drawer and looked at the storage unit key. Unit 47. She'd been back three times since Mary disappeared. Each time expecting something different. Each time finding the same things: Mary's jacket on the hook by the door. Her phone, dead. Her car keys sitting on a cardboard box.

And the folder. The thick manila folder stuffed with documents Nora hadn't let herself read.

She should have burned everything. Should have taken it out to the fire pit behind her house and stirred the ashes until nothing was left. Made it disappear.

Instead, she'd kept it. The package and the folder and the key. Just in case Mary came back. Or didn't.

* * *

Her phone buzzed.

Local number, 910 area code, not one she recognized.

"Banks."

"Nora." A man's voice, gravelly, old. "It's Dutch. We need to talk."

Dutch Petersen. Seventy-three years old, worked the Southport docks since Eisenhower, knew where every body was buried because he'd helped bury half of them. He'd been on the *Miss Carolina* the night it went down. One of the three survivors—him, Leo Marks, and Russell Banks. Leo had moved to Jacksonville six months later and never came back. Russell had died five years after, eaten up by guilt and cancer.

That left Dutch as the only living witness to what had really happened.

"It's late, Dutch."

"I know what time it is." A pause, the sound of a television in the background, laugh track from some late-night rerun. "I saw him, Nora. That man. The one asking about the girl."

"You talked to Grady Pruitt?"

"He came by my place this afternoon. Sat on my porch for an hour, asking questions. Showed me a picture of the Galloway girl." Dutch's voice dropped. "He knows things, Nora. Things he shouldn't know. Things nobody should know."

A cough on the other end. Wet, rattling. Dutch had been smoking since Korea.

"What did you tell him?"

"Nothing. Told him I was an old man with a bad memory. Told him to find someone else to bother." The

TV went silent—Dutch had muted it, or turned it off. When he spoke again, his voice was different. Smaller. "But he'll be back. His kind always comes back. And I'm too old to keep lying, Nora. Too old and too tired."

"Dutch—"

"I can't do this no more. You understand? I wake up every night seeing their faces. Iris. Tommy Pruitt. That Rodriguez girl. I see them in the water, and I hear your daddy yelling, and I—" He stopped. Breathed. The sound of it was ragged, wet. "We need to talk. In person. Not on the phone."

"When?"

"Tomorrow. Noon. You know where."

The line went dead.

Outside, the wind had shifted, blowing rain against the windows in gusts that sounded like handfuls of gravel. The storm was here now, or the edge of it. She could hear the boats shifting at their slips, the groan of dock lines taking strain, the clatter of loose halyards nobody had tied off. Tomorrow the harbor would be full of broken cleats and chafed lines and skippers complaining about the weather like it was her fault.

Tomorrow she would meet Dutch at the fish house and find out how much longer she had before everything came apart.

She looked at the photograph on the wall. The *Miss Carolina* at anchor, shot the summer before it went down. Her father in the wheelhouse, squinting into the lens, hand raised in a wave that looked like it might also be warding something off. She'd thought that was humility when she was a girl. Now she knew it for what it was: a man who spent fifteen years expecting the knock on the door that never came, braced for it even in photographs, even when someone was just pointing a camera at him on a nice afternoon.

Dutch's voice. I wake up every night seeing their faces.

Iris Galloway's name was on the plaque because her father had needed crew and Iris had needed work and nobody had told Iris what she was getting onto. Elena Rodriguez the same. They'd trusted him with their lives because he was the captain, because that was what you did when you stepped onto someone's boat. You put yourself in their hands.

He'd put them in the water.

Not what he'd intended. She knew that. Not what anyone had intended. But the way a thing turns out is the thing you carry, not the way you meant it. Russell Banks had meant to scuttle an empty boat for insurance money and walk away clean, and instead he'd walked away from two women who drowned trusting him, and he'd carried that for fifteen years, and it had killed him as surely as the cancer. Just slower.

She'd known some of this. Not all of it, not the shape of it, not the names of who else was involved. But she'd known enough to understand why he'd looked at her sometimes like he was trying to memorize her face. Like he wasn't sure how many more times he'd get to see it.

Nora set the phone on the desk. The shaking in her hands had spread to her arms, her shoulders. She hadn't eaten since breakfast. Hadn't slept more than three hours in the last two days. She tried to stand and her legs wouldn't hold. She sat back down.

You know where.

The old fish house. Dutch had worked there for forty years before it closed, back when there was still money in buying catch off the day boats and shipping it north on ice. He'd had a spot on the loading dock where he ate his lunch, watching the trawlers come in, and he'd taken Nora there when she was a girl. Told her stories about her father when Russell Banks was young, before the debt and the bad decisions and the men who'd shown up one night with a proposal he couldn't refuse.

The wind was dying down now. The worst of the weather pushing east, out past the shoals, out toward the open Atlantic where it couldn't hurt anyone. By morning, the Cape Fear would be flat. The sun would come up over Battery Island. The tourists would line up at Fishy Fishy for lunch, and the charter boats would head out for the morning bite, and Southport would look exactly as it always looked—quiet, quaint, a nice place to raise a family or retire or forget about whatever you were running from.

By morning, Grady Pruitt would still be in town. Dutch would tell her something she didn't want to hear. Everything she'd built—the job, the reputation, the careful lie of her life—could start to come apart.

Nora picked up the storage unit key and closed her fist around it. The metal edge bit into her palm. Hard enough to leave a mark. Hard enough to remind her that she was still here, still breathing, still in control of something. Even if that something was only a key to a storage unit full of evidence that could destroy her.

Where is she?

She didn't know. She was going to find out.

Outside, the Cape Fear ran black and silent toward the sea, carrying its secrets with the tide.

Nora sat in her office and waited for the sun.

Wilmington, 2015

The hospice smelled like Pine-Sol and urine. Nora had been sitting in the vinyl chair beside her father's bed for six hours, maybe seven. She'd stopped checking her phone. The battery had died around suppertime and she'd left the charger in the truck and hadn't gone back for it because every time she stood up his breathing changed and she sat back down.

The room was on the second floor, east-facing, and at some point the light from the parking lot had replaced the daylight without her noticing. Orange sodium through the blinds. The same color as the Southport waterfront at night, though she tried not to think about that. She tried not to think about anything. She listened to the machines and she watched her father's chest rise and fall and she peeled a hangnail on her left thumb until it bled.

Russell Banks was fifty-eight years old and looked eighty. The cancer had started in his liver and gone everywhere. His arms on the blanket were the color of old newspaper. His hands were what she couldn't look at. The bones showed through. The skin moved over them like cloth.

He'd been under for two days. The morphine drip ran continuously, a clear line into the back of his left hand where the vein still held, and the nurse—Linda, the one with the Lumbee accent and the squeaky shoes—had told Nora this morning that it could be hours or it could be days and there was no way to know and she should eat something. Nora had not eaten something.

She was thinking about the water bill. The water bill at the harbormaster's office was past due because she'd been driving to Wilmington every other day for three weeks and the mail was piling up and she needed to call the town clerk before they sent a notice. She was thinking about the water bill and not about her father dying because the water bill was a thing she could fix.

His hand moved.

She almost missed it. A twitch in the fingers, the kind that could be reflex, the kind Linda said didn't mean anything. But then his wrist turned and his fingers opened and closed and his head moved on the pillow and Nora's hand was on his before she'd decided to reach for it.

"Daddy?"

His eyes opened. Not the half-lidded drifting she'd seen the last few days, the morphine gaze that looked through her and past her and into whatever the dying watch instead of the living. These were open. Present. His pupils were pinprick-small but tracking, and when they found her face they locked on and didn't let go.

"Nora." His voice was a scrape. Something down in his throat that used to be a baritone. "Nora-girl."

"I'm here, Daddy. I'm right here."

His hand found her wrist. The grip was wrong—too hard, desperate, the bones of his fingers digging into the tendons above her pulse. She tried to adjust her hand and he pulled her closer, pulling her down toward the bed rail, and his breath was sour and chemical and his eyes were wide.

"Listen to me." The whisper came out hard. "You have to listen."

"I'm listening."

"They made me do it." His grip tightened. She could feel her pulse beating against his fingers. "They said they'd hurt you and your mama and your sister. Said it was just insurance money. Nobody gets hurt, Russell. Just scuttle the boat and collect. That's what they said."

"Daddy, it's okay—"

"It's not okay." He pulled her closer. The bed rail pressed into her ribs. A monitor beeped twice, something changing in his vitals, and she heard footsteps in the hallway that didn't stop. "The fire. The fire caught faster than they said it would. I tried to get the pumps going and they wouldn't start and I could hear them, Nora, I could hear them below—"

His voice broke.

"I could hear them in the water. Screaming. And I couldn't get to them. The smoke was—I couldn't see. I went over the side and Leo was already in the water and Dutch had the cooler and I could hear Iris and Tom and the other one, the kid, I could hear—"

He stopped. His eyes went somewhere else. Somewhere she couldn't follow. His grip on her wrist hadn't loosened.

"The boat," he said.

"What boat, Daddy?"

"They were watching. From the boat. No lights. Just sitting out there in the dark, watching it burn. Watching people die." His head turned on the pillow and his eyes came back to her face but they weren't seeing her anymore. "Sarah. Sarah, you have to believe me, I didn't know anyone would get hurt. They told me it would be clean."

The name hit her in the chest. Her mother. Three hours south in Southport, probably asleep, and her father was talking to her like she was sitting in this chair. "Daddy, it's Nora. It's me."

"Sarah, the boat—they were watching—you have to take the girls and go. Take Nora and the baby and go somewhere he can't find you. He'll come for us. He'll—"

"Daddy." She put her other hand on his face. His jaw was sharp under her palm, no flesh left to soften it. His skin was hot. "It's Nora. Mama's not here. You're in the hospital."

He stared at her. Something behind his eyes shifted, recalibrated, and for a moment he was back. He saw her. His daughter. Not his wife.

"Nora." Quieter now. The grip on her wrist easing by a fraction. "I'm running out of time."

"You need to rest."

"No. Listen. The boat that was watching—he sent it. He sent all of it. The insurance, the money, he set the whole thing up and we were—I was—" His hand trembled against her wrist. "I was just the one dumb enough to do it."

She didn't understand. She heard the words—boat, fire, insurance, watching—and they didn't arrange themselves into anything that made sense. Her father had run a shrimp boat. The *Miss Carolina* had caught fire and sunk. Three people died. It was an accident. It was five years ago and it was an accident and her father was dying and the morphine was wearing off and he was confused and frightened and none of this was real.

"I know, Daddy." She smoothed the blanket over his chest. Her voice was the voice she used for drunks at the dock, for tourists who'd run aground on the shoal, for anyone who needed to be told the world was still working. "I know. It wasn't your fault."

"It was my fault. That's what I'm telling you. Nora-girl, it was my—"

"It's okay." She reached for the call button on the bed rail. "It's going to be okay. Let me get the nurse."

"No." His grip found its strength again, one last surge, pulling her hand away from the button. "Don't. You have to hear this. He's still out there. The man on the boat. He's—"

"Daddy, nobody's out there. You're safe. I'm right here."

He looked at her like someone who won't open a door you're pounding on. Then something in his face gave way. Not surrender. He knew she wasn't going to hear him. He could see it.

His hand opened. Her wrist slid free. His fingers had left marks, red ovals that would purple by morning.

Nora pressed the call button.

Linda came in forty-five seconds later, squeaky shoes on the linoleum, and Nora stood by the window while the nurse checked his vitals and adjusted the line and asked

Nora if he'd been agitated and Nora said yes, he'd been talking, he seemed confused, he was upset, and could they increase the dosage because he was in pain, he was clearly in pain.

Linda looked at Russell. Russell looked at the ceiling. Whatever had brought him to the surface was draining away, the morphine pulling him back under, and his mouth was still moving but no sound came out. His lips forming words nobody would hear.

"We can adjust it," Linda said. "I'll call Dr. Patel."

"Thank you."

Linda left. The room was quiet except for the monitors and the air conditioning and the soft, wet sound of Russell's breathing through his open mouth. Nora sat back down in the vinyl chair. She picked up his hand—gently this time, careful with it.

His eyes were half-open. Glassy. Whatever window had opened was closed.

"It's okay, Daddy," she said, to the room, to no one. "You can rest now."

He died thirty-one hours later without waking up again. Nora was in the hallway getting coffee from the machine when it happened. She came back to the room and the monitor was flatlined and Linda was already there, and Russell Banks was still and yellow and lighter somehow, like the weight had been the living and now the living was done.

She drove back to Southport that afternoon with the windows down because the truck's AC had quit and the September heat wouldn't break. The bruises on her wrist had gone the color of plums. She kept touching them at red lights, pressing her thumb into the marks, feeling the ache. She didn't know why.

She would not understand for ten years.

CHAPTER 2

The Key

She hadn't slept.

The salvage shop behind her house had come with the property—a former marine salvage operation she'd kept running because the structure was already there. Steel I-beam across the ceiling, chain hoist on its trolley, large sliding doors that opened to the side street. She'd been there since midnight, the hoist clicking as she lowered a corroded propeller bracket to the workbench. Classical music played low from the corner radio. Goldberg Variations.

The music stopped when she heard footsteps on the side street outside.

She waited. The footsteps passed.

The music came back on. She ran her fingers along the bracket's corrosion pattern, testing the stress points. Saltwater always left a signature. You could read how long something had been down, what depth, what currents. She'd learned young: nothing stays lost. It just stays hidden.

She tagged it with grease pencil: *November 7. Incoming tide. NE wind 15.*

The sky through the shop windows had gone from black to gray. She turned off the music, locked the doors, and walked back through to the house. The work helped. Gave her something to focus on besides Dutch's voice in her head, that ragged breathing. *I can't do this no more.*

The storm had passed by dawn, leaving the marina wrecked.

Nora walked the docks at first light, clipboard in hand, cataloging the damage. A sailboat had broken loose from D-dock and drifted into the fuel pier, leaving a gash in its gelcoat and a dent in the pump housing. Three cleats had pulled free from the boards, their bolts rusted through. Someone's dinghy had flipped and was floating upside down in the yacht basin, its oars gone. The commercial dock had fared better—those boats knew how to tie off for weather—but even there she found chafed lines, a snapped halyard, and a crab pot that had somehow ended up on the roof of the bait shack. On C-dock, a trawler named *Patience* had ridden out the storm without a scratch. A woman lay face-down on the foredeck, bikini top untied, a bottle of rosé sweating on the deck beside her. Mid-morning. Half the marina in shambles. Nora shook her head and kept walking.

The air smelled like churned mud and salt and the green stink of seaweed rotting in piles along the waterline. Fiddler crabs had come out of their burrows by the thousands, scuttling across the exposed mud flats in waves that rippled and shifted whenever Nora's shadow passed over them. A great blue heron stood motionless at the end of the fuel dock, watching the water with the patience of something that had been doing this for a million years.

Noon. The fish house. She had four hours to figure out what she was going to say to him.

She didn't know. Didn't know what Dutch wanted, what he was planning, what he might have already told Grady Pruitt. Fifteen years of silence, and now everything was cracking open at once. Mary gone. Grady in town. Dutch calling in the middle of the night, talking about faces in the water.

Nora stopped at the end of C-dock and looked out across the Cape Fear. The river was brown and swollen from the runoff, carrying branches and trash and the occasional dead fish past the channel markers. A pelican dove for something near the far shore and came up empty. The sun was already hot, burning off the last of the clouds, and by noon the humidity would be thick enough to chew.

She wrote *D-14: loose piling, check bolts* on her clipboard and kept walking.

* * *

Marla Hutchins was waiting in the office when Nora got back, a Styrofoam cup of coffee in each hand.

"You look like death," Marla said.

"Thanks."

"Didn't sleep, did you."

Nora took the coffee. It was from the coffee shop on Howe Street, the good stuff they kept behind the counter for locals. Marla had been bringing her coffee for twelve years, ever since Nora took over as harbormaster. Neither of them acknowledged what it meant.

"Storm kept me up," Nora said.

"Storm my ass. I saw your lights on at three in the morning." Marla settled into the chair across from Nora's desk, the one with the cracked vinyl seat that nobody ever replaced. "That's twice this week."

"Inventory."

Marla's eyes narrowed. "You said that last time."

Nora didn't answer.

Marla was sixty-three, built low and solid, with gray hair she kept short and eyes that didn't miss much. "That man was here again this morning. The one from last night."

"Grady Pruitt."

"Showed up at seven, before I even had the lights on. Asked if you were here. Asked about Mary Galloway. Asked about the *Miss Carolina*." Marla's eyes narrowed. "Asked about your daddy."

"What did you tell him?"

"Told him you weren't here and I didn't know when you'd be back. Told him the *Miss Carolina* was ancient history and he should let the dead rest." Marla paused. "He didn't seem inclined to take my advice."

Nora sat down behind her desk with her coffee. The cup was too hot, burning her palms through the Styrofoam, and she didn't move to set it down.

"What's going on, Nora?"

"Nothing."

"Don't bullshit me. I've known you since you were fourteen years old, running errands for your daddy on this dock. I know when something's wrong." Marla leaned forward. "That man, Pruitt, he's not going away. And the way he talks about Mary Galloway..." She shook her head. "He thinks something happened to her. Something bad."

"Mary left town. People do that."

"People leave forwarding addresses. They tell their landlords. They don't vanish in the middle of the night and leave their car keys behind."

Nora looked up. "How do you know about the car keys?"

Marla's face didn't change. "I know everything that happens in this town. You should know that by now."

"What else do you know, Marla?"

The older woman's fingers drummed on the arm of the chair—a nervous habit Nora had never seen before.

"I know your daddy wasn't the only one who owed money to the wrong people. I know there are men in this town who've been getting rich off other people's misery for longer than you've been alive. And I know that when those men feel threatened, bad things happen to the people asking questions." Marla stood up, smoothing the front of her blouse. "Whatever's going on, you need to get ahead of it. That Pruitt man is going to keep digging until he finds something. And from the look on your face, I'd say there's plenty to find."

She walked toward the door, then stopped with her hand on the frame.

"Whatever you find out about your daddy—remember he was trying to protect his family."

She left without waiting for a response.

The screen door banged shut behind her, and Nora sat alone in the office, listening to the creak of the building and the slap of water against the pilings.

Marla knew something. Had known for years, maybe. Another secret in a town full of them.

Three hours until noon.

* * *

The fish house sat at the end of a dirt road that hadn't been graded since the plant closed. Nora took her truck, a ten-year-old Tacoma she'd bought used from a shrimper's widow, bouncing over ruts and potholes while dust billowed up behind her. The road ran through a stand of loblolly pines, their needles brown from the summer heat, then opened onto the shell-covered lot where the workers used to park.

The building looked worse in daylight than it had from the water. Rusted corrugated steel, the red paint long since faded to a dull brown. The loading dock had collapsed on one end, boards rotted through and hanging over the water at crazy angles. A chain-link fence that someone had cut through years ago, the gap wide enough to drive a truck through.

Nora parked in the shade of a water oak and got out. The heat was immediate and heavy. Cicadas screamed in the trees, that rising and falling drone that meant summer in the South. The air smelled like hot metal and old fish and the sulfur stink of the marsh at low tide.

Dutch's truck was already there. A rusted-out Chevy older than Nora, parked near the gap in the fence. He was sitting on the edge of the loading dock, his legs dangling over the water, a cigarette in his hand.

She walked across the shell lot, her boots crunching on the oyster fragments. A black snake slithered out of her path and disappeared into the weeds along the fence line. In the marsh, a rail called—that harsh *kek-kek-kek.*

Dutch didn't turn around when she climbed up onto the dock. He was looking out at the water, at the place where Dutchman Creek bent toward the river. From here you couldn't see the spot where the *Miss Carolina* had gone down—it was around the bend, past the old channel marker—but she knew he was looking at it anyway. He'd been looking at it for fifteen years.

"You came," he said.

"You asked."

She sat down beside him, leaving a few feet of space. The boards were soft with rot, and she could feel them give slightly under her weight. Below, the water was brown and thick with runoff from the storm, carrying leaves and sticks past the pilings.

Dutch was seventy-three but looked older. Skin like cracked leather, hands spotted with age, a tremor in his fingers when he raised the cigarette to his lips. He'd been a big man once—Nora remembered him from childhood, hauling crates off the shrimp boats, arms like dock pilings—but the years had shrunk him. The cigarettes hadn't helped. Neither had the drinking.

"How long you been sitting here?" Nora asked.

"Couple hours. Couldn't sleep." He took a drag, let the smoke out slow. "Couldn't sleep for fifteen years, you want the truth."

"Dutch—"

"I know why you're here. You want to know what I told that man. Pruitt." He spat the name. "You want to know if I gave you up."

"Did you?"

Dutch laughed. It turned into a cough, wet and rattling, and he spat into the water below. "Not yet."

The words hung there. Nora watched a dragonfly hover over the water, its wings catching the light.

She looked at Dutch. The tremor in his hands. The way he held the cigarette. Everything cracked somewhere. The question was whether you could see it coming.

"What did he ask you?"

"Everything." Dutch flicked ash into the water. "How the fire started. How your daddy got off the boat. Why three people died and three people didn't." He turned to look at her, and his eyes were red-rimmed. "He knows it wasn't an accident, Nora. He's got papers. Documents. I don't know where he got them, but he's got them."

Mary. Mary had been feeding him something before she disappeared. Had to be.

"What did you tell him?"

"Told him I was drunk that night. Told him I don't remember much." Dutch's mouth twisted. "Same lie I've been telling for fifteen years. Same lie I told the Coast Guard, the insurance people, Judge Cranston. Same lie I told your mama at your daddy's funeral."

"What else does he know?"

Dutch's cigarette burned down between his fingers. A blue crab surfaced below them, claws working at something dead in the shallows, then sank back into the murk.

"There was something I never told you," he said. "Something your daddy made me swear to keep quiet."

Nora waited.

"There was another boat out there that night. About a quarter mile off, running without lights. I saw it when I came up out of the water. Saw it sitting there, watching, while we were screaming for help." Dutch's voice dropped. "And then I saw it turn and head for shore."

The words landed somewhere deep, somewhere she'd kept locked for fifteen years.

"Nobody ever said anything about another boat."

"No. It wasn't." Dutch dropped the cigarette and ground it out with his heel. "Your daddy told me to keep my mouth shut. Said it was for my own good. Said if I talked about what I saw, I'd end up like Tommy Pruitt and Iris and Elena."

"You never told me."

"Russell asked me not to. Said you were safer not knowing." Dutch looked at her. "I told Mary, though. Three weeks before she disappeared. Told her everything."

Three weeks. Before the storage unit key. Before *you know what to do*.

"What did she say?"

"She said she already knew about the boat. Said she had photographs." Dutch's cigarette had burned down to his fingers. He dropped it in the water. "I don't know where she got them. She wouldn't tell me. Said it was better if I didn't know who her sources were."

Nora's mind was racing. Photographs of a boat that was supposed to be invisible. Someone else had been watching that night. Someone who kept records.

"Did she tell you who was on that boat?"

"No. She said she was close to finding out. Said she had one more piece to track down, and then she'd have enough to go to the FBI." Dutch's hands were shaking. "That was the last time I saw her. Two days later, she was gone."

The cicadas had gone quiet. The only sound was the water moving below them and the distant hum of a boat motor on the river.

"There's more," Dutch said. "Things I haven't told anyone."

Nora waited.

"The night of the sinking, before everything went wrong, your daddy pulled me aside. Told me that if anything happened, I should get to shore and find a man named Delacroix. Said Delacroix would know what to do."

"Who's Delacroix?"

"I never found out. Your daddy died before I could ask him, and I was too scared to go looking on my own." Dutch's face was gray in the harsh light. "Mary asked about him too. Said she'd found the name in some old documents. She was trying to track him down when she disappeared."

Delacroix. A new name. A new thread to pull.

"Why are you telling me this now?"

"Because Pruitt knows about the boat. I didn't tell him—Mary must have, before she disappeared. And if he knows about the boat, then he knows there's a witness out there. Someone who can identify whoever was watching that night." Dutch looked at her. "Whoever took Mary, they're going to come for that witness next. And if they find out I've been talking..."

He didn't finish the sentence. He didn't need to.

"Who was on that boat, Dutch? You must have some idea."

"I've spent fifteen years trying not to think about it." He pulled another cigarette from his pack. His hands were shaking so badly it took three tries to light it. "Cranston had a boat back then. So did half the county commission. Could have been any of them."

"Could have been someone else. Someone we don't know about."

"Could have been." Dutch exhaled smoke. "That's what scares me. The men I know about, Cranston and his people—they're bad, but they're predictable. They want money and power and they don't care who they hurt to get it. But if there's someone else, someone who's been hiding in the shadows all this time..." He shook his head. "That's the kind of person who makes people disappear."

They sat in silence for a while. The tide was turning, the water starting to push back up the creek. An osprey circled overhead, scanning for fish. Dutch's hands had steadied some, though not completely.

"You know what I think about most?" he said. "Not the fire. Not the screaming. Not even the faces. It's the quiet after. When Leo and me were hanging onto that cooler, waiting for the Coast Guard, and there wasn't any sound except the water and the wind. It was so quiet,

Nora. Like the whole world had stopped to look at what we'd done."

Nora didn't say anything. There was nothing to say.

"Iris was a good woman. Worked harder than most men, never complained, always had a joke to tell when things got bad." Dutch exhaled smoke. "She had a grown daughter by then. Mary's mother. And a granddaughter—Mary couldn't have been more than ten or eleven when it happened."

"I know."

"That little girl lost her grandmother because of us. Because your daddy trusted the wrong people and I was too much of a coward to stop him." Dutch's voice cracked. "And now her daughter is out there somewhere, maybe dead, and I'm still sitting here feeling sorry for myself."

"Dutch—"

"Let me finish." He turned to look at her, his hands braced on his knees. "I'm tired of lying."

"What are you going to do?"

"Tell the truth." Dutch said it simply, without drama. "I'm too old to keep lying. Too tired. Pruitt's going to find out eventually—might as well hear it from me."

"If you talk to Pruitt, you're not just putting yourself at risk. You're putting everyone at risk. My family. My sister. Everyone connected to this."

"Your family made their choices. Same as I made mine." Dutch stood up, his knees cracking. "I'm done protecting men who wouldn't piss on me if I was on fire. Done waking up every night hearing them scream."

"Give me time. A week. Let me find Mary and figure out what's really going on."

Dutch looked down at her, his face unreadable in the harsh noon light. A bead of sweat ran down his temple and dropped onto the rotted boards.

"One week," he said finally. "That's all you get. After that, I'm talking. To Pruitt, to the FBI, to anyone who'll listen."

He turned and walked back across the shell lot to his truck. Nora watched him go. The Chevy started with a rattle, backed out of the lot, and disappeared down the dirt road in a cloud of dust.

She sat on the loading dock for a long time after the Chevy disappeared down the dirt road.

The water below her was still brown from the storm. A plastic bottle drifted past on the current, caught in the eddy behind a piling, circled twice, and moved on. The osprey was still working the creek, patient and methodical, dropping and rising and dropping again. She watched it without seeing it. Her mind was somewhere else.

Iris had a grown daughter. And a granddaughter—Mary couldn't have been more than ten or eleven.

She'd known this. Had known it in the abstract, the way you know a fact without letting it land. But Dutch had said it like a man who'd been carrying the specific weight of it for fifteen years, and now it was landing in her.

Mary had been ten years old. Her grandmother had gone to work one morning on Russell Banks's boat and hadn't come home, and nobody had ever told Mary or her mother or anyone else what had actually happened. The official story—engine fire, tragic accident—had stood for fifteen years because everyone who knew the truth had too much to lose by telling it.

Including Nora.

She'd told herself she was protecting her mother. Protecting the family name. Protecting the careful order of her life in this town, the job, the house, the morning walks past the plaque she'd learned not to read. She'd told herself silence was the only option because her father was dead and the men behind it were powerful and there was nothing left to do but keep the peace.

She'd believed it too. Mostly.

The loading dock had been full of workers once. She remembered coming here with her father when she was small—the smell of ice and raw fish, the shrimp boats tied three-deep at the pier, the men moving crates in the August heat. Dutch had worked these docks for forty years. Had known her father since before she was born. Had sat on this same rotted planking and watched three people drown and kept quiet about the boat he'd seen in the dark because Russell Banks had told him to.

Because they were all trying to protect something.

Iris Galloway had a granddaughter who'd grown up without knowing the truth. Elena Rodriguez had a family, somewhere, who'd been told the same story about an accident, a tragedy, nothing to be done. Thomas Pruitt had a son who'd spent two years of his life and everything he had trying to find out what had really happened to his father.

And Nora had spent fifteen years walking past a plaque that lied.

She thought about her father's hand on her wrist in the hospice room. The bruises she'd pressed her thumb into all the way home on 17. It was my fault. That's what I'm telling you.

He'd known what he was asking her not to do. Had known and had asked anyway, and she'd complied, and now Mary was gone and Dutch was ready to break and Grady Pruitt was in town with two years of documents and a dead man's letter, and all of it was coming apart regardless of what she did.

Dutch was right. She'd been protecting men who wouldn't have protected her.

She got up off the rotted boards. Her legs were stiff. The shell lot glittered in the noon heat, white and sharp underfoot. She walked to her truck, opened the door, and sat for a moment with both hands on the wheel.

A week. She'd told Dutch she needed a week.

She didn't know if that was enough. She didn't know if anything would be enough. But she had the storage unit key in her pocket and a package in her boat and a man named Grady Pruitt in town who was very good at digging up secrets.

She started the engine and pulled out of the lot.

* * *

The drive back to town took less than half an hour, but Nora barely noticed the road. Her mind kept circling back to what Dutch had said. A boat without lights, watching while three people drowned. Someone on that boat who had seen everything. Someone who had photographs.

And a name: Delacroix.

She'd never followed up on it. Her father had said the name on his deathbed—Delacroix—and she'd filed it away with everything else he'd said that night, too raw to pull at that particular thread. Dutch had heard it, though. And Mary had found it in old documents. It meant something.

The road wound through marshland and pine forest, past the ruins of old rice plantations and the earthworks where Confederate soldiers had dug in a hundred and sixty years ago. History everywhere in this part of the South, layer on layer of it, blood and money and secrets going back centuries. Her father's crime was another layer. Another story the land would swallow and forget.

The marina parking lot was half-empty when Nora pulled in. The storm had scared off most of the tourists, and the regulars were still dealing with damage to their boats. Good. She didn't want to talk to anyone. Didn't want to explain where she'd been or what she'd learned.

Grady Pruitt's truck was parked by the fuel dock.

She saw him before he saw her. He was sitting on the seawall, eating something out of a paper bag, but his eyes weren't on the food. He was watching the harbor. His gaze moving from boat to boat, slip to slip, cataloging details and filing them somewhere behind those gray eyes. His posture was loose, legs crossed, shoulders easy, but Nora could see the tension in his hands. A man who'd learned to look comfortable while expecting trouble.

When he spotted her truck, he stood up and started walking toward her. He moved well. Balanced. Like someone who'd spent time on water, where the floor shifted under you.

Nora got out and met him halfway. The dock boards were warm, still drying from last night's rain. A pelican sat on one of the pilings, watching them with prehistoric indifference.

"Ms. Banks." He nodded, polite but not friendly. "I was hoping we could talk."

"I have work to do."

"This won't take long." He fell into step beside her as she walked toward the office. "I spoke with Dutch Petersen this morning. Before you did."

Nora kept walking. Didn't let her pace change.

"He told me about the second boat."

She stopped. Turned to face him. The sun was behind her, throwing her shadow across the dock boards. She could smell the harbor on the air—diesel and salt and the faint rot of seaweed baking on the rocks.

"Dutch is an old man with a guilty conscience. He sees things that aren't there."

"He saw a boat. Running without lights, a quarter mile off, the night the *Miss Carolina* went down. He saw it watching while three people drowned. And then he saw it head for shore. Mary knew about that boat. She had photographs. And now she's gone."

"I don't know where Mary is."

"I believe you." He said it simply, without accusation. "I don't think you know where she is. But I think you know more than you're telling me."

"What do you want, Mr. Pruitt?"

"I want to find out what happened to my father. I want to know who was on that boat. And I want to find Mary Galloway before whoever took her decides she's more trouble than she's worth." He let that sit. "You can help me, or you can stand in my way. But I'm not leaving until I have answers."

A boat motored past the fuel dock, its wake slapping against the seawall. The pelican took off, wings beating heavy against the air. Nora watched it go.

"Why did you come here?" she asked. "Not to Southport. Here. To my dock, in the middle of the day, where everyone can see us."

"Because I want them to see us." He glanced toward the marina, where a handful of boat owners were watching from their decks. "I want whoever's watching to know that I'm not going away. That I'm talking to people. That I'm getting close."

"That's a good way to get yourself killed."

He glanced down at his hands, picked at a cuticle with his thumb. "Maybe. But it's also a good way to flush out whoever's been hiding. Pressure makes people careless. And I want whoever took Mary to make a mistake."

Nora looked at him for a long moment. At the gray eyes and the scar above his eyebrow and the stubborn set of his mouth. He reminded her of someone.

"You're using yourself as bait."

"If that's what it takes."

"And you think I'm going to help you."

"I think you're going to do whatever you have to do to protect your family. And right now, helping me is the best way to do that." He reached into his pocket and pulled out a business card. Plain white, black text. A phone number and nothing else. "Day or night. When you're ready to talk."

He held it out. Nora didn't take it. He set it on the railing of the dock and stepped back.

"One more thing. I know about the storage unit. Unit 47, out on Fish Factory Road. I haven't been inside yet. Wanted to give you a chance to do the right thing first."

He turned and walked back toward his truck, boots heavy on the boards. Nora watched him go.

He knew about the storage unit. He knew about the second boat. He knew more than she did.

She looked down at the business card. Picked it up. The paper was cheap, the ink slightly smeared.

She put it in her pocket.

* * *

Unit 47 was exactly as she'd left it. Mary's jacket still on the hook. Her phone dead on the shelf. Her car keys on the cardboard box, waiting for hands that hadn't come back for them. The sticky note on the banker's box still read EVIDENCE THAT'LL RUIN THANKSGIVING in Mary's neat block print. Nora had smiled the first time she'd seen it. She couldn't smile now.

She pulled the door down behind her and picked up the folder.

She picked up the folder and opened it.

The first page was a photocopy of an insurance document. Maritime policy, Lloyd's of London, dated March 2010. The *Miss Carolina* had been insured for $1.2 million: three times what the boat was worth. The beneficiary was listed as Cape Fear Maritime Holdings.

She flipped through more pages. Bank records showing payments to names she recognized—council members, port authority officials, people who'd been running this town for decades. A deed transfer for property on Bald Head Island, signed by Ward Cranston. Meeting minutes from the county commission with whole sections blacked out.

And photographs. Surveillance shots of men meeting in parking lots, on docks, in back rooms. She recognized some of the faces. Cranston. The current mayor. The port authority director. Men she'd known her whole life, men who came to the marina for boat shows and ribbon cuttings and Fourth of July parades.

In one photo, standing at the edge of the frame: her father. Russell Banks, looking younger than she remembered, shoulders hunched, eyes on the ground. The posture of a man who knew he was in over his head.

They made me do it, Nora-girl.

She kept flipping. More documents. More photographs. A map of the harbor with locations marked in red ink—the spot where the *Miss Carolina* went down, the route the second boat had taken, a third location she didn't recognize.

And then she found it. A photograph of a boat, grainy and dark, shot from what looked like the deck of the *Miss Carolina.* A white hull, no running lights, maybe forty feet. A figure standing at the helm, face obscured by shadow.

Mary had found the second boat. Had found a photograph of whoever was watching that night.

Nora stared at the image, trying to make out details. The boat's lines were familiar—something about the shape of the cabin, the angle of the flybridge. She'd seen this boat before. Or one like it.

There was a note clipped to the photograph, written in Mary's careful handwriting:

Vessel identified as Lady Justice. *Registered to Cape Fear Maritime Holdings. Same company that held the insurance policy. Follow the money.*

Lady Justice. Nora knew that boat. It was tied up at the Bald Head marina—she'd seen it a dozen times, coming and going, always crewed by men who didn't talk and didn't look anyone in the eye.

Cranston's boat. It had to be.

Her phone buzzed. She pulled it out, expecting Marla or Dutch.

Unknown number.

"Banks."

"Ms. Banks." A man's voice, unhurried and flat. Not cold—flat. "You arrived at the U-Store-It at two-seventeen this afternoon. Blue Tacoma, Brunswick County plates. You parked in the third row, walked to unit forty-seven, and you've been inside for approximately eleven minutes."

The temperature in the storage unit dropped ten degrees.

"Who is this?"

"That's not a productive question." He paused, and she could hear something in the background—ice shifting in a glass, maybe, or the creak of a chair. "You're holding a folder. Inside that folder is a photograph of a vessel called the *Lady Justice*, along with financial documents and a handwritten note. The woman who assembled that material made a series of choices over a period of months, and those choices led to an unfortunate outcome."

She looked around the storage unit. The walls were thin—corrugated metal over a steel frame. No windows. One door. If someone came through that door, she had nowhere to go.

"What do you want?"

"I want to save you some time." Reasonable. Almost helpful. "The material in that folder represents a version of events. An incomplete version. The woman who compiled it was working from assumptions, and those assumptions were wrong. Pursuing them further would be a waste of your energy, and frankly, it would complicate things for people who don't need complications."

"Is Mary Galloway alive?"

A beat. "At the moment."

"What does that mean?"

"It means the situation is manageable. It means people are making reasonable decisions, and nobody else needs to get caught up in it." Another pause. "Your father was in a similar position, once. He had information he didn't fully understand, and he had a choice about what to do with it. He chose to go back to his life. His family. His work at the marina. It was the right decision. He had fifteen good years because of it."

Had. Past tense. Her hand tightened on the folder.

"You're threatening me."

"I'm describing how things work." His voice didn't change. No edge, no heat. "You have a life, Ms. Banks. A good one, from what I understand. The harbormaster position. Your mother in Southport. The house out by the marsh. The one with the salvage shop out back." He let each detail land. "None of that needs to change. Destroy the folder. Forget the storage unit. Go home."

"And if I don't?"

"Then you're making a choice. And choices have costs." The calm didn't waver. "Your father learned that. I would rather you didn't have to."

Outside, she could hear a car passing on the road, the crunch of tires on gravel.

"You have twenty-four hours to think it over. That's generous. Use them."

The line went dead.

Nora stood in the storage unit, the folder clutched in her hands, and listened to the silence. Her mouth had gone dry.

Twenty-four hours.

She looked down at the folder. At the photograph of the *Lady Justice*. At the shadow at the helm who might be the key to everything.

The man on the phone hadn't raised his voice. Hadn't needed to. She stood there, folder in her hands, and her arms were loose at her sides. Not shaking. Just loose. A match and ten minutes and her life goes back to what it was yesterday.

She closed the folder, tucked it under her arm, and walked back to her truck.

* * *

She drove without thinking, taking back roads she hadn't used since high school, looping around the edges of town until she was sure nobody was following her. The sun was going down by the time she pulled into her driveway—cracked concrete that led to a small house with a the salvage shop dark behind it.

The house was dark. She hadn't been home in two days—hadn't wanted to be alone with her thoughts in a place that held so many memories. The porch light was burned out, and the screens on the windows needed replacing, and the whole place had that abandoned look of somewhere nobody cared about anymore.

She sat in the truck, watching the last light fade over the marsh. Egrets were settling in the live oaks along the water, their white shapes ghostly against the darkening sky. A fish jumped in the shallows—mullet, probably, running from something bigger.

You have twenty-four hours to decide.

She thought about destroying the folder. Thought about burning the package, dumping the ashes in the river, pretending none of this had ever happened. She could do it. Could walk away, keep her head down, let the dead stay buried.

Her father had tried that. Had spent five years trying to outrun what he'd done, and it had eaten him alive.

Mary had tried to find the truth, and now she was gone.

Grady Pruitt was trying to find the truth, and someone had threatened to kill him.

Dutch was going to tell the truth, whether Nora helped him or not.

The truth would come out. The question was whether Nora would be standing when it did.

She got out of the truck and walked to the end of the dock behind her house. The wood was soft under her feet, warped by years of salt and weather. The marsh stretched out in front of her, silver-gray in the fading light, the spartina waving in a breeze she couldn't feel. A night heron called from the reeds.

Her father had loved this dock. Had stood here a thousand times. Had watched the same sunset, smelled the same salt air, listened to the same sounds of water and insects and birds. Had he known, even then, that it would all come crashing down eventually? Had he understood that secrets don't stay buried forever?

The tide was going out, exposing the mud flats where fiddler crabs would emerge by the thousands when the sun came up. She could smell the rich, sulfurous smell of the mud that tourists hated and locals learned to love. The smell of home. The smell of everything she'd built and everything she stood to lose.

She pulled out her phone and looked at Grady Pruitt's business card. The paper was soft from being in her pocket, the edges already curling.

Day or night. When you're ready to talk.

She wasn't ready. She might never be ready. But ready or not, the truth was coming. Dutch would talk. Grady would dig. Whoever had Mary would come for Nora eventually. The only question was whether she'd be standing when it hit.

She could run. Could pack a bag, empty her bank account, disappear. Start over somewhere nobody knew her name or her father's crimes. Leave the whole mess for someone else to clean up.

Nora dialed the number.

It rang twice before he answered.

"Pruitt."

"It's Nora Banks. We need to meet."

A pause. She could hear traffic in the background—he was on the road somewhere, still hunting.

"When?"

"Tonight. There's a boat ramp off Fish Factory Road, past the Wildlife Grill. I'll be there at ten."

"I'll find it."

She hung up before she could change her mind. Before she could think about what she was doing, who she was betraying, how many lives might come apart because of this one phone call.

The last of the light was gone now. The marsh was dark, the night heron silent, the only sound the whisper of water against the pilings and the distant rumble of a truck on the highway. Stars were coming out overhead—the same stars her father had watched from this dock, the same stars that had shone down on the *Miss Carolina* the night it burned.

Nora stood on the dock and waited for whatever came next.

* * *

The phone call came at 10:47 PM.

Ward Cranston answered on the second ring. He was in his home office in Wilmington, the windows dark, a tumbler of bourbon on the leather blotter beside a stack of unsigned warrants. He listened without speaking.

"Banks made contact with the Pruitt man," the voice said. "Boat ramp. Fish Factory Road. Twenty minutes ago."

Cranston set down his pen. "They meet?"

"Talking now. Looks cooperative."

Through the phone, Cranston could hear traffic. The caller was mobile, watching from a distance.

"Stay on them. I want to know where Pruitt goes after." He picked up the bourbon, didn't drink. "And find out if Banks has the key."

"Understood."

The line went dead.

Cranston sat for a moment in the silence. Then he opened his desk drawer, pulled out a different phone, and dialed a number he'd memorized thirty years ago. It rang four times before connecting. No greeting. Just the sound of breathing on the other end.

"We have a problem," Cranston said. "The Banks girl is moving."

A pause. Then: "Handle it."

The line went dead.

Cranston finished the bourbon in one swallow and reached for the unsigned warrants.

CHAPTER 3

The Ramp

The boat ramp off Fish Factory Road was a slab of concrete that disappeared into black water. Street lights at the lot's edge, but the trees screened it from the houses across Fish Factory Road. The kind of place fishermen used at dawn and teenagers used after dark, and nobody came to at ten o'clock on a Tuesday night in late August.

Nora parked at the edge of the lot, where the gravel gave way to scrub oak and wax myrtle. She killed the engine but left the keys in the ignition. The folder from the storage unit was on the passenger seat, along with a flashlight and the snub-nosed .38 she kept in her glovebox. She hadn't fired it in three years. Hadn't needed to.

She hoped she wouldn't need to tonight.

The night was thick and close, the air heavy with moisture that would turn to fog by morning. She could hear the water lapping against the concrete, the chirp of tree frogs in the marsh, the distant rumble of a truck on Highway 133. No other cars in the lot. No headlights on the road. She was early. She was always early, a habit from her father, who'd said that the only time you should arrive on time was when you wanted someone to know you were coming.

The ramp was clean concrete, well maintained, the county lot lined with trees that blocked the view from the houses across Fish Factory Road. During the day it was busy—bass fishermen, kayakers, families putting johnboats in Dutchman Creek. At ten o'clock on a Tuesday night, it was empty. The street lights threw circles on the asphalt but the trees held the darkness between them.

Nora had launched her father's boat from this ramp a hundred times as a kid. Had learned to back a trailer here, learned to read the current by the way the water swirled around the concrete, learned to tie a bowline and a cleat hitch while her father smoked cigarettes and told her stories about the old days. Before everything went wrong. Before the fire and the lies and the slow, grinding death of a man who couldn't live with what he'd done.

Ten minutes passed. Fifteen. A raccoon emerged from the brush and waddled across the boat ramp, pausing to look at her truck before disappearing into the darkness on the other side. An owl called from the pines—a great horned, by the sound of it, hunting the marsh edges where the rabbits ran.

At 10:07, headlights appeared on the road.

Nora watched the vehicle approach. Gray Dodge Ram, moving slow, no turn signal. It pulled into the lot and parked thirty feet away, angled so its headlights weren't pointing directly at her. Smart. The engine cut off, but the driver didn't get out. He sat there behind the wheel, watching her the same way she was watching him.

A minute passed. Two.

Nora opened her door and stepped out. The humidity wrapped around her immediately, pressing against her skin, filling her lungs with air that tasted of salt and mud. She left the .38 in the glovebox. If this went wrong, a gun wasn't going to save her anyway.

Grady Pruitt got out of his truck. He was wearing the same canvas jacket he'd worn at the marina, the same boots, the same look of exhausted determination. He walked toward her, stopping about ten feet away. The distance between them felt deliberate.

"Ms. Banks."

"Mr. Pruitt."

"You came alone."

"So did you."

He nodded, a small movement, barely visible in the dark. "You said you wanted to meet. So let's meet."

Nora looked at him. At the scar above his eyebrow, the stubble on his jaw, the way he held himself—weight forward, balanced, ready to move. Careful. Watchful.

"I read the folder," she said. "The one Mary put together."

"And?"

"And you were right. The insurance policy. The bank records. The photographs. The boat."

Grady's expression didn't change, but his shoulders loosened slightly.

"The *Lady Justice*," he said.

"You know about it."

"I've known for six months. Mary found the registration records back in February. Cape Fear

Maritime Holdings. Same shell company that held the insurance policy on the *Miss Carolina.* Same company that made payments to half the county commission. What I didn't have was proof that the boat was there that night. Dutch gave me that."

"Dutch told you about the second boat."

"He told me he saw it. Saw it watching while three people drowned. Saw it turn and head for shore." Grady's voice was flat, controlled. "He didn't tell me who was on it. Said he didn't know. Said your father never told him."

Nora thought about the photograph in Mary's folder. The grainy image of the *Lady Justice*, shot from the deck of the *Miss Carolina.* The shadow at the helm.

"My father didn't tell me either," she said. "Not directly. But he mentioned a name, on his deathbed. Delacroix."

Grady went still. "Delacroix."

"You know it?"

"I've heard it." His voice had changed. Harder now. More careful. "Where did your father hear it?"

"He told Dutch to find a man named Delacroix if anything went wrong. Said Delacroix would know what to do."

"And Dutch never followed up."

"Dutch was scared. My father died. Everyone kept their mouths shut." Nora spread her hands. "Until Mary showed up."

The owl called again, closer this time. Grady glanced toward the sound, then back at her.

"Delacroix isn't a person," he said. "It's a place."

* * *

They moved to his truck, sitting in the cab with the windows down and the dome light off. Grady had a laptop open on the center console, the screen dimmed to preserve their night vision. He pulled up a folder and scrolled through documents.

"I've been at this for two years," he said. "Started right after my mother died. She had a box of my father's things—letters, photographs, his Coast Guard papers. I went through it looking for something to hold onto. He died when I was twelve. I barely knew him."

"What did you find?"

"A letter. Addressed to my mother, but never sent. He wrote it the week before the *Miss Carolina* went down." Grady clicked on a file, and a scanned image appeared on the screen. Handwritten, the ink faded, the paper yellowed. "He knew something was going to happen. Didn't know what exactly."

He was staring at the letter on the screen. When he spoke again, his voice was different. Rougher.

"I was twelve years old when he died. I remember my mother sitting me down in the kitchen—we lived in a little house in Wilmington, nothing fancy—and telling me that there had been an accident. A fire on the boat. She said my father was a hero, that he'd tried to save the others. That's what the Coast Guard told her. That's what everyone told her."

"She believed it?"

"She wanted to believe it. We all did." Grady rubbed his face with his hand. "The insurance company paid out. Not a lot, my father wasn't the captain, but enough to keep us going for a while. My mother went back to work, waitressing at a place on Market Street. I grew up. Went to school, got a job, got married. Tried to forget."

"What changed?"

"My mother got sick. Pancreatic cancer, the kind that doesn't give you time. Six weeks from diagnosis to the end." He closed the laptop halfway, the screen casting a faint glow on his face. "She was in hospice when she told me. Said she'd always known something was wrong about the way my father died. Said she'd been too scared to dig into it. Asked me to find out the truth, if I could."

"And you promised."

"I promised." Grady opened the laptop again and pulled up another file. "She died three days later. I went through her things, found the box with my father's stuff. Found the letter."

Nora leaned closer. The handwriting was cramped, difficult to read in the dim light.

Louise—

If you're reading this, something's gone wrong. I can't tell you everything, but I need you to know that I didn't have a choice. They came to me with an offer. Said if I didn't help, they'd hurt you and the boy. I thought I could play along, find a way out. I was wrong.

There's a man named Russell Banks. He's the captain. He's in the same position I am. If something happens to me, find him. He'll know what to do.

I'm sorry. I'm so sorry.

Tom

Nora read it twice. Her father's name, in a dead man's handwriting. The same coercion, the same threats. They'd been trapped together, her father and Thomas Pruitt, and neither of them had known how to get out.

"He never sent it," Grady said. "My mother found it in his sea bag after the Coast Guard returned his effects. She didn't understand what it meant. Neither did I, until I started digging."

"Your mother never talked about it?"

"My mother spent fifteen years trying to forget. She remarried when I was fifteen—a good man, a high school teacher named David who treated me like his own. We moved to Raleigh, I finished school, got a degree in business. Life moved on." Grady closed the file. "But she kept the letter. Kept it hidden in a shoebox in her closet, along with my father's Coast Guard papers and a photograph of him on the deck of the *Miss Carolina*, taken the week before he died. She never threw any of it away."

"She was waiting for someone to find it."

"Maybe. Or maybe she couldn't let go." Grady shrugged. "When she died, I inherited the box. And I started asking questions."

"Two years of questions."

"Two years. I quit my job—I was a project manager at a construction firm, good salary, benefits, the whole deal. Told my boss I needed time off to deal with family matters. He gave me two weeks. I took two months. When I came back, they'd already replaced me."

"And your wife?"

Grady's hand moved to his other hand, thumbnail picking at the cuticle of his index finger. He didn't notice he was doing it.

"Laura died three years ago. Breast cancer." He said it flat. "She was thirty-eight."

"I'm sorry."

"Everyone is." He let the silence sit for a beat, then turned back to the laptop screen. "After she died, I needed something to be about. Something that had an answer. Her death didn't have that—cells dividing wrong, bad luck. But my father's death had a name attached to it. Someone made a choice. Someone could be held accountable." He scrolled through the files. "I made my choice. I'd make it again."

"Two years. Dozens of FOIA requests. Interviews with anyone who'd talk to me. Insurance records, bank statements, property transfers." He scrolled to another folder, and the laptop screen threw blue light across the cab of the truck. Outside, the boat ramp was empty, the water black beyond the concrete. Nora could hear the river against the pilings of the dock—a slow, rhythmic slap, patient and indifferent. "I traced Cape Fear Maritime Holdings back through three shell companies to a trust registered in the Cayman Islands. Dead end. But the trust made payments to a property management company in Wilmington, and that company managed a piece of land on the Cape Fear River."

"Shell companies." Nora looked at him. "That's tax strategy. Half the boat owners at my marina run their insurance through LLCs."

"This isn't tax strategy."

"How do you know?"

He held up a hand. "I should say: the paper trail is solid through the shell companies. The connection to the property is documented. What I can't prove yet is who controls the trust. That part is inference."

"Inference." She let the word sit. A stranger's truck. A stranger's laptop. A stranger's two-year obsession. She checked the side mirror. Nothing on the road behind them.

He clicked on a map. A satellite image appeared—dense trees, a narrow road that wound through marshland, and a building near the water. The building was large, two stories with a dormer attic, with a wide porch facing the river and a dock jutting out into the current.

"Delacroix," Grady said. "It's an old hunting lodge about fifteen miles upriver from Southport. Built in the 1920s by a lumber baron named Etienne Delacroix, French Canadian, made his money logging cypress down in Louisiana before moving east. The family used it for duck hunting and fishing parties until the 1980s, when the last Delacroix died without heirs. The property sat vacant for a few years, then it was sold to—"

"Cape Fear Maritime Holdings."

"The same shell company that insured the *Miss Carolina*. The same one that owns the *Lady Justice*."

Nora looked at the screen. Trees. A building. A dock. She'd lived in Southport her whole life. There were a hundred places like this along the river—old lodges, fish camps, hunting clubs with gates and no-trespassing signs. Half of them were owned by people in Wilmington or Raleigh who showed up twice a year to shoot ducks. A satellite photo didn't prove anything.

"So someone bought a lodge through a shell company. That's not a crime."

Grady's jaw shifted. He zoomed in on the image. The building was barely visible through the trees: weathered wood, dark windows, a sagging roofline that suggested decades of neglect. "I drove out there six weeks ago. The road is gated—new gate, heavy steel, security cameras mounted on the posts. The property is fenced with razor wire, the kind you see at industrial sites. Not exactly what you'd expect for an abandoned hunting lodge."

"You think someone's using it."

"I know someone's using it. Look at this." He switched to a different image—the same building, but taken from a different angle. In this one, Nora could see lights in the windows. A pickup truck parked near the dock. A man standing on the porch, face turned away from the camera. "I took this with a telephoto lens from across the river. That truck has been there every time I've checked. Same model, same license plate, registered to a company called Coastal Security Solutions."

"Never heard of them."

"Neither had I. But I traced them back through the state business registry. Coastal Security Solutions is a subsidiary of Tidewater Holdings, which is a subsidiary of Cape Fear Maritime Holdings." Grady rubbed his face with both hands, hard. When his hands came down, the lines around his eyes looked deeper in the laptop light. "It's all the same people, Nora. Same companies, same money."

"Or it's one rich guy with a real estate hobby and a security contract." She said it and watched his face. Watched him decide whether to argue.

"You don't believe that."

"I don't know what I believe. I've known you for four hours."

The truck was quiet. The river against the pilings. A truck passed on the road behind them—headlights sweeping across the rearview mirror, gone.

Nora studied the image. Fifteen miles upriver. Close enough to reach by boat in under an hour. Close enough that a man at Delacroix could have watched the *Miss Carolina* burn and been back on shore before anyone started asking questions.

"You think this is where they operated from."

"I think it's where they still operate from." Grady switched to another image—a photograph of the *Lady Justice* tied up at a private dock, its white hull gleaming in the afternoon sun. "I took this three weeks ago. The boat is registered to Cape Fear Maritime, but it's moored at Bald Head. I've been watching it. It makes runs upriver every few days, always at night, always without running lights."

"To Delacroix."

"That's my guess. I've never been able to follow it—they'd spot my boat a mile away. But if the pattern holds, they'll make another run tomorrow night."

Nora looked at him. At the laptop screen, the maps, the documents. Two years of work, laid out in folders and files.

"Why are you showing me this?"

Grady closed the laptop. The cab went dark. The river was still there—she could hear it, smell it, salt and mud. Her eyes adjusted. His face. The boat ramp beyond the windshield, the concrete disappearing into black water.

"Because I can't do this alone," he said. "I've been trying for two years. Every time I get close, something blocks me. Lawyers, county clerks, people who suddenly don't remember what they told me last week. I can't fight that by myself."

"And you think I can help."

"I think you know things I don't. I think you have access I don't. And I think—" He stopped. "I think you're ready to stop protecting a dead man's secrets."

Nora didn't argue.

"There's something else," she said. "Someone called me today. After I left the storage unit. They knew about the package in my boat. They knew about the unit on Fish Factory Road."

Grady's posture changed. "What did they say?"

"Destroy everything. Forget Mary's name. Or end up like my father." She paused. "They gave me twenty-four hours."

"How long ago was that?"

"Six hours. Give or take."

The tree frogs had gone quiet. The only sound was the water against the boat ramp and the distant hum of insects in the marsh.

"Did you recognize the voice?"

"No. Male. Calm. Like he was placing an order at a drive-through." Nora shook her head. "He said Mary wasn't dead. Said whether she stayed that way depended on what I did next."

* * *

They talked for another hour, comparing notes, filling in gaps. Grady had court records Nora had never seen—testimony from the original investigation, statements that had been sealed by order of Judge Ward Cranston. Nora had the folder from Mary's storage unit, the photographs and documents that Mary had spent eight months collecting.

"This is the witness list from the Coast Guard hearing," Grady said, pulling up another document. "Five people testified. Your father, Dutch Petersen, Leo Marks—the three survivors. Plus the insurance adjuster and a marine surveyor who examined what was left of the hull."

"I remember the hearing. I was eighteen. My mother made me stay home."

"The testimony is sealed. Cranston issued the order three days after the hearing concluded. No explanation, no justification. A signature and a stamp." Grady scrolled through the document. "I had to file four separate requests to get even a redacted copy. Half the pages are blacked out."

"What's left?"

* * *

The next night, they took Nora's boat.

She'd told herself it was reconnaissance. That before she committed to anything, before she helped a man she'd known four days go up the Cape Fear River toward a property owned by people who had already threatened her life, she needed to see it herself. Not Grady's telephoto photographs. Not a satellite image on a laptop screen. The actual water. The actual boat.

They launched from the public ramp on Dutchman Creek at ten o'clock, Nora at the helm of her father's old Carolina Skiff—sixteen feet, center console, a thirty-horsepower Yamaha that she'd rebuilt herself the spring after he died. She ran it without lights, the way he'd taught her, watching the channel markers by the phosphorescence the bow wave kicked up in the dark water.

Grady sat in the bow with the binoculars and didn't ask questions about where they were going. She gave him credit for that.

The Cape Fear ran wide and slow here, the current weaker in the summer's low water. The river smelled of salt and mud and the faint petroleum of the shipping lanes, and above them the sky was clear for the first time in days, the stars thick overhead, the Milky Way visible as a pale smear above the tree line. The night was warm and still. Somewhere in the marsh a chuck-will's-widow called—once, twice—and went quiet.

She cut the engine half a mile downriver from Delacroix and let the current carry them.

From the water, the property was barely visible. The live oaks overhung the bank, their branches reaching low over the surface, and behind them the lodge sat dark and high on its bluff, no lights showing. The dock jutted out into the current—she could see its shape against the reflection of the stars on the water. Empty.

"Not here yet," Grady said quietly.

"Not yet."

They drifted. Nora kept them in the current's center, using the paddle to make small corrections, holding them in place without engine noise. Grady had the binoculars up, scanning the dock, the bank, the tree line. A great horned owl called from somewhere in the oaks. Below the hull, the river moved around them, dark and patient, carrying them slowly south.

The *Lady Justice* came upriver at eleven forty-three.

She heard it before she saw it—the low rumble of twin diesels, running slow, no exhaust lights. Then the white hull materializing out of the darkness upstream, forty feet, flybridge, moving without running lights the way Grady had described. It passed maybe seventy yards off their position, close enough that Nora could see the figure at the helm—a man, silhouetted against the faint glow of the instrument panel. He was watching the channel ahead without scanning, without caution. A man who'd made this run before and expected no surprises.

Grady had the binoculars on it. His breathing had gone very controlled.

The *Lady Justice* reduced throttle and turned toward the Delacroix dock. Nora heard the engines drop to idle, heard a line thrown and caught, heard voices—two men, low and businesslike. A flashlight swept the dock once. Then the lights went out.

"Three men at the dock," Grady said quietly. "One came from the house. Two off the boat."

"What are they transferring?"

"Can't tell from here. Too dark. But they're moving something." He lowered the binoculars. "Happens every three to four days, according to my records. Same crew, same boat, same hour."

Nora looked at the dock. At the dark lodge behind it, set back from the river, its windows black. The *Lady Justice* was tied up now, the men moving with practiced efficiency between the boat and the dock. No hurry. No lookouts. They weren't worried about being seen out here.

She understood why. This was fifteen miles from the nearest marina. The channel was too shallow at night for anyone who didn't know it. And the people who fished these waters—the crabbers, the trawlers, the shrimpers who ran before dawn—had been giving this stretch of river a wide berth for a long time. You learned which questions got answered and which ones got you a visit from someone who wasn't police.

She and Grady drifted south with the current, silent, letting the distance grow between them and the dock until they were around the bend and she could start the engine without the sound carrying back. The Yamaha caught on the first pull.

They were a mile downriver before either of them spoke.

"I need to call someone," Grady said. "A source at the U.S. Marshal's office. If Cape Fear Maritime has federal exposure, there might already be a file."

"How long will that take?"

"Two days. Maybe three."

Two or three days meant Mary had two or three more days wherever she was. It meant the voice on the phone might decide her deadline wasn't generous enough. It meant more nights lying awake in her father's house listening to the tide come in.

"Make the call," she said.

She pushed the throttle up and ran south toward the lights of Southport, the bow lifting and the water black on either side, and behind her the river ran on in the dark.

* * *

"Enough to know that someone was lying." He pointed to a section of text. "This is Dutch's testimony. He says the fire started in the engine compartment, spread to the fuel tanks, and the boat went down in less than ten minutes. Standard story—mechanical failure, tragic accident, nobody's fault."

"That's what he told me."

"That's what he told everyone. But look at this." Grady pulled up another document—a technical diagram, covered in handwritten annotations. "This is the marine surveyor's report. He examined the hull fragments that washed up on Oak Island two weeks after the sinking. The burn patterns were wrong for a mechanical engine fire—too clean, too even. And he found chemical residue on two separate fragments. Accelerant. The kind that doesn't come from a fuel line rupture."

"Someone poured it."

"Someone poured it. Which means either the *Miss Carolina* was the unluckiest boat in history, or someone set it up to burn."

Grady closed the file. "The surveyor's report was never made public. It was submitted to the Coast Guard, then sealed along with everything else. I only found it because someone in the Wilmington office made a clerical error and filed a copy in the wrong folder."

Together, they had enough to see the shape of it.

The *Miss Carolina* had been deliberately sunk for insurance money. Russell Banks had been coerced into doing it, threatened with harm to his family. Thomas Pruitt had been coerced the same way. The plan was simple: engine failure, controlled fire, everyone off the boat before it went down. No one was supposed to die.

Something had gone wrong. The fire had spread too fast, the fuel had ignited before the crew was clear, and three people had burned or drowned while the survivors watched from the water.

The men behind it—Cranston and whoever else was involved—had covered it up. Paid off witnesses, buried evidence, made sure the official story was the only story. For fifteen years, it had worked.

Then Mary Galloway had started asking questions. And now she was gone.

"The *Lady Justice* is the key," Grady said. "If we can prove that boat was at the scene, we can tie it to Cape Fear Maritime. And if we can tie Cape Fear Maritime to Cranston—"

"We need someone who saw the boat that night. Someone who can identify it."

"Dutch."

"Dutch is a drunk with a guilty conscience. A defense attorney would tear him apart." Nora thought about the photograph in Mary's folder. "But if there's photographic evidence—if Mary found a way to prove the *Lady Justice* was there—"

"Then we have something." Grady nodded. "Did you bring the folder?"

She reached for the door handle. He didn't move to open his.

"Two years," he said. "Every time I get close, the same wall. Different faces, same wall." He was looking at the water, not at her. "I've been trying to make this mine to finish. It isn't."

She didn't ask what he meant. She understood enough—that the silence ran through her bloodline, not his. That whatever was waiting at the end of this, it had her name on it in ways it never would have his.

She got out.

Nora walked back to her own vehicle. The night air was cooler now, the fog starting to creep in from the water. She could smell the pluff mud, thick and sulfurous, mixing with the salt. The tree frogs had started up again, their chorus filling the darkness.

She opened the passenger door of her truck and reached for the folder.

Something was wrong.

The folder was where she'd left it, on the seat. But it was open. The pages were out of order, some of them bent. Someone had rifled through them quickly. And the photograph of the *Lady Justice*—the one Mary had labeled, the one that showed the boat without lights, the shadow at the helm—was gone.

"Grady."

He was out of his truck in seconds, moving toward her with his hand on his pistol. She held up a hand to stop him.

"Someone was here. The photo of the boat—it's gone."

Grady scanned the darkness around them. The scrub oak, the marsh, the road. The fog was thickening, visibility down to maybe fifty feet. Beyond that, nothing but white and shadow.

"You're sure you had it?"

"I had it. I looked at it before I came here. It was right on top."

Grady turned in a slow circle, his eyes searching the fog. His hand hadn't moved from his pistol. "They were watching us. The whole time. Probably followed you from the storage unit." He looked at her. "They knew what you had. And they took exactly what they needed to take."

She thought about the .38 in her glovebox—useless against someone who could move through fog without making a sound. Thought about the voice on the phone, calm and certain. *You have twenty-four hours*.

Eighteen hours now. Give or take.

Grady was already moving back toward his truck. "Follow me. Don't stop for anything."

They pulled out of the lot, Grady leading, Nora close behind. The road was empty, the fog so thick the headlights barely cut through it. Nora kept checking her mirrors, looking for other headlights, any sign they were being followed.

Nothing. The road behind her was dark.

But someone had been at that boat ramp. Someone who could move through the night without being seen, who could get into her truck without making a sound.

* * *

They reconvened at a 24-hour diner on the edge of Southport, a place that catered to fishermen and truckers. The building was a converted gas station from the 1950s, the old pumps still rusted solid out front. Inside, the booths were cracked vinyl, and the jukebox in the corner hadn't worked since the Reagan administration.

The waitress took their order without looking at them, scratched it on a pad, and shuffled back to the kitchen. The coffee came in mugs thick enough to stop a bullet.

Nora wrapped her hands around her cup and stared out the window. The parking lot was empty except for their trucks and a semi with Georgia plates. The fog had thickened, turning the streetlights into yellow smears.

"They're sending a message," Grady said. "They want us to know they can get to us whenever they want."

"They already made that clear when they called me."

"This is different. They walked right up to your truck while we were sitting fifty feet away, took what they wanted, and vanished." He shook his head. "These aren't amateurs."

The waitress came back with Grady's eggs. She set the plate down hard enough to rattle the silverware, refilled their coffee without being asked, and disappeared again. The eggs were overcooked, the toast cold.

Grady pushed the food around his plate. "I keep thinking about what they took. Why that photograph specifically."

"It was the strongest piece of evidence Mary had. A direct link between the *Lady Justice* and the sinking."

"But they left everything else. The insurance documents, the bank records, the property transfers. All of that is still in your folder." He looked up at her. "Why take one photograph and leave the rest?"

Nora hadn't thought about that. She'd been too shaken by someone reaching into her truck without her knowing.

"Maybe they didn't have time to take everything."

"Or maybe they didn't need to." Grady pushed his plate away. "Think about it. The documents prove that Cape Fear Maritime Holdings insured the boat, owned the *Lady Justice*, and made payments to county officials. That's enough to raise questions, but it's not enough to convict anyone. It's circumstantial."

"The photograph was direct evidence."

"The photograph placed the *Lady Justice* at the scene of the crime. It proved that whoever owned that boat was watching while three people died." He leaned forward. "Without the photograph, we have a theory. With it, we had proof."

The surface of her coffee was dark and still, reflecting the fluorescent lights overhead.

"Mary would have made copies," she said. "She was too careful not to."

"Then we need to find them. Her apartment, her computer, wherever she kept her backups." Grady pulled out his phone and scrolled through his contacts. "I have a friend in Raleigh who does digital forensics. If Mary uploaded anything to the cloud, he might be able to find it."

"That could take weeks."

"We don't have weeks. We have—" He checked his watch. "Seventeen hours, give or take. Until your deadline runs out."

The deadline. Nora had almost forgotten. Twenty-four hours to destroy the evidence and walk away. Seventeen hours now. By tomorrow evening, whoever had called her would know she wasn't going to cooperate.

"We need to move faster," Grady said. "The *Lady Justice* makes a run tomorrow night. If we can follow it to Delacroix, get photographs, maybe get close enough to see who's on board—"

"That's suicide. You said yourself they'd spot your boat a mile away."

"I wasn't planning to use my boat."

Nora looked at him. He was watching her with an expression she couldn't read.

"You want to use mine."

"You're the harbormaster. You have a legitimate reason to be on the water at night. Checking channel markers, responding to calls—whatever cover story you want." He leaned forward. "And you know these waters better than anyone. You grew up here. You know every shortcut, every creek, every place to hide."

"I know every way to get killed, too."

"Then help me not get killed."

He'd been at this for two years. Had sacrificed his job, his marriage, God knew what else. And now he was asking her to risk everything she had left.

She thought about Mary, who'd done the same thing and was now missing.

She thought about Dutch, who was going to talk whether she helped him or not.

She thought about her father, dying in that hospice bed, his hand like paper in hers.

Protect this family, Nora. Whatever it takes.

Mary was family too.

"Tomorrow night," she said. "We'll take the Whaler. But if things go wrong—if they spot us, if we get separated—you're on your own."

"Understood."

"And we need backup. Someone who knows we're going, someone who can call for help if we don't come back."

"Who do you have in mind?"

Nora thought about Marla, who knew everything that happened in this town. Thought about Dutch, too scared and fragile to trust with something like this.

"Marla Hutchins," she said. "She's worked the marina desk for forty years. If anyone knows who's been running these boats in and out of Southport, it's her."

"Can she be trusted?"

"I don't know." Nora met his eyes.

Grady pulled a worn leather notebook from his jacket pocket and slid it across the table.

"This is everything I have. Two years of research—names, dates, account numbers. If something happens to me tomorrow night, I want someone else to have it."

Nora looked at the notebook. The leather was cracked and stained, the pages swollen from years of handling.

"You're giving this to me."

"I'm trusting you with it." He held her gaze. "That's different."

She took the notebook. It was heavier than she expected.

* * *

The fog was thick by the time they left the diner, rolling in from the river in waves that swallowed the streetlights. The air was wet and cold, a sharp contrast to the heat of the day, and Nora could feel the moisture beading on her skin.

Grady walked her to her truck, his boots crunching on the gravel. "Get some sleep," he said. "Tomorrow's going to be long."

"I haven't slept in three days."

"Then do whatever you have to do." He stopped by her driver's side door. "We get one shot at this. If we blow it, they'll know we're coming, and everything disappears. Evidence, witnesses, all of it."

"I know."

"Do you?" He was looking at her steadily, the sympathy plain on his face. "You've been living with this for fifteen years. Telling yourself it was the only way. But it's not, Nora."

She said nothing. There wasn't anything to say that wouldn't sound like an excuse.

"Eight o'clock tomorrow morning. Meet me at the marina. We'll go over the plan, check the boat, make sure we're ready. And talk to Marla. We need someone who knows what we're doing. Someone who can raise the alarm if we don't come back."

"And if Marla can't be trusted?"

"Then we're already dead." He said it simply, without drama. "At this point, we either trust someone or we go it alone. And alone isn't working."

He walked back to his truck, climbed in, started the engine. The headlights cut through the fog, creating a tunnel of yellow light that seemed to go nowhere. He backed out of the lot and pulled onto the road, and then the fog swallowed him whole.

Nora stood in the parking lot, listening to the engine fade into silence. The notebook was in her hand, the leather warm from Grady's pocket. Two years of work. Two years of sacrifice. All of it resting in her palm.

She got in her truck and drove home.

The fog had closed everything down to the cone of her headlights and the road immediately ahead.

She drove through Southport the way she'd driven it a thousand times—the turn past the Methodist church, the straight shot down Moore Street, the right onto Yacht Basin, the harbor a darkness she could smell but not see through the white. The bar at Provision Company had closed already, the waterfront empty except for a security light at the fuel dock and the distant blink of the buoy at the channel mouth. At two in the morning, even in

August, this town went to sleep. Had always gone to sleep. Had always trusted that what was buried would stay buried.

The notebook was on the passenger seat. She kept glancing at it. Cracked leather, pages swollen from years of handling. Two years of a man's life—his marriage, his job, his whole settled existence—reduced to something that fit in a jacket pocket.

She thought about what Grady had said. You've been living with this for fifteen years. Telling yourself it was the only way.

She had been. She'd told herself the story so many times it had stopped feeling like a lie. Her father had made a mistake under duress. Three people died. He had spent the rest of his life paying for it. The men who'd coerced him were powerful, entrenched, connected to every institution in the county. Coming forward wouldn't bring anyone back. It would only destroy what was left.

That's what she'd told herself.

But Mary had been ten years old when her grandmother went to the bottom of the Cape Fear. She'd grown up without that woman. Had grown up with a mother who'd been told it was an accident, a tragedy, nobody's fault. Had spent years not knowing and then more years finding out, and had come to Southport anyway, alone, and had spent eight months pulling thread after thread until someone put her in a van.

And Nora had stood in her office that afternoon in July and thought she shouldn't be here and given her the address for Provision Company anyway, because she hadn't been able to make herself say go home, this town will hurt you.

Because she'd wanted to be found.

That was the thing she hadn't admitted until right now, driving through fog at two in the morning with Grady Pruitt's notebook on the seat beside her. She'd been waiting fifteen years. Waiting for someone to come to town and ask the right questions. Waiting for someone to give her a reason to stop carrying it alone.

Mary had come. Grady had come. Dutch was ready to break. Everything was moving whether she was part of it or not.

The road turned off 133 and ran south along the marsh, the headlights catching the tops of the spartina in the fog, the whole wet world pressing in on both sides. She could hear the tide, that soft persistent push of water against the bank, and she rolled the window down despite the fog and let it in—the smell of pluff mud and salt air and the faint petroleum of the boats, the smell that had been underneath every moment of her life in this place, the smell she sometimes thought she'd carry out of here in her bones.

She turned into her driveway. The gravel was wet and quiet under the tires.

Her headlights swept the porch and then the house and she saw the dark windows and her hand went to the door handle before the engine was off.

* * *

She'd left a light on in the kitchen—she was certain of it. The bulb over the sink, the one she always left burning when she knew she'd be coming home late. But the windows were black, the porch empty, the whole place looking abandoned.

She sat in the truck, engine running, and stared at the house.

Could be a blown fuse. Could be the bulb burned out. Could be the power company finally cutting off the electricity she'd been three weeks late paying. Could be nothing.

Could be someone waiting inside.

She reached into the glovebox and took out the .38. Checked the cylinder—six rounds, all in place. She hadn't fired the gun in three years, but she'd cleaned it last month. Habit from her father, who'd cleaned his guns every Sunday whether he'd used them or not.

Nora got out and walked toward the house. The gravel crunched under her boots, loud in the fog-muffled silence. The marsh was invisible beyond the dock, the spartina hidden by white, the only sound the slow drip of water condensing on the live oak branches overhead.

She climbed the porch steps. The third step creaked, the one she kept meaning to fix, the one her father had promised to fix a dozen times before he got sick. The screen door was closed but not latched. She always latched it. Had latched it this morning before she left.

The front door was unlocked.

She pushed it open with her left hand, the .38 raised in her right, and stepped inside. The hallway was dark. The kitchen darker. The smell of the house was wrong—not the usual must of old wood and salt air, but something sharper. Sweat. Adrenaline. Someone had been here recently. Someone might still be here.

She moved down the hallway, her back to the wall, her eyes adjusting to the darkness. The living room was ahead, the door half-open. She could see the edge of her father's old armchair, the one he'd sat in every night to watch the news and drink his bourbon. The one she'd kept after he died, even though it was worn and stained and she should have thrown it out years ago.

The light came on.

Nora swung the gun toward the switch, finger tightening on the trigger.

"Easy." A woman's voice. Familiar. "It's me."

Mary Galloway was sitting in the armchair, her face pale and gaunt, her hair shorter than Nora remembered, hacked off unevenly. Her left arm was in a makeshift sling, the fabric stained with something dark. Her eyes were sunken and ringed with bruises.

She looked at Nora. At the gun. At the house around them.

"Nice armchair," she said. "Smells like bourbon and regret. I feel right at home."

She lowered the .38.

"Close the door," Mary said. Her voice was hoarse, cracked. "We need to talk."

CHAPTER 4

The Safehouse

Nine Days Before Present Day

The bag smelled like motor oil and someone else's sweat.

Mary counted seconds after they put it over her head. An old habit from her research days—when you can't see, you measure time. She'd been outside her apartment, phone still warm in her hand from the voicemail she'd left Grady, when the van door slid open. Two men. Big hands, no words. One grabbed her arms, the other her legs, and she was inside the van before she could scream.

She got to forty-seven before the van stopped.

They carried her through what sounded like woods—branches snapping underfoot, ground uneven beneath their boots—and down a set of stairs. Wooden stairs first, then concrete. When they pulled the bag off, she was in a room with no windows. Concrete walls, concrete floor, a cot with a thin mattress, a plastic bucket in the corner. A single lightbulb behind a wire cage in the ceiling. The door was steel, new, bolted into an old wooden frame. The house around it was falling apart—she could hear the wind moving through gaps in the siding, could smell mildew and rot—but that door was professional.

They'd done this before.

She could hear boat traffic somewhere above and to the east. Could smell the river through the walls—that brackish tidal smell, mud and salt. Somewhere upriver, she thought. Somewhere along the Cape Fear, in one of the dozens of old houses that sat back from the water in the pines, the kind nobody visited and nobody missed.

The first day was questions. A voice on the other side of the steel door—calm, educated, patient. She never saw his face. He asked about her research. Where had she found the documents? Who had she shown them to? Where were the copies?

Mary sat on the cot with her back against the wall and said nothing.

The voice asked the same questions again. And again. Hours passed, or what felt like hours—the lightbulb never changed, the room never changed, and without her phone she had no way to mark time except by the meals they slid through a slot in the door. Bread. Water. A bruised apple.

She didn't eat. Couldn't make herself.

The second day, the steel door opened.

The man who walked in was older, maybe sixty. Gray hair cropped short, calm eyes behind wire-rimmed glasses, the build of someone who'd stayed fit out of discipline rather than vanity. He wore a button-down shirt, no tie, sleeves rolled to the elbows. He carried a folding chair under one arm and a small leather case in his other hand.

He set the chair down across from her cot, sat, and crossed his legs.

"My name isn't important," he said. His voice was polite, almost warm. The voice of a man who might sell you insurance or teach your Sunday school class. "I'm a consultant. I specialize in extracting information from difficult subjects."

Mary pressed her back harder against the wall.

"I want you to understand something." He set the leather case on his knee and unzipped it slowly. Inside, there were tools—pliers, a small hammer, zip ties, things she couldn't name and didn't want to. He didn't take any of them out. He just wanted her to see them. "I don't enjoy this work. Some people in my line do, and I find that distasteful. I'm a professional. I want to get the information I need and leave. How long that takes is entirely up to you."

"I don't know what you're talking about."

"You do." He smiled. It was a kind smile. That was the worst part. "You've spent eight months pulling documents from county records, photographing files in the Brunswick County clerk's office, cross-referencing property deeds with corporate filings. You found the connection between Cape Fear Maritime Holdings and Judge Ward Cranston. You found the insurance records from the *Miss Carolina*. And three days ago, you found something else. Something that scared you enough to call a man named Grady Pruitt and leave a voicemail at two in the morning."

He knew everything.

"Where are the copies?" he asked.

Mary stayed quiet.

He had expected that. He reached forward and took her left hand. His grip was gentle, almost tender.

Then he bent her index finger backward until she heard it pop.

The pain was white and total. She screamed—couldn't help it, the sound torn out of her before she could clamp her jaw shut. He held the finger there, bent at an angle fingers don't go, and waited.

"Where are the copies?"

She shook her head. Tears ran down her face and she couldn't speak even if she'd wanted to.

He let go. The relief was so sudden it was almost worse—her whole body shuddered, and she curled forward over her hand, cradling it against her chest.

"We have time," he said. "I cleared my whole day."

He moved to the next finger.

By the time he'd worked through her left hand, Mary's legs were kicking against the cot frame in short, involuntary spasms. Her fingers were swollen, two of them bent wrong, the pain a constant shriek underneath everything. She'd stopped screaming. Didn't have the air for it anymore.

"You're tougher than I expected," he said. He sounded genuinely impressed. "Most people give me what I want after the second finger. I respect that." He tilted his head. "But I should tell you—fingers are where I start. Not where I finish."

He took her right arm. Gripped the wrist with one hand and the shoulder with the other. She knew what was coming and tried to pull away, but he was stronger and she was already broken in too many places.

He dislocated her shoulder with a single, practiced motion.

A wet pop, then the grinding of bone. The pain was different from her fingers—deeper, more complete, the kind that turned the world gray at the edges.

He put it back. Waited thirty seconds. Dislocated it again.

By the fourth time, she started talking.

Not everything. Not the storage unit, not the flash drive, not all three locations where she'd hidden copies. She gave him pieces—enough to make him think she was breaking, not enough to give up what mattered. The documents in the county clerk's office. The photographs she'd taken of Cranston's property records. Names he probably already knew.

He listened. Nodded. Wrote things down in a small notebook with neat handwriting.

"That's a good start," he said. "We'll continue tomorrow."

He left. The steel door closed. The bolt shot home.

Mary lay on the cot, her shoulder a fire that wouldn't go out, her fingers throbbing in time with her heartbeat, and looking at the wire cage around the lightbulb. The concrete ceiling was water-stained, the marks spreading outward from a crack in one corner.

She was going to die here. She knew that. Whether she talked or not, whether she gave them everything or nothing, the ending was the same. People who built rooms like this, who hired men like this—they didn't let you walk away after.

But not yet. Not today.

She reached down with her right hand and felt along the underside of the cot frame. The welds were old, the metal rusted in the damp. One of the crossbars had a seam where the spot weld had started to fail. She worked at it with her fingers—the only hand she had, the shoulder above it grinding with every movement, every degree of rotation a separate negotiation with the pain. She couldn't grip hard. Couldn't torque. Could only push and pull in the narrow range of motion the shoulder allowed, millimeter by millimeter. The sweat ran into her eyes. She blinked it away. When the shoulder caught wrong she bit down on her lip until she tasted blood, held still, breathed through it, and started again. She did not make a sound. She wasn't going to give them a sound.

Her broken fingers were useless. Her good arm wasn't good. But the seam had moved a fraction of an inch.

* * *

The consultant came back on the third day. More questions, more pressure—the shoulder again, and this time her ribs, a knee driven into her side while he asked the same questions in the same polite voice. She gave him more pieces, enough to keep him working, never the whole picture.

Then his phone rang.

He stepped outside the door. She could hear his voice—low, clipped, irritated. Something had come up that required him elsewhere.

When he came back in, he was already putting on his jacket.

"I have to leave for a few hours," he said. "We'll pick this up when I return."

The steel door closed. She heard voices—the consultant giving instructions to someone. A single guard. Young, from the sound of his voice. She heard the consultant's car start, heard it pull away on a gravel road, heard the engine fade to nothing.

Mary went to work on the crossbar.

It took two hours. The metal cut her right hand, and the rust worked into the wounds, but she didn't stop. When the bar finally came free—eighteen inches of steel, thin but solid—she slid it under the mattress and lay back on the cot and waited.

The guard opened the door at what she guessed was evening. He was young—mid-twenties, thick neck, the body of someone who spent too much time in a gym and not enough time thinking. He carried a bottle of water in one hand and a paper plate with bread in the other. No weapon drawn. He looked at her without fear.

She was curled on the cot, facing the wall, her body slack. Broken. Done. That's what he saw.

He set the water on the floor and bent to put the plate beside it.

Mary came off the cot in one motion. The crossbar caught him across the throat—not a swing, a thrust, the end of the bar driven into his Adam's apple. He went down with both hands at his neck, eyes wide, legs kicking against the concrete.

She took his keys. His phone. Stepped over him and through the steel door.

The house was old, sagging, surrounded by loblolly pines and darkness. She could smell the river close. She didn't know where she was and didn't have time to figure it out.

She ran.

* * *

They caught her again on the seventh day.

She'd been hiding in tobacco barns and hunting camp outbuildings, eating what she could find, moving at night, sleeping in daylight in whatever cover presented itself. Her arm was useless. She'd been sleeping in the loft of a tobacco barn off Highway 87 when she heard the van on the gravel below. Someone had seen her the night before—at the gas station, maybe, or on the road—and made a call. That was the thing about this county. Someone was always watching. Someone was always loyal to the wrong people.

This time they didn't take her to the house. They took her to a boat.

She could feel it—the motion of the deck beneath her, the rumble of diesel engines, the slap of water against the hull. Not a fishing boat. Something bigger, cleaner, the kind of boat that cost money. They zip-tied her wrists and ankles and left her in a cabin below deck. The porthole was a little larger than a dinner plate, bolted shut. Through the glass she could see fog and darkness, the waterline lapping a foot below the frame. Close. Too close for comfort if the boat took on any kind of chop.

She heard them talking above her. Voices she didn't recognize, except one—the consultant was back. She heard the word *Delacroix*. She heard someone say *move her upriver at first light*.

Then the engines cut. The boat settled into a slow rock, anchor chain rattling through the hawsehole. Whatever they were waiting for—a tide, a signal, instructions from someone higher up—they weren't in a hurry.

They were going to kill her. Wherever Delacroix was, whatever was upriver, she wasn't coming back from it.

The zip ties were the cheap kind—smooth plastic, no teeth on the locking tab. She worked at them for hours, twisting her wrists back and forth, the plastic cutting deeper each time, the skin opening in thin lines that stung first and then went past stinging into something that didn't have a name. The blood helped—slicked the plastic enough that she could feel the tie shift a fraction. She worked that fraction. Her shoulder screamed with every rotation of her wrists, the joint grinding, the dislocated socket a white-hot pressure that radiated down her arm and up into her neck. More than once she stopped and pressed her forehead to the cot frame and breathed through her teeth until the world came back. Then she started again. She had learned in that room to put pain in a place—a closed door at the back of her mind, something she could acknowledge without letting it run her. The door kept wanting to blow open. She kept pushing it shut.

The first tie gave way just after midnight. She worked her free hand around to the others. She could hear snoring from the cabin above.

The porthole was secured with wing nuts, four of them, rusted from salt air. She worked them with her fingers—slow, agonizing, the broken ones on her left hand useless, her right doing everything. Two came free. The third wouldn't move. She used her shoe, tapping the wing nut in the right direction until it broke loose. The fourth came free with her palm flat against it, her whole body leaning into it.

The porthole was barely wide enough for her shoulders. She went headfirst, and her good shoulder caught on the frame—too tight, not going to fit. She twisted, leading with the bad side, the shoulder that still wasn't set right, that hung loose and wrong in ways shoulders shouldn't. The joint ground against itself as she forced her body through the opening. She bit down on her own forearm to keep from screaming. The pain whited out her vision, but the shoulder compressed, folded, gave her the inches she needed.

Something in the metal frame caught her forearm as she went through. She felt it bite—a hot line from elbow to wrist—but she was already falling, already committed, and then she was through and dropping.

She hit the Cape Fear River.

The cold was total. Not cold the way a swimming pool is cold, or the way the Outer Banks surf is cold in April—this was a different thing entirely, a physical fact that landed on her like a wall and took everything. The water closed over her head and her body forgot what it was supposed to do. Her lungs seized. Her muscles locked. The arm wound—open, raw, the porthole frame having ripped open the length of her forearm—sent a white scream up through her shoulder and into her teeth. She sank for several seconds, the dark water pressing in from all sides, the cold already working past her skin and into the muscle, into the bone, her thoughts beginning to slow and flatten at the edges the way they did when the consultant had kept her awake for two days. Some older part of her brain sent the signal. Her legs kicked. She came up gasping.

She had maybe thirty minutes before the cold made the decision for her.

The current had her immediately.

She didn't fight it. Couldn't, with one arm, with the shoulder grinding every time she moved—and fighting the Cape Fear at night in November with a dislocated joint wasn't surviving, it was dying in a different direction. She let the water take her. Let herself be moved. Every yard of river between her and that boat was a yard closer to alive.

For a while she could hear the boat behind her. The anchor chain. The low hum of the generator running below decks. A door slamming—someone checking the porthole, maybe, or just going below for another beer. The sound faded as the current pulled her around a bend, and then there was only the water and the dark and the sound of her own breathing, ragged and too loud.

The river was wide here. She couldn't see either bank—couldn't see anything at all. The sky above was clouded over, no moon, no stars, just a uniform darkness that made it impossible to tell where the water ended and the air began. She kept her face tilted up, watching for the horizon to differentiate itself, watching for the silhouette of a tree or a dock or anything that would tell her where she was.

Nothing. Just the dark and the current and the cold that was working its way deeper with every passing minute.

Her left arm wasn't working. She'd known that going through the porthole, had planned for it—lead with the bad side, compress the joint, don't scream. She hadn't screamed. She'd bitten through her own lip instead, tasted blood all the way down, but she hadn't made a sound and that was what mattered. Now the arm hung at her side, moving with the current, useless. The shoulder felt wrong in a way she couldn't fully process—a grinding looseness, bone seated wrong against bone, pain so constant she'd stopped feeling it.

She kicked. Kept her face above water. Tried to think.

She'd been on the Cape Fear once before, on a kayak tour out of Southport, two summers ago, before she'd started following the thread that had led to the storage unit and the eight months of research and this. The guide had told them that the Cape Fear drained forty-four percent of North Carolina's land area, that it ran 202 miles from its headwaters to the sea, that it was one of the few rivers on the East Coast that ran relatively straight—no major meanders, just that persistent southerly push toward the Atlantic. She'd thought that was interesting, then. A historical footnote. Now she was in it, in the dark, in November, with one functioning arm and no idea how far the nearest bank was.

The cold kept going deeper. It had moved through her skin, through her muscles, and was now working on her core—she could feel her thinking getting slow and soft at the edges, the way it had felt on the third night in the room when the consultant had been asking the same questions and she'd been trying to keep track of what she'd given him and what she'd held back. She'd learned in that room to recognize the signs of her mind trying to quit. To notice when the thoughts started getting heavy, to force them to move.

Iris Galloway, she thought. Your grandmother's name was Iris Galloway. She worked on Russell Banks's boat. She had a daughter named Louise and a granddaughter who is currently drowning in the Cape Fear River. Iris Galloway went to work one morning and didn't come home because a man she trusted had made a deal with men he shouldn't have trusted, and the river she's floating in right now covered those men's tracks for fifteen years. So swim.

She swam. Or something like it—a one-armed crawl, more rolling than stroking, the kick doing most of the work. She couldn't sustain it. The shoulder wouldn't let her do anything that rotated the left side of her body, and every kick sent vibration up through her spine and into the joint. But she could do thirty seconds of it, rest, do thirty more.

Thirty on, thirty off. Thirty on, thirty off.

She started counting to keep her mind working. Had learned that in the room too—when you can't see, you measure time. She'd gotten to forty-seven when the van stopped. She'd counted 847 seconds before the consultant came back on the third day. She counted now, and the counting kept the numbers moving through her head, and the numbers kept her thinking, and the thinking kept her swimming.

The current was taking her south and east, she thought. She had no way to confirm it—no stars, no landmarks—but the Cape Fear ran southeast toward the mouth, and the guide had said the current ran at two to four knots in normal conditions. She'd been in the water maybe twenty minutes. Half a mile, maybe more if the current was running strong from the rain.

Something brushed her leg.

She thrashed, pure instinct, the bad shoulder lighting up with a full-voltage shock that took her breath. Not a hand—too soft, too yielding. Marsh grass, or a floating branch, or one of the jellyfish that clustered in the river mouth this time of year. She held still and let herself be carried, waiting to see if it came again.

It didn't.

After a while she heard the marsh.

Not the river—she'd been hearing the river this whole time, the slip and surge of moving water. This was different. Spartina moving in a breeze she couldn't feel from the surface. The high electric sound of insects. A great blue heron somewhere close, its alarm call cutting through the dark once and then going silent. The marsh smell was different from the river smell—wetter, more sulfurous, the rot of organic material trapped in the mud and slowly becoming part of the river.

She was near a bank.

She turned toward the sound and swam. It took longer than she expected—the bank kept not materializing, the marsh sounds staying close but the ground staying absent beneath her feet. She was about to turn back to the current when her knee hit something and she pitched forward and her good hand found mud.

She stayed there for a while, half in and half out of the water, her face against the mud, the cold river running over her legs. The mud smelled like rot and iron, and it was warm compared to the water—or not warm exactly, but less cold, the cold of earth instead of the cold of moving water, and the difference was enough.

She pulled herself forward. Got her knees under her. Got her one working arm under her. The mud sucked at her hands and knees, the deep pluff mud of a tidal flat, the kind that went down three feet before it hit anything solid. She'd read about people getting stuck in it. Had thought that was hyperbole.

It wasn't.

Every time she moved a hand forward, the arm sank to the elbow before finding purchase. The mud closed around her wrist and held, and pulling free made a sound like a boot being pried loose, and she was burning calories she didn't have on a process that wasn't getting her anywhere.

She stopped. Breathed. Looked up.

The clouds had thinned slightly to the south. There was no moon, but the sky was lighter in that direction—the glow of Wilmington, or Southport, or some combination of civilization that existed to the south of wherever she was. She turned so the light was ahead of her and began to move, not forward on her hands and knees, but sideways, working along the edge of the mud flat where the ground was firmer, where the spartina roots gave her something to grab.

It took twenty minutes to travel maybe a hundred yards. When the mud finally firmed into solid ground, she stopped and lay flat on her back and looked at the sky and did an inventory.

Right shoulder: unusable. Left arm: seeping from the porthole gash, nothing on it, the river water having done whatever the river water does. Left hand: three fingers broken, swollen to twice their size, useless. Right hand: functional, blistered from the zip ties and the seawater, but functional. Legs: working, cold, shaking.

Core temperature: falling. She could feel it in the way her thoughts kept wanting to simplify, to reduce themselves to the immediate and let the larger picture go. She recognized the feeling from the third night in the room. She pushed back against it.

Iris Galloway, she thought again. Thomas Pruitt. Elena Rodriguez. Three people at the bottom of the Cape Fear because a man called Pilot decided the math was acceptable. Those three people need a witness. Get up.

She got up.

The sandbar extended maybe forty yards, a tongue of silt and shell deposited by the current, the spartina already colonizing its upriver end. Beyond it, inland, she could see the dark shapes of loblolly pines against the slightly lighter sky. A barn maybe, or a house—some human structure, set back from the water.

She started walking toward the pines. Her boots were gone—left on the boat, or lost in the river. She felt every shell and broken root through her socks, but she kept her weight forward and kept moving and did not stop to count the things she didn't have.

The pine needles were soft underfoot when she reached them. The trees cut the wind, and the temperature dropped another two degrees in their shadow, but she was out of the water and on solid ground and that was enough for now.

She found the barn a quarter mile inland.

The arm was bleeding badly—she could feel it with every step, the warmth running down to her fingers despite the cold water, that had slowed it some. She made the hayloft on will alone, climbing with her one good hand and her teeth and her knees, and collapsed into the hay. The bleeding. She needed to deal with the bleeding. But the rafters went soft above her and then there was nothing.

Dawn came gray through the gaps in the siding.

She found a feed sack on a nail by the barn door. Tore a strip from it with her teeth and her one working hand and bound the wound as tight as she could manage. It wasn't enough. It would have to be.

Then she went looking for clothes.

She stole a man's canvas jacket off a line and a pair of boots two sizes too big from a porch. Back in the barn she bound the wound tighter with what was left of the feed sack, pressing the cloth hard against the worst of it.

She hitched a ride with a trucker heading south on 87. He took one look at her and didn't ask questions.

Three days she hid. Moving between barns and abandoned buildings, stealing food from gardens and gas station dumpsters. Three days of trying to figure out who she could trust, who wasn't already bought or scared or compromised. She started moving south on the fourth day, making two miles before her arm forced her to stop. Two miles the next day. Less the day after that.

She kept coming back to the same name.

* * *

"How did you get in?"

Nora stood in the doorway of the living room, the .38 still in her hand, her heart hammering against her ribs. Mary looked like a different person from the woman who'd pressed a storage unit key into her hand outside Fishy Fishy. That woman had been confident, sharp-eyed, moving with purpose. This woman was hollowed out. The bones of her face stood out under skin that had gone gray and papery. Her lips were cracked. Her right hand—the good one—lay still in her lap, but the fingers twitched every few seconds.

"Back door. You left it unlocked." Mary shifted in the armchair, her face tight as her injured arm moved.

"You've been gone for ten days. Everyone thinks you're dead."

"I almost was."

Nora set the .38 on the side table. She crossed to the kitchen, filled a glass with water from the tap, and brought it back to Mary. Water slopped over the rim when Mary took it.

"Drink slow. You'll make yourself sick."

Mary took a sip. Then another. Her eyes closed.

"I thought I was going to die in that room," she said quietly. She opened her eyes. "They knew everything, Nora. They knew about the storage unit, about Grady, about you. They knew I'd been to see Dutch."

"How?"

"I don't know. Someone's been watching. Someone's been listening." Mary set the glass down on the side table. "They wanted the photograph. The one of the boat. I told them I'd hidden it somewhere they'd never find it. That's the only reason I'm still alive."

Nora thought about the photograph that had been stolen from her truck earlier tonight. The one Mary had hidden. The one that was now in the hands of whoever had taken her.

"They found it," Nora said. "Tonight. Someone took it from my truck while I was meeting with Grady."

What little color Mary had in her face drained away, leaving her waxy. Her right arm crossed her body, fingers gripping her own elbow.

"Then they don't need me anymore."

"They let you go?"

"I escaped. They moved me to a boat. I heard them talking about some place called Delacroix—said they were taking me upriver at first light. I got my hands free and went through a porthole into the river."

"The *Lady Justice*?"

"Maybe. I couldn't see—they kept me blindfolded most of the time. But it was big. Diesel engines. It wasn't a fishing boat."

"Delacroix is a hunting lodge upriver. Cape Fear Maritime Holdings bought it in '85. Grady found it in the property records—thinks it's their base of operations." Nora paused. "We were going to follow the *Lady Justice* there tomorrow night."

"Don't." The word came out sharp. Mary leaned forward in the chair, and Nora could see the effort it cost her. "That's where they were taking me to kill me, Nora. I heard them talking—they've done it before. People go up that river and don't come back. Whatever you're planning, whatever Grady thinks he's going to find there, it's not worth dying for."

"Three people died on that boat. Your grandmother. Grady's father—"

"And your father spent five years dying of guilt over it. I know." Mary's voice was flat. "I've been living with this longer than you have. But I didn't spend eight months building this case and ten days being tortured to watch you throw it away walking into their front door."

Nora didn't argue. She looked at her cousin—the makeshift sling, the porthole wound binding visible at her wrist, the bruises yellowing along her jaw.

"What do you want to do?"

Mary reached into the pocket of the canvas jacket—too big for her, a stranger's coat—and pulled out a USB drive. Small, black, unremarkable. The plastic casing was scratched and water-stained from the river, but intact.

"Everything I found. Scanned documents, photographs, recorded conversations. I made copies and hid them in three different places." She held it out. "This is the last one."

Nora looked at the drive. Such a small thing to have caused so much trouble.

"What's on it?"

"Proof that the *Miss Carolina* was deliberately sunk. Proof that Ward Cranston orchestrated the cover-up." Mary paused, pressing the heel of her palm against her forehead. "And there's a name. Someone above Cranston, someone who's been pulling strings in this county for decades." Her hand dropped. "It's all on the drive. I wrote everything down because I knew—the fever, the pills—I knew I'd lose track of it."

"What name?"

"Pilot." Mary's eyes were unfocused, the word coming slow. "They call him Pilot. I found references going back forty years, buried in the property records, the shell company filings. Cranston reports to him. The county commission, the state reps who've been blocking investigations—they all report to someone called Pilot."

"How does it work?"

"Layers. Cranston handles the county. Dutch—harbor. Bennett—street level." She swallowed, her voice fading. "All reporting up. None of them know... the whole thing. Bottom level—expendable. No one talks."

"Who is he?"

"I don't know. I was getting close when they grabbed me." She gestured weakly at the drive. "It's on there. Everything I had. Property holdings, financial records, the pattern of how he moves money through the system. If we can get it to someone outside the county—FBI, state attorney general, a reporter who isn't on the payroll—"

"Then what?"

"Then we bring them down. All of them."

Nora took the drive. It was warm from Mary's pocket, the plastic smooth against her fingers.

"And if we can't?"

Mary's eyes had closed, her head tipping back against the chair.

"Mary."

"I'm awake." But she didn't open her eyes. "We have until morning. Maybe less. When they figure out I'm gone, the first place they'll look is here."

Nora got up and went to the window. She pulled the curtain aside an inch and looked out at the driveway, the road beyond, the darkness pressing in from all sides. No headlights. No movement.

"Grady Pruitt," she said. "You called him before they grabbed you."

"I left him a voicemail. Told him I'd found something, that I knew who was on the second boat." Mary's voice was thick. "I was supposed to meet him the next morning. I never made it."

"He's here. In Southport. He's been looking for you."

"I figured he'd come. After the voicemail." Mary's words were slurring, the painkillers or the exhaustion or both. "Couldn't risk reaching out. Couldn't risk leading them to him."

"He's got a motel room. The Pine Grove, out on 17. He said I could come there if I needed somewhere safe."

"You trust him?"

Nora considered the question. She thought about Grady's gray eyes, his worn notebook, the letter from his dead father.

"He's been at this longer than either of us. And he's got as much to lose."

"His father died on that boat." Mary nodded slowly, her eyes still closed. "He remembers. Actual memories of the man they killed. That's different from growing up with stories and photographs and a hole where someone should have been."

"Your father and my grandmother were friends," Mary said. "Did you know that? Before the *Miss Carolina*. They worked together on other boats, ran in the same circles. She used to talk about him—said he was one of the good ones. Honest. Hardworking. The kind of man who'd stay late to help you fix your engine and never mention it after."

"He was." Nora's voice was rough. "Before."

"Before Cranston got his hooks into him." Mary's eyes were still closed. "That's what they do. They find people who are vulnerable—people with debts, or secrets, or just families they're trying to keep fed—and they squeeze. Your father wasn't a criminal, Nora. He was a victim. Same as my grandmother. Same as Tommy Pruitt. Same as everyone else they've chewed up."

"That doesn't make it better."

"No. But it might make it easier to understand."

Nora thought about her father in those last years. The drinking, the silence, the way he'd shrink into himself whenever anyone mentioned the *Miss Carolina*. The way he'd sit on the dock at dusk, staring out at the water, his face slack and empty. She'd thought it was grief. It wasn't. Or not only.

"He tried to tell me," she said. "At the end. When the morphine wore off. He kept talking about the fire, about people in the water. About a boat that was watching."

"The *Lady Justice*."

"He never said the name. Just kept saying 'the boat, they were watching from the boat.'" Nora shook her head. "I thought he was hallucinating. I told the nurses to increase his dosage."

"You couldn't have known."

Nora let the curtain fall closed.

"We need to move. Can you walk?"

"Not fast." Mary opened her eyes. "But I can move."

"I'll get you some clothes. Something that isn't torn and bloody."

While Mary cleaned up in the bathroom, Nora gathered what they might need. She retrieved the .38 from the side table where she'd set it, checked the cylinder—six rounds—and slid it into her waistband. The USB drive went into her pocket. She grabbed a change of clothes, a flashlight, the remainder of the first aid kit. Her father's old binoculars. A hunting knife she'd inherited and never used. The emergency cash from the coffee can above the refrigerator—three hundred dollars in twenties.

The last thing she grabbed was a photograph from the mantel. Her father and mother on their wedding day, young and smiling. Her mother in a simple white dress, her father in a suit that didn't quite fit. She didn't know why she took it. She did.

Mary was waiting by the back door when Nora came out of the bedroom. She looked steadier now—the food and the pills doing their work—but she was still pale, still moving like every step cost her.

"Ready?"

"No." Mary managed a thin smile. "But let's go anyway."

They went out the back, through the laundry room. The fog swallowed them immediately, reducing visibility to maybe twenty feet. Nora led the way across the yard, past the dock where her father's old Whaler was tied up, to the edge of the property where the marsh began.

"My truck is in the driveway," Nora said, keeping her voice low. "If they're watching the house, they'll see us leave."

"Is there another way?"

Nora looked at the boat. At the marsh. At the fog that hid everything beyond arm's reach.

"We take the boat. Go by water, come up on the marina from the back side. My truck stays here—they might think we're still inside."

"Can you navigate in this fog?"

"I've been running these waters since I was twelve." Nora started toward the dock. "My father used to take me out in the middle of the night, kill the engine, and make me tell him exactly where we were—just from sound and smell alone. Said a real waterman could find himself on any water blindfolded."

"Did it work?"

"Eventually. I ran us aground about a dozen times first."

They made their way down to the dock. The boards were slick with condensation, and Mary stumbled twice before Nora took her uninjured arm. The Whaler was a dark shape at the end of the dock, its lines disappearing into the fog.

Nora climbed in first, then helped Mary down. The boat rocked under their weight, water lapping against the hull.

"Sit in the bow," Nora said. "Keep your head down. If you see anything—lights, another boat, anything—tell me."

Mary moved forward, bracing herself against the gunwale. Nora cast off the lines and pushed them away from the dock with an oar. The current caught them immediately, pulling them out into the channel.

She didn't start the engine. The sound would carry in this fog, and if anyone was listening, they'd know exactly where she was. Instead, she dropped the trolling motor and let it pull them through at idle, nearly silent on the black water, guiding them through the maze of creeks and channels she'd memorized over a lifetime on the water.

The fog was absolute. Nora couldn't see the bow of the boat, couldn't see Mary huddled in the forward seat. She navigated by feel and memory—the way the current shifted at certain bends, the sound of water moving over oyster beds and around dock pilings. Her father had taught her this, back when she was young enough to think he knew everything.

The marsh was alive around them, even in the darkness. She could hear the rustle of a night heron taking flight, the splash of a mullet jumping, the low grunt of an alligator in the reeds. The pluff mud smell was thick and sulfurous, mixing with the salt, and every few minutes she'd catch a whiff of honeysuckle from the bank, diesel from a distant boat, the faint chemical tang of the paper mill fifteen miles upriver.

They drifted for a while. The dark water carried them through a world reduced to sound and smell and the cold that crept through Nora's jacket. Once, she heard the low thrum of a boat engine in the distance, and she cut the trolling motor and held them still until the sound faded.

"Someone's out here," Mary whispered.

"Could be anybody. Fishermen running early, shrimpers checking their nets." But Nora didn't believe it. Not at three in the morning, not in this fog. She adjusted their course, angling toward a side channel that would add ten minutes to their journey but would keep them away from the main river.

The fog began to thin as they approached the marina. Nora could see the glow of lights ahead—the security lamps on the fuel dock, the dim bulbs over the office door. She started the engine, keeping it low, and motored the last hundred yards into the yacht basin.

The marina was quiet. A few boats rocked at their slips, their owners asleep or gone. The office was dark. But there was a car in the lot. Not Marla's blue Ford. Something else. A dark sedan, new, the kind of car that didn't belong at a working marina at three in the morning.

"Someone's here," Mary whispered.

"I see it." Nora killed the engine and let the boat drift. They were fifty yards from the dock, hidden by the fog and the darkness. The car was clearer now—black or dark blue, four doors, no plates visible from this angle.

"We should go," Mary said. "Find another way to the motel."

"No." Nora was staring at her office. The door was ajar, a crack of light spilling out. Two keys existed—hers and Marla's. Marla's car wasn't in the lot.

"Nora, don't—"

"Stay here." Nora was already tying off at a slip on the far side of the basin, away from the office and the strange car. "If I'm not back in five minutes, take the boat and get out of here. Go to the motel, find Grady, tell him what happened."

"Nora—"

"Five minutes."

She climbed out, keeping low, and made her way along the dock toward the parking lot. She could smell diesel fuel and old bait, the familiar scent of the marina, but underneath it something else—metal and old blood.

The car was empty. She checked the plates—North Carolina, standard issue, nothing distinctive. Could be anyone's car. Could be a late-night fisherman who'd parked here and walked to one of the boats.

But the office door was open. And Marla never left the office door open.

Nora moved toward the building, her hand on the .38 in her waistband. The dock boards creaked under her feet, and she froze, listening. No response. No sound from inside the office. The lap of water against the pilings and the distant cry of a night bird in the marsh.

She moved through the front office, past the counter where she'd stood a thousand times checking in boats and handing out slip assignments. Past the coffee machine and the rack of charts and the bulletin board covered with notices.

The back room door was ajar. Light spilled through the crack.

Nora pushed it open.

Marla Hutchins was on the floor beside the desk. Her reading glasses were still on. A coffee cup had gone over with her.

Then she saw the blood.

It had pooled beneath her, spread in a dark stain across the floorboards. Still bright. This had happened recently.

She reached out and touched Marla's shoulder. The body was warm.

"I'm sorry." The voice came from behind her.

Nora spun, the .38 coming up.

A man stood in the doorway. Tall, broad-shouldered, wearing a dark jacket and gloves. His face was unremarkable—the kind of face you'd forget. Bland features, thinning hair, eyes that were gray or blue or some color in between. In his hand was a pistol with a suppressor.

"Put the gun down, Ms. Banks."

"You killed her."

"She knew too much." He gestured with the suppressed pistol. "Put it down. I won't ask again."

He wasn't worried. She could see it in the way he stood—weight easy, no urgency. He'd done this before.

"Who are you?"

"Someone who cleans up messes." He took a step forward, casual, unhurried.

"You've been watching me."

"For years. Since your father died." His eyes didn't change. "I was there at the end. Not to kill him—he was doing that fine on his own. Just making sure he kept his mouth shut."

"Who do you work for?"

"You know the answer to that."

"Cranston."

"The judge is useful. But he's not the one giving orders." The man tilted his head. "Pilot is. And Pilot is right here in Brunswick County. You've probably met him a dozen times and never known."

Nora kept the .38 level. Her hand wasn't steady, but at this range it didn't need to be.

"Last chance," the man said. "Put down the gun, and I'll make it quick. Keep pointing it at me, and I won't."

A sound came from outside. A pelican hitting the water, close and loud in the silence.

The man's eyes flicked toward the door. For a second.

Nora fired.

The shot was deafening in the small room. The man staggered backward, hand going to his shoulder. His gun came up, and Nora dove behind the desk as he fired—a muffled crack that punched a hole in the wall where her head had been.

She scrambled for the door and burst out into the fog. Behind her, she heard the man cursing, heard his footsteps coming after her.

"Mary!" she screamed. "Run!"

She sprinted across the marina, not looking back. The fog swallowed her, turned the world into a gray blur of shapes and shadows. She couldn't see the boat. Couldn't see anything except the dock beneath her feet and the darkness ahead.

A gunshot cracked behind her—he didn't care about noise anymore. The sound echoed across the water. Then another. Wood splintered somewhere to her left.

Nora reached the slip where she'd tied the Whaler. The boat was gone. The lines were hanging loose in the water, and the slip was empty.

Mary had run. Good. That was good.

Another shot. This one closer. Nora felt the air move past her ear.

She turned left, heading for the commercial dock, for the maze of boats and equipment that might offer cover. Shrimp boats, charter boats, a stack of crab pots, the fuel storage tanks. Any of them might hide her long enough to figure out what to do next.

Her lungs burned. Her legs screamed. She could hear the man behind her, his footsteps heavy on the boards, gaining with every stride. He was faster than she was, and she'd barely slept in three days.

Another shot. Something tugged at her sleeve, and she felt a burning pain in her left arm. A graze—the kind that would bleed and hurt but wouldn't stop her. She'd deal with it later. If there was a later.

She ducked between two shrimp boats, squeezed through a gap barely wide enough for her body, and came out on the other side of the dock. The nets were hanging overhead, still wet from the previous day's haul, and she had to push through them to keep moving. The stench of fish and salt and old bait was overwhelming.

Ahead, was the bait shack, the fuel pumps, the road beyond. If she could reach the road. If she could flag down a car.

Headlights cut through the fog. A truck, coming fast, the engine roaring.

Nora ran toward it, waving her good arm.

The truck slammed to a stop. The door flew open.

Grady Pruitt stepped out, a shotgun in his hands. He'd dressed in a hurry—jeans, boots, a t-shirt that was inside out—but his hands were steady and his eyes were clear.

"Get behind me," he said.

Nora dove past him, putting the truck between herself and the dock.

The man in the dark jacket emerged from the fog. He saw Grady, saw the shotgun, and stopped. For a moment, nobody moved. The fog swirled around them, muffling sound, blurring edges.

"Walk away," Grady said. "Right now. Or I put a hole in you the doctors won't be able to fix."

The man's mouth twisted. Blood was running down his arm where Nora's bullet had hit him, soaking through his jacket, dripping onto the pavement.

"This isn't over," he said. "You know that. Wherever you go, we'll find you. Whatever you do, we'll know."

"Maybe. But not tonight." Grady racked the shotgun.

The man looked at Nora. At Grady. At the shotgun pointed at his chest, mentally calculating odds and angles.

Then it passed.

"We'll be in touch," he said.

He turned and walked back into the fog. His footsteps faded. Then there was only the sound of the water and the distant cry of a bird and Nora's own breathing.

Grady kept the shotgun raised until the footsteps disappeared entirely. Then he lowered it. His eyes moved to her arm.

"You're bleeding."

"It's nothing. Marla's dead." Nora's voice was rough. "He killed her. And Mary—"

"Mary's in my truck. She just showed up at the motel in your boat. Told me you were in trouble."

Nora looked. Mary's pale face was barely visible through the fog-streaked window, her right hand pressed against the glass.

"We have to go," Nora said. "They'll send more."

"I know." Grady opened the driver's door. "Get in. We'll figure out the rest on the road."

Nora climbed into the back seat. The truck started moving before she'd closed the door, Grady pulling a U-turn and accelerating into the fog. The marina disappeared behind them—the boats, the docks, the office where Marla lay on the floor.

Marla. Forty years at that desk, and now she was gone.

Nora pressed her hand against her wounded arm. Ahead, the road was empty.

CHAPTER 5

The Noose

They drove north on Highway 17, the fog thinning as the sun rose behind the clouds. Grady kept the speedometer at exactly fifty-five—fast enough to make distance, slow enough to avoid attention. The shotgun lay across the back seat next to Nora.

Mary was in the passenger seat, her head resting against the window, her eyes closed. She hadn't spoken since they'd left the marina. Her breathing was shallow, rapid, and every few minutes she'd shift in her seat and wince, her good hand pressing against her injured arm.

"She needs a hospital," Nora said.

"She needs to not be dead." Grady's eyes didn't leave the road. "Hospital means paperwork. Paperwork means questions. Questions mean Cranston finds out where we are inside of an hour."

"Look at her. She's burning up."

"I know." Grady paused. "I know a guy in Wilmington. Not a doctor—a vet. He owes me a favor. He can look at her arm, give her antibiotics, keep his mouth shut."

"A vet."

"You got a better idea?"

Nora didn't. She leaned forward between the seats and pressed the back of her hand against Mary's forehead. The skin was hot and dry, feverish. The infection was spreading.

"How far to Wilmington?"

"Forty minutes. Maybe less if traffic stays light."

Mary's eyes fluttered open. She looked at Nora, then at Grady, then at the road ahead. It took her a moment to remember where she was.

"What happened?" Her voice was a croak.

"We got out. You came to the motel, remember? Told Grady I was in trouble."

"The marina." Mary's face tightened. "What happened there. I waited five minutes."

"Marla's dead."

Mary closed her eyes again. "I'm sorry."

"It's not your fault."

"It's all my fault. I started this. I brought this down on everyone." Mary's voice was barely a whisper. "I should have left it alone. Should have let the dead stay buried."

"The dead weren't staying buried. They never do." Nora sat back in her seat. "Cranston's been running this county for thirty years. Someone was going to find out eventually. Better it was you than someone who'd sell the information to the highest bidder."

"I might still do that. If I live long enough."

It was a joke, Nora realized. A weak one, but a joke. Mary was still fighting.

"You're going to live," she said. "We're going to get you fixed up, and then we're going to burn these bastards to the ground."

Mary was silent. Her eyes had closed again, and her breathing had evened out. Sleep or unconsciousness—Nora couldn't tell which.

They drove in silence for a while. The landscape outside the window shifted from marsh to pine forest, the trees pressing close to the road, their branches heavy with Spanish moss. A few other cars passed them going the other direction—early commuters, probably, heading to jobs in Southport or Shallotte. Normal people living normal lives, unaware of the violence that had unfolded a few miles away.

"The man at the marina," Grady said finally. "What did he tell you?"

Nora had been thinking about that. About the things the cleaner had said, the casual way he'd described watching her father die.

"He said he'd been watching me for years. Said he was there when my father died—not to kill him, just to make sure he didn't talk." She paused. "He mentioned a name. Pilot."

"Mary told me about that. Someone above Cranston."

"He said Pilot is here. In Brunswick County. Someone I've probably met."

"That narrows it down to about ten thousand people."

In the passenger seat, Mary made a sound—low, involuntary. Her head slid against the window and she shifted uneasily. Nora reached forward and eased her shoulder back. Mary's skin was damp through her shirt.

"She's getting worse."

"Twenty minutes." Grady checked the mirror. Checked it again.

Nora sat back. The thought she'd been building had broken apart. She had to find it again.

"It narrows it down more than that. Forty years, Mary said. So he's old. Sixty, probably older. And he's running a judge, the county commission—that's not some businessman. That's real power."

"Old money," Grady said. "Old family."

"Maybe. Or someone who built it."

A car came up behind them, fast, and Grady's eyes went to the mirror and stayed there. His hands shifted on the wheel. The car—a white sedan, nobody they recognized—passed on the left without slowing. Grady watched it go. Nora watched him watch it. Neither of them said anything until it was around the curve and gone.

They passed a sign for Wilmington—twenty miles.

Grady pulled off at the next exit without warning, taking the ramp at the last second.

"What are you doing?" Nora's hand went to the .38 at her waist.

"We need burners." He nodded toward a strip mall ahead—a Dollar General, a tanning salon, a bait shop with a hand-painted sign advertising live shrimp. "Our phones are traceable. They'll know where we are the second we power them on."

"I haven't turned mine on since the marina."

"Doesn't matter. If it's on, they can triangulate. Even without a call." Grady pulled into the bait shop parking lot. The gravel lot was empty except for a rusted-out Silverado on blocks. "Stay with Mary. I'll be two minutes."

He was back in three, carrying two burner phones in plastic clamshell packaging.

"Prepaid," he said, sliding one across to Nora. "Forty dollars each at the Dollar General. Can't trace them unless we give them time."

Nora turned the phone over in her hands. Basic flip phone, no camera, no data. Just calls and texts. "They can still triangulate."

"Only if we're stupid about it." Grady pulled back onto the highway, merging into sparse traffic heading north. "Rule: only these phones from now on. Two-minute calls maximum. Power them off between uses. Never make two calls from the same location."

"And our old phones?" "In a dumpster behind the Dollar General." He glanced at her. "Memorize this number."

He read it off the packaging, and Nora committed it to memory. Seven digits. No saved contacts. No call history worth finding. If they got caught, these phones would be empty.

"How long do you think we have?" she asked.

"Until they figure out we're not where we said we'd be?" Grady checked the mirror again. "Six hours. Maybe eight if we're lucky."

The sun was fully up now, burning through the clouds, turning the fog to steam on the asphalt.

"I keep thinking about what he said." Nora's voice was quieter now. The analytical edge gone. "That my father almost told me everything. A few times toward the end. But he didn't."

"He was protecting you."

"He was protecting himself. His memory. The story he wanted me to believe." She stopped. Started again. "I spent five years thinking he died of guilt. That the cancer was his body giving up because his mind already had. But that man at the marina—he was watching. Making sure my father stayed quiet. Making sure his confession stayed private."

"You think they would have killed him if he'd talked?"

"I think they would have killed me." She said it flat. Looking at the back of Mary's head, the gray-streaked hair matted against the glass. "That's what he was afraid of. That's why he kept his mouth shut. Same as Iris Galloway. Same as your father. They weren't victims—they were prisoners."

Grady's hands tightened on the steering wheel.

"My father wrote a letter. Before the sinking. He never sent it, but he wrote it." He took a curve too fast. The truck drifted toward the center line and Mary's head rolled against the window and she made that sound again, and Grady corrected, and for a few seconds the only noise was the tires finding the lane and Mary's breathing, shallow and wrong. "Said he didn't have a choice. Said they'd threatened my mother and me." His voice was rough. "I was twelve years old. I didn't know anything. But he was dying to protect me from people I'd never even met."

Nora didn't respond. The road. The trees. A flatbed truck carrying lumber passed going south.

"They find your weakness and they squeeze," she said. "And they never let go."

The road curved east, following the river. Nora could see the water through the trees—brown and slow, dotted with fishing boats heading out for the morning catch. In the passenger seat, Mary's breathing had gone uneven again, catching.

"We need to talk about Dutch," she said.

Grady's expression didn't change. His shoulders dropped half an inch.

"What about him?"

"Mary thinks he's compromised. She showed him the Cranston photograph. Two days later someone broke into her apartment."

"That could be coincidence."

"Could be. But someone knew we were meeting at the boat ramp. Someone knew what was in my truck. Someone's been feeding information to Cranston, and Dutch is the only person who knew everything. He came to you, Grady. He volunteered information. That's not what scared witnesses do. That's what informants do."

When Grady spoke, his voice was careful, controlled.

"I've known Dutch for two years. He's told me things—things about the sinking, about your father, about what happened that night—that only someone who was there could know. He's not making it up. He's not lying."

"I'm not saying he's lying. I'm saying he might be playing both sides. Telling you enough to seem credible while feeding Cranston everything he needs to stay ahead of us."

"That's a hell of an accusation."

"It's not an accusation. It's a possibility." Nora met his eyes in the rearview mirror. "I'm not asking you to believe it. I'm asking you to consider it. Because if Dutch is compromised, then everything we've planned—everything we're about to do—is already known to the people who want us dead."

Grady watched the road. Nora could see him turning it over in his mind. Dutch had been his source, his ally, his only connection to the truth about his father's death. Accepting that Dutch might be a traitor meant accepting that two years of work had been built on a lie.

She didn't say anything. There was nothing to say that the silence didn't already hold.

"I need to talk to him," Grady said finally. "Face to face. Look him in the eye and ask him directly."

"And if he lies?"

"Then I'll know. I've gotten pretty good at spotting liars." He glanced at her in the mirror. "Present company excepted."

"I haven't lied to you."

"No. But you held back. About your father, about what you knew." His voice softened. "I'm not blaming you. I understand why you did it. But we're past that now. If we're going to survive this, we need to be honest with each other. Completely honest. No more secrets."

Nora thought about the USB drive in her pocket. The files Mary had collected, the evidence of thirty years of corruption. The name "Pilot" and the mystery of who he really was.

"No more secrets," she said.

* * *

The vet's name was Carl Reeves, and he operated out of a converted garage behind his house off Route 133, north of Bolivia, in the kind of rural stretch where nobody asked questions about what you did or who came through your door. The house was small and unremarkable—single-story cinder block, metal roof, a gravel drive running through wiregrass and sand. Exactly the kind of place you'd drive past a thousand times without noticing.

Grady pulled into the driveway and killed the engine. The garage door was closed, the windows dark. A hand-painted sign on the side of the building read "Reeves Veterinary—By Appointment Only."

"Wait here."

He got out and walked to the side door of the garage. Knocked three times, paused, knocked twice more. A moment later, the door opened and a man appeared—big, broad-shouldered, with gray hair and a deeply creased face. He was wearing a faded Duke sweatshirt and cargo pants, and there was something in his posture that suggested he'd been awake for a while.

They talked for a minute, too quietly for Nora to hear. Carl glanced toward the truck, saw Mary slumped in the passenger seat, and his expression shifted from caution to concern. Then Grady waved her over.

"Help me with Mary."

They got Mary out of the truck and half-carried her into the garage. Inside, the space had been converted into a makeshift clinic—an examination table in the center, cabinets full of supplies along the walls, a sink with a hose attachment in the corner. Fluorescent lights buzzed overhead, casting everything in a harsh white glow. It smelled like antiseptic and animal fur.

"Put her on the table," Carl said. He was already pulling on latex gloves, his movements quick and professional. "How long has she been like this?"

"She was coherent an hour ago. She's been in and out since then."

Carl unwrapped the makeshift sling and examined Mary's arm. His face was impassive, but Nora saw his lips tighten when he saw the wound. The gash ran from elbow to wrist where the porthole frame had torn through.

"This is infected. Badly. Whatever she used to bind it trapped bacteria inside. She needs IV antibiotics and probably surgery to clean out the dead tissue."

"Can you do that here?"

"I can do the antibiotics. I can clean the wound, debride what needs to be debrided, close it properly." Carl looked at Grady. "But she needs a real hospital, eventually. If this spreads to her blood, she'll go septic. And I can't treat sepsis with a bottle of penicillin and a prayer."

"How long do we have?"

"Twenty-four hours. Maybe forty-eight if she's lucky and I'm good." Carl was already reaching for supplies—a bag of saline, tubing, a needle. "I'm going to sedate her for this. She's not going to want to be awake."

Nora watched as Carl worked. He was efficient, his attention focused entirely on the patient. Whatever he'd done before becoming a veterinarian, he'd clearly had training. Military, maybe. Or something less official.

At some point he looked up, noticed her arm, and said nothing—just handed her a roll of gauze and a bottle of antiseptic. She cleaned and wrapped it herself, one-handed, while he finished closing Mary's wound.

"How do you know him?" she asked Grady quietly.

"He patched me up a couple years ago. I got into some trouble in Fayetteville, needed stitches and couldn't go to a hospital. A friend of a friend sent me here." Grady leaned against the wall, his arms crossed. "Carl doesn't ask questions. And he doesn't talk to anyone about who comes through his door."

"That's a useful skill."

"It's kept him alive this long."

Mary was unconscious now, the sedative pulling her under. Carl had started an IV line and was cleaning the wound with something that smelled like iodine. The flesh underneath was red and swollen, streaked with lines of infection that ran up toward her elbow.

"She's strong," Carl said without looking up. "Most people would have passed out from the pain days ago. Whatever happened to her, she's been fighting through it."

"She's a fighter," Nora agreed.

"She'll need to be." Carl set aside the cleaning solution and picked up a scalpel. "This is going to take a while. There's coffee in the house if you want it. Kitchen's through the back door, first room on the left."

* * *

Carl had been working on Mary for twenty minutes. Through the thin walls, Nora could hear murmured reassurances, the clink of instruments, Mary's occasional sharp intake of breath even through the sedation.

Grady leaned against the wall near the door, his arms crossed, staring at nothing. He hadn't spoken since Carl started.

Nora paced. Three steps to the window, three steps back. The blinds were drawn, but she kept checking anyway, looking for headlights in the driveway, for shapes moving in the darkness outside.

"You're going to wear a groove in the concrete," Grady said.

"Better than standing still."

"Is it?"

She stopped pacing. Looked at him. He was still staring at the wall, but he wasn't seeing it anymore.

"My wife used to pace," he said. "When she was worried. Back and forth across the kitchen while I was on assignment. She said it helped her think. I always thought it made her more anxious."

Nora sat down on a metal stool near the supply cabinet. "Laura?"

"Yeah." He didn't look at her. "She taught fourth grade in Raleigh. Had this thing where she'd bring home the kids' drawings and hang them on our refrigerator. Said it reminded her why she did it."

Nora waited. The fluorescent lights buzzed.

"She was thirty-eight. Breast cancer, the fast kind." His voice was flat, practiced. "I was in New Orleans when she got the diagnosis. Chasing a lead on my father's case. She called me and I could hear it in her voice before she said a word."

"Grady—"

"I drove straight through. Fourteen hours. When I got to the hospital, she looked at me and said, 'You're late.'" He almost smiled. "Like she'd been waiting. Like she was annoyed I'd kept her. That was Laura. Even at the end."

He was quiet for a moment.

"She died three years ago. I told you that. But I didn't tell you—" He stopped. Rubbed his face with his hand. "After she was gone, everyone was so gentle. I'm sorry, I'm so sorry, let me know if there's anything I can do." He shook his head. "And I wanted—I don't know how to say this. I wanted someone to be angry. Not careful. Not whispering. I wanted someone to—" He broke off. Looked at his hands. "Everyone whispered. Like if they were quiet enough, it wouldn't hurt."

"Is that why you're here? Why you're really here?"

"My father is why I'm here. But Laura is why I can't stop. Her death didn't have a name attached to it. Cells dividing wrong, bad luck." He spread his hands. "My father's death has a name. Someone made a choice. Someone can be held accountable."

"And that helps?"

"I think it's bullshit," Nora said. "What happened to your wife. What happened to your father. None of it should have happened."

"Yeah," he said. "It is."

The fluorescent light buzzed. Somewhere outside, a car backed out of a driveway and headed down the street, the sound ordinary and very far away.

Nora looked at her hands in her lap. The brass key from the storage unit was still in her right front pocket.

She could feel the flat of it through the denim. A week ago she'd been doing inventory counts, arguing with a charter captain about his overdue slip fees. She'd known Dutch Petersen her whole life.

She turned her hand over. The key had left a mark in her palm.

From the garage: Mary's breathing, the IV drip, Carl moving between the table and the cabinet.

"She's going to make it," Nora said.

Grady looked at the door. Then back at his hands.

He pushed off from the wall. "Go get the coffee. I'll stay here in case Carl needs anything."

"You sure?"

"Yeah." He almost smiled. "I've done enough waiting rooms. Go."

She went.

* * *

The kitchen was small and cluttered, every surface covered with stacks of veterinary journals and half-empty coffee cups. A cat was sleeping on the windowsill, orange and fat, one eye opening lazily as Nora entered.

She found the coffee maker and started a fresh pot. While it brewed, she pulled out the USB drive and turned it over in her fingers. The plastic was warm from her pocket, smooth and unremarkable.

Nora found a laptop on the kitchen table, half-buried under a pile of junk mail and veterinary supply catalogs. She opened it and was surprised to find it unlocked—no password, no security. Carl either trusted his neighbors or didn't care about his privacy. Given what she'd seen of his operation, she suspected the latter.

She plugged in the USB drive and waited for it to load.

The files appeared one by one. Hundreds of them, organized into folders with labels like "Insurance," "Property," "Payments," "Witnesses." Mary had been thorough—more thorough than Nora had realized. This wasn't evidence of the *Miss Carolina* sinking. This was a comprehensive record of corruption going back decades.

She clicked on the folder labeled "Pilot."

Inside were a dozen documents—scanned letters, financial records, photographs. Nora opened the first one and began to read.

The document was a letter, typed on plain paper with no letterhead. It was dated March 1987 and addressed to "W. Cranston."

Ward—

The property transfer is complete. Cape Fear Maritime Holdings now controls the parcel we discussed. The previous owners have been compensated and have agreed to relocate. I trust you'll handle the county paperwork with your usual efficiency.

Regarding the other matter: our friends in Raleigh have confirmed that the investigation will not proceed. The committee has been persuaded that there is insufficient evidence to warrant further inquiry. You may consider that problem solved.

As always, destroy this letter after reading.

—P

Nora stared at the signature. A single letter. P for Pilot.

She opened the next document. Another letter, this one from 1992.

Ward—

The insurance matter is becoming complicated. The adjusters are asking questions we'd rather not answer. The Carolina project will need to wait—our window has closed for now. Keep Banks and the crew on retainer. When the time is right, we'll proceed.

Russell Banks has been briefed and understands his role. His family situation makes him cooperative. I trust you've made similar arrangements with the crew.

—P

The Carolina project. The *Miss Carolina.* This was a letter from eighteen years before the sinking—proof that the plan had been in motion for almost two decades, waiting for the right moment.

Nora opened the next document. A financial record, this one showing a wire transfer from Cape Fear Maritime Holdings to an offshore account in the Cayman Islands. The amount was $2.3 million. The date was June 2010—one month after the sinking.

The next document was a list of names. Witnesses, it was labeled. Next to each name was a dollar amount and a status: "Paid," "Pending," or "Handled."

She scanned it. Fourteen names. Some she recognized—dock workers, a harbor official, a Brunswick County commissioner who'd retired quietly in 2012. Each one accounted for. Each one resolved.

Dutch Petersen wasn't on it.

Nora read through the list again, slower. His name wasn't there. Not paid. Not handled. Not pending. Not mentioned at all.

She closed the laptop and the room came back—Carl's kitchen, the fluorescent light humming above the stove, the faint antiseptic smell drifting from the garage where Mary was still under. She put her hand flat on the table. The Formica was cold and slightly sticky under her palm.

Fourteen names. Not Dutch.

Dutch on the phone at two in the morning, ice clinking in his glass. I see them sometimes, Nora-girl. Out on the water. His voice cracking on the word water. She'd sat in her truck in the marina parking lot with the phone pressed to her ear and the tide going out and she'd believed him. Believed the shaking in his voice. Believed the guilt was real.

If he was on their payroll, his name would be here. Unless they kept him off the list on purpose. Unless his arrangement was different—older, verbal, the kind you didn't put in writing.

Or unless he wasn't theirs at all.

Dutch at her father's funeral. That big weathered hand on her shoulder, the weight of it, the scents of Old Spice and cigarettes. He'd stood next to her mother through the whole service and his eyes were red and Nora had thought: This man loved my father. And maybe he had.

She didn't know which was worse. A name on the list would have been clean. This was grief with nowhere to go.

She had to tell Grady.

* * *

She found him in the garage, standing by the operating table while Carl finished closing Mary's wound. The flesh was cleaner now, the infection scraped away, the edges held together with neat rows of stitches.

"She'll live," Carl said. "Assuming she doesn't do anything stupid in the next few days. She needs rest, fluids, and antibiotics. And she needs to stay off that arm."

"Thank you." Grady's voice was rough with relief.

"Thank me by not coming back for a while. I like you, Grady, but you attract a certain kind of trouble I can do without." Carl stripped off his gloves and dropped them in a biohazard container. "There's a room in the back where she can sleep. You're welcome to stay until she's strong enough to move."

"We can't stay long. A few hours at most."

"Then make them count." Carl looked at Nora. "You found the coffee?"

"I did. Thank you."

"Help yourself to whatever else you need. Food's in the fridge, towels in the hall closet. The bathroom's at the end of the hall." He picked up a jacket from a hook by the door. "I've got appointments this afternoon. Real ones, with actual animals. I'll be back by five. Try not to burn the place down."

He left. The door closed behind him, and they were alone.

Nora waited until she heard his car start and pull away. Then she turned to Grady.

"I found something. On the USB drive."

She told him about the letters. About the wire transfers, the list of witnesses, the single-letter signature. And she told him about Dutch.

Grady's face went still as she talked. When she finished, he didn't speak. He walked to the window and stood there, running it back—every conversation with Dutch, every piece of information, testing each one against this new fact. What held up. What didn't. What he'd missed.

"He's not on it," Grady said finally.

"No."

"That could mean they kept him off deliberately. Verbal arrangement. Someone they trusted enough not to document." He paused. "Or it means he was never theirs."

"I know."

"Two years, Nora. He gave me things nobody else would have known. Details about the fire. About what happened on that boat." Grady's voice was careful, controlled. "Either he was feeding me just enough to keep me busy. Or he was telling me the truth, and someone in Cranston's operation knew enough about Dutch to use him against us without him ever knowing."

Nora kept her voice steady. "Either way, we can't tell him where we're going tonight."

"No." He didn't move from the window. His expression was hard, but the certainty was gone. "We can't."

His hands were still in his pockets. He'd stopped looking at the backyard. He was looking at something closer—the glass, maybe, or his own reflection in it. His shoulders were drawn in, the posture of a man who'd taken a hit and hadn't straightened yet.

Nora watched him. She didn't speak.

On the operating table behind them, Mary's breathing kept its slow sedated rhythm. The IV bag Carl had hung from a coat rack dripped at measured intervals. Outside, the warbler was still going—three notes, a pause, three notes again, going about its business on the other side of the glass.

"Two years," Grady said. Not to her. To the window. "Every lead he gave me. Every name. Every time he said *you're getting close, son.*" His voice caught on the last word. He pulled his hands from his pockets and pressed them flat against the windowsill, leaning his weight into it.

Nora gave it time. The warbler. The IV drip. The hum of the refrigerator in the other room.

"Maybe he is," she said. "Maybe he's both things—a man who feels genuine guilt and a man who's been compromised. People are complicated. They can want to tell the truth and be too scared to do it. They can hate what they've become and still keep doing it because they don't see any other way."

"That doesn't make it better."

"No. It doesn't."

They stood in silence. Mary's breathing. The warbler outside. Grady at the window, his weight on his hands, not moving.

"What do we do?" He said it without turning around. Not determination. Just a man with nothing left to ask.

"We can't trust him. We can't tell him anything about where we are or what we're planning, but we might be able to use him."

"Use him how?"

"If Dutch is feeding information to Cranston, then he's a channel. A way to send messages without them knowing we know." Nora came to stand beside him at the window. "We tell Dutch we're going one place, and then we go somewhere else. We let him think we've given up, and then we hit them where they're not expecting."

"You want to use him as a decoy."

"I want to use their own weapon against them. They've been playing us for months—years, in your case. It's time we started playing them."

"I'll need to contact him. Make it seem natural, like I'm updating him on the situation."

"Tell him we're running. Tell him we're scared and we're heading north, maybe to Virginia or D.C. Tell him Mary's hurt and we need to find somewhere safe to hide."

"And while he's telling Cranston to watch the highways heading north—"

"We'll be going somewhere else entirely."

Grady turned to face her. His expression was hard, determined, but underneath it Nora could see the pain. Dutch had been his friend—or at least, he'd thought so. Learning the truth was like losing him twice.

"This doesn't feel right," he said. "Using a man I trusted, turning his betrayal into a weapon."

"Nothing about this feels right. It hasn't felt right since my father died." She set her hands flat on the table. "But feeling right isn't the goal. Surviving is."

"Sentiment is what makes us human."

"My father had plenty of sentiment. It didn't save him."

She stepped back from the window.

"I'm going to check on the files. We need to know everything that's on that drive before tonight."

* * *

Mary woke up around noon.

She came back slowly, blinking against the light, her good hand reaching for her injured arm. When she found the bandages—clean now, properly dressed—she relaxed slightly.

"Where am I?"

"Wilmington. A friend's place." Nora was sitting beside the table, a cup of cold coffee in her hand. "How do you feel?"

"Like someone scraped the inside of my arm with a cheese grater." Mary tried to sit up and winced. "What happened?"

"Carl—the vet—cleaned out the infection. You've got about a hundred stitches and enough antibiotics in you to cure a small army." Nora helped her into a sitting position. "He says you'll live, as long as you don't do anything stupid."

"I specialize in stupid." Mary looked around the garage, taking in the examination table, the cabinets, the general veterinary chaos. "A vet?"

"It's a long story."

"We seem to have a lot of those." Mary swung her legs over the edge of the table and sat there, breathing slowly, getting her bearings. "Where's Grady?"

"In the house. Making some calls."

"To who?"

Nora hesitated. She'd been dreading this conversation, but Mary deserved to know.

"I looked at the files on the USB drive. The ones in the 'Pilot' folder."

Mary's expression sharpened. "And?"

"I found a list of witnesses. People who've been paid or 'handled' over the years." Nora paused. "Dutch Petersen isn't on it."

Mary closed her eyes. When she opened them again, her face was still.

"That doesn't mean he's clean."

"No. It doesn't."

"I knew something was wrong the moment he looked at that photograph. He wasn't surprised. He'd seen it before." Mary's laugh was short and humorless. "Or he's been set up to look that way. Either way I don't trust him."

"Grady's contacting him now. Feeding him false information—telling him we're running north, trying to get out of the state."

"And where are we actually going?"

"Delacroix," Nora said. "Tonight."

Mary was quiet for a moment. Then she nodded.

"They'll be expecting us to run. They'll be watching the highways, the airports, the train stations. They won't be expecting us to come straight at them." Nora stood up and began pacing. "You said you knew the layout of the compound. The security patterns, the guard rotations. Is that still true?"

"A concrete room at Delacroix and a cabin below deck on the *Lady Justice*—I never saw much. I tried to track the guard rotations, count footsteps, figure out when shifts changed. Whether any of that is still accurate, I don't know."

"We'll work with what we have." Nora stopped pacing and faced her. "The files in Cranston's safe—you said they were everything. Account numbers, witness lists, the names of everyone he's paid off. Is that true?"

"That's what they showed me. They were bragging, trying to break me. They wanted me to know how powerful they were, how untouchable. It backfired. All they did was give me a target."

"Then that's our play. We go to Delacroix, we find out who Pilot is, and we end this. The drive goes to Torres regardless—but if we don't identify Pilot now, he walks away clean while Cranston takes the fall alone."

Mary was thinking it through. "It's a good plan. Risky as hell, but good."

"Can you make it? With your arm?"

"I can make it." Mary's voice was hard. "I didn't crawl through a porthole and swim for miles down the Cape Fear to die in some vet's garage. I'm seeing this through."

"Then we leave at dark. Eight o'clock. That gives us six hours to rest, plan, and figure out how we're getting onto that property without getting killed."

The door opened and Grady came in. He looked tired—more tired than Nora had seen him. His eyes were hard.

"It's done," he said. "I called Dutch. Told him we were heading to Richmond, that Mary was hurt and we needed to disappear for a while. He sounded concerned. Sympathetic." His mouth twisted. "He's good. I'll give him that. I almost believed him myself."

"Did he ask where we were calling from?"

"I told him a rest stop on I-95. He won't be able to trace it—I used a burner phone and kept the call under two minutes."

"Good." Nora looked at both of them. "We've got six hours. I suggest we use them."

"I made another call," Grady said. He didn't sit down. "There's a contact at the FBI field office in Wilmington. Special Agent Torres. She's been working maritime racketeering on the Carolina coast for three years. I've crossed paths with her twice—she knows my name, and I know she's not county."

"You trust her?"

"I trust that she has no reason to protect Cranston. That's about as far as trust goes right now." He leaned against the doorframe. "I didn't tell her where we were or what we were doing tonight. But I left a message. Told her we had evidence of a federal case and that if she didn't hear from me by tomorrow morning, she should start asking questions about Delacroix."

* * *

They spent the afternoon planning.

Carl had maps in his study—topographic maps of the Cape Fear region, detailed enough to show individual buildings and roads. The kind of maps hunters and surveyors used, with elevation lines, water features, and tiny symbols for structures that weren't on any GPS. They spread them across the kitchen table and Grady and Mary walked them through what they each knew about Delacroix.

The compound was larger than Nora had expected. The main house—the old hunting lodge—sat on a bluff overlooking the river, surrounded by acres of pine forest and marsh. The building itself was two stories, built in the 1920s from cypress and heart pine, with a wide wraparound porch and a steep tin roof that would be murder in a storm. There was a dock at the waterfront with a boathouse at its end. The *Lady Justice* tied up alongside it when she wasn't at Bald Head. A service road ran along the back of the property, through the wildlife refuge, connecting to a county highway about three miles to the west.

"The perimeter is fenced," Grady said, his finger tracing the boundary on the map. "Razor wire on top, security cameras every hundred yards. The main gate is here, on the east side—" He tapped the spot twice. "—with a guardhouse manned twenty-four hours a day. Spike strip barrier if you try to run it."

"How many guards total?"

"I counted six on my surveillance runs, but there could be more. Two at the gate, two patrolling the perimeter, two at the house." Grady's hand swept a clockwise circle on the map. "Perimeter guys drive golf carts with spotlights. Circuit every thirty minutes, clockwise."

"What about the house itself?"

"That's where it gets easier. The house is used for entertaining—Cranston's political friends, business associates. It has to look legitimate. There are no guards inside, no obvious security. A lot of expensive furniture and a safe in Cranston's private office on the second floor."

"Do you know the combination?"

"No. But I know it's a Gardall—I saw the brand when they opened it. Seven-digit combination, electronic keypad." Mary shrugged. "We'll have to crack it or find another way in."

Nora thought about the tools they had. A shotgun, a .38, a hunting knife. Not exactly a safecracking kit.

"What about the service road? The one you used to escape?"

"It's gated, but the lock is a padlock. I slipped around the gate when I ran—there's a gap in the fence line just wide enough. It's not serious security." The road runs through the wildlife refuge, so there's no cell service and no regular patrols. If we can get past the gate, we can drive most of the way to the compound without being seen."

"And then what?"

"There's a spot where the road comes within a quarter mile of the house. Dense trees, good cover. We can leave the vehicle there and approach on foot."

Grady was studying the map, his brow furrowed.

"The dock," he said. "If the *Lady Justice* is there, that means Cranston's there too. He wouldn't leave his boat unattended."

"Probably. Or someone high up in the organization." Mary's eyes were distant, calculating. "If we're lucky, we might catch more than files."

Nora put her finger on the dock marked on the map. The bluff position, the bend in the river.

"What's the tide doing tonight?"

Grady looked up.

"The Cape Fear floods on an incoming tide," Nora said. "If the *Lady Justice* is at the dock and the tide's running in, she's sitting in four feet under the hull. Running out, maybe three or less." She traced the bend with her finger. "A boat that size needs to swing at anchor before she can get under way. She can't back into a running current without stalling. Storm conditions, disorganized crew—they're spending fifteen minutes just getting off the dock."

"So she's not a quick exit."

"Not in a storm. Not with an outgoing tide." Nora sat back. "Cranston has money. Money doesn't mean good sailors."

Mary had been listening. "There's a fuel shutoff on the dock. Manual lever, close side of the pump house. I saw it when they brought me in by water."

"They cut the fuel, nobody goes anywhere fast." Nora looked at both of them. "It's not the plan. But it's useful."

"And if we're unlucky, we walk into a room full of armed men who've been expecting us."

"That's always a possibility."

"This isn't a safe plan, Grady. It's a desperate one. But it's the only one we've got."

They argued about details for another hour. Entry points, exit routes, contingencies if things went wrong. Grady wanted to scout the property first, get eyes on the security before committing. Nora thought that was too risky—every hour they waited was another hour for Cranston to find them.

They'd approach the property from the service road, park at the spot Mary had identified, and observe for a while. If everything looked clear, they'd move in. If not, they'd fall back and reassess.

It wasn't a great plan. But it was a plan.

By late afternoon, the weather had turned. Clouds rolled in from the west, heavy and dark, and the wind picked up, rattling the windows of Carl's house. A storm was coming—the remnants of something that had formed in the Gulf and was now tracking up the coast.

"That could work in our favor," Grady said, watching the sky through the kitchen window. "Rain and wind will cover noise, make it harder for them to see us coming."

"It'll also make it harder for us to see them." Nora was cleaning the .38, checking the cylinder, making sure everything was in working order. "And if we have to run, wet ground is going to slow us down."

"We won't have to run. We go in quiet, we get the files, we get out. Nobody sees us, nobody gets hurt."

"That's the plan. Plans don't always survive contact with reality."

Mary was resting on the couch in the living room, her eyes closed, her breathing regular. The antibiotics were working—her fever had dropped, her color was better. But she was still weak, still recovering. Nora worried about bringing her along. But Mary knew the approach, the fence gap, the service road. She'd stay with the truck—but they needed her to get there.

At six o'clock, Carl returned. He checked on Mary, changed her bandages, gave her another dose of antibiotics.

"She shouldn't be moving around," he said to Nora quietly. "Another day of rest and she'd be in much better shape."

"We don't have another day."

He didn't ask any questions—that wasn't his style—but Nora could see the concern in his eyes.

"Be careful," he said. "Whatever you're doing, be careful."

"We will."

They ate a quick meal—sandwiches from Carl's fridge, washed down with more coffee—and then it was time to go. Grady loaded the truck while Nora helped Mary into the back seat. The shotgun went on the floor, covered with a blanket. The .38 went in Nora's waistband.

"Thank you," she said to Carl as they pulled out of the driveway. "For everything."

"Just don't come back," he said. But he was smiling slightly as he said it.

They drove south on Highway 17, then cut west on a county road that wound through farmland and forest. The storm was closer now, the clouds black and swollen, lightning flickering in the distance. The first drops of rain began to fall as they crossed the Brunswick County line.

"About an hour out," Grady said.

Nora watched the darkness outside the window. The trees were bending in the wind, their branches whipping back and forth. The rain was coming harder now, drumming on the roof of the truck, streaking the windshield.

The night of the sinking, fifteen years ago. Had it been raining then? Had he stood on the deck of the *Miss Carolina* and watched the storm roll in, knowing what was about to happen?

Grady's phone buzzed. He glanced at the screen, handed it across. Unknown number. Nora answered.

"Hello?"

"Nora Banks.

"The voice was familiar—smooth, unhurried. The same voice she'd heard at the marina. The cleaner. "I'm impressed. You're harder to kill than I expected."

"I'm full of surprises."

"So I've noticed. But here's the thing, Nora. We know where you're going. We've known since your friend Grady called his informant this afternoon. Dutch may be compromised, but he's not the only source we have."

She looked at Grady, who was watching her in the rearview mirror, his face tense.

"You're lying."

"Am I? Then tell me—how do I know you're thirty minutes from Delacroix, approaching from the west on County Road 211? How do I know you've got a wounded woman in the back seat and a shotgun on the floor? How do I know you're planning to use the service road through the wildlife refuge?"

The line went silent for a moment. Then the voice continued, softer now.

"We see everything, Nora. We hear everything. You can't run, you can't hide, and you definitely can't sneak up on us." A pause. "Turn around. Go back to wherever you came from. Forget you ever heard the name Pilot. This is your last warning."

The line went dead.

Nora's mind was racing, trying to figure out how they'd known. Dutch, obviously—but the cleaner had said Dutch wasn't the only source. What else? Who else?

Then she remembered.

The phone. She'd made calls on this phone. To Grady, to Anna—the first time she'd dialed that number in two years—to half a dozen other people over the past few days. If Cranston had access to the cell towers, if he had someone at the phone company—

"Stop the truck," she said.

Grady pulled over to the side of the road. The rain was hammering down now, visibility reduced to almost nothing.

"What is it?"

"They're tracking our phones. They've been tracking us the whole time." Nora opened the door and stepped out into the rain. She walked to the edge of the road, wound up, and threw her phone as far as she could into the darkness.

When she got back in the truck, Grady was already reaching for his own phone.

"How long do you think they've been listening?"

"Long enough. They knew our route, our plan, everything." Nora wiped rain from her face. "Throw it. Now."

Grady threw his phone out the window. Mary was awake in the back seat, her eyes wide.

"What do we do now?"

Nora looked at the road ahead. The rain, the darkness, the storm that was only getting worse. They were less than an hour from Delacroix, and Cranston knew they were coming.

"We keep going," she said.

"They're expecting us."

"They're expecting us to run. They gave us a warning because they thought we'd turn around." Nora shook her head. "That's their mistake. They think we're scared. They don't understand that we've got nothing left to lose."

Grady put the truck in gear.

"All right," he said. "Delacroix."

The truck pulled back onto the road, its headlights cutting through the rain. Lightning flashed overhead, illuminating the trees for a split second before plunging everything back into darkness.

"They'll have the main entrance covered," Mary said from the back seat. Her voice was stronger now, sharpened by adrenaline. "If they know we're coming, they'll be waiting."

"Then we don't use the main entrance." Nora was thinking fast, running through the layout Mary had described. "You said the service road comes within a quarter mile of the house. What's between the road and the compound?"

"Forest. Dense pine, some undergrowth. The fence runs along the property line, but there's a section near the river where it's older—chain link instead of razor wire. I noticed it when I was escaping."

"Can we cut through it?"

"With the right tools. It's rusty, hasn't been maintained." Mary leaned forward between the seats. "But they'll have patrols. If they're expecting us, they'll have people watching the perimeter."

"The storm will help with that. Hard to see in this rain, hard to hear over the wind." Grady was driving faster now, the speedometer climbing toward sixty. "We come in fast, hit the fence, get to the house before they can react."

"And if we can't get to the house?"

"Then we improvise." Nora checked the .38, made sure it was loaded. "Whatever happens, we don't stop. We don't turn back. We've come too far."

The rain was hammering the windshield so hard the wipers could barely keep up. Through the gaps between sweeps, Nora could see the road unwinding ahead of them—black asphalt through the storm and the trees, no other cars, no lights.

Twenty minutes to Delacroix.

The wipers beat back and forth. Nobody spoke. The rain came down.

CHAPTER 6

Delacroix

The service road was a river of mud.

Grady's truck crawled along at fifteen miles an hour, the tires slipping and grabbing, the headlights cutting through sheets of rain that came down so hard Nora couldn't see more than twenty feet ahead. Trees pressed in on both sides, loblolly pines bent almost double by the wind, their branches scraping against the windows like fingers trying to get in.

"Quarter mile to the turnoff," Mary said from the back seat. She was hunched over the map, Grady's flashlight clamped between her teeth, tracing the route with one finger. "There's a pullout on the left where we can leave the truck. From there it's maybe three hundred yards through the woods to the fence."

"And the fence section you mentioned? The old one?"

"Straight shot from the pullout. Follow the creek bed south and you'll hit it."

The truck lurched as the right rear tire dropped into a rut. Grady wrestled the wheel, fighting for traction, and for a moment Nora thought they were going to slide off the road entirely. Then the tire caught and they were moving again, slower now, the engine whining in protest.

"This is insane," Grady said. He wasn't complaining. Stating a fact.

"Probably." Nora checked the .38 for the third time, making sure the cylinder was dry. "But we're here."

The turnoff appeared out of the rain, a gap in the trees wide enough for a vehicle, marked by a rusted metal post that had once held a sign. Grady pulled in and killed the engine. The headlights died. The only light was the occasional flash of lightning, turning the world white and purple before plunging it back into darkness.

The rain came down so hard it sounded like gravel on the roof.

They sat in the darkness, the compound invisible through the storm. Mary was in the back seat, her good arm crossed tight against her body, fingers gripping her own elbow, pulling against her ribs. Grady's phone glow illuminated her face as she studied the satellite images one more time.

But she wasn't looking at the screen anymore. She was staring past it, into the dark.

"You okay?" Nora asked.

"My grandmother used to hate storms." Mary kept her eyes down. "She'd make me sit with her in the hallway closet when the thunder got bad. Said it was the safest place in the house. I think she didn't want to be alone."

Nora waited.

"Iris Galloway." Mary said the name slowly, like she was tasting it. "Everyone calls her the victim. The woman who drowned. The witness who had to die. But she was a person, you know? She had a life before all of this."

"What was she like?"

"Stubborn." Mary almost smiled. "God, she was stubborn. She used to argue with the preacher after Sunday service, walk right up to him and tell him everything he'd gotten wrong in the sermon. He hated her. Half the congregation hated her. But she didn't care."

Lightning flashed. For a moment, the compound was visible through the trees, the dark bulk of buildings, the glint of the fence.

"She taught me to play poker when I was eight," Mary said. "Real poker, not the kid version. She said a woman who couldn't bluff was a woman who'd get walked over her whole life. My mother was furious when she found out." She paused. "She made the best pie crust in Brunswick County. Buttermilk. She'd let me help roll it out, and I'd always make a mess, and she'd pretend to be annoyed but she never really was."

"She sounds like someone worth knowing."

"And she died on that boat because the plan went wrong. Because she was in the wrong place at the wrong time. Because the men running that operation cared more about money than about who got hurt."

The rain kept falling. In the distance, thunder rolled.

"I was eleven when she died," Mary said. "I remember the funeral. I remember my mother crying, and my father standing there with his head bowed like he was trying to hold something in. I remember everyone saying it was an accident. A tragedy. Three people lost in a boat fire. A tragic accident. Nothing to investigate."

"But you knew."

"I didn't know. Not then. I knew something was wrong. The way people looked at each other. The way they stopped talking when I walked into a room." Mary finally met Nora's eyes. "I've spent eight months trying to prove what happened to her. Eight months of dead ends and sealed records and people who suddenly can't remember anything. And now we're sitting in a truck in the rain, about to break into the compound of the man who had her killed."

"Scared?"

"Terrified. But she would have done it. If it were me who'd been killed, if it were her sitting here, she would have driven right through that fence without thinking twice."

"Runs in the family."

Mary laughed. It was a short, sharp sound, almost lost in the rain.

"Yeah," she said. "I guess it does."

She turned toward the compound, toward the fence, toward whatever was waiting. Her hand lay flat on her knee, her breathing slow and even.

"Let's go get the bastards who killed my grandmother."

* * *

They'd been over it a dozen times on the drive, but Nora went through it again anyway. Mary would stay with the truck, her arm made her a liability in a physical confrontation, and someone needed to be ready to drive if they had to leave fast. Nora and Grady would approach the house through the woods, cut through the fence, and make their way to the main building. The safe was in Cranston's office on the second floor, east side of the house. They'd get the files, get out, and be back at the truck within the hour.

"If we're not back in an hour, leave," Nora said. "Drive to Wilmington, go straight to the FBI field office, ask for Torres, and give her the drive. Tell her everything."

"I'm not leaving you."

"You are if we're not back. The information is what matters. If we don't make it, someone has to finish this."

"They'll be watching the main gate and the dock road," Mary said. "That's how people get in—by car or by boat. But the storm's going to pull their patrols back. Nobody stands a perimeter in lightning like this. That's our window."

"Are their motion sensors?" Grady asked.

"Yes, but half of them are dead—I clocked that on my surveillance runs. The ones that work are along the main approaches, not the fence line. We go through the weak section near the creek, we're in their blind spot. I walked the creek bed approach twice. I know the route."

"Mary reached out with her good hand and found Nora's in the darkness and squeezed.

"Be careful."

"Always."

Nora and Grady stepped out into the storm.

The rain hit her immediately. Within seconds she was soaked through, her clothes plastered to her skin, water running into her eyes and down the back of her neck. The wind was worse, gusts that came out of nowhere and nearly knocked her off her feet, carrying leaves and pine needles and the smell of the swamp.

Grady was already moving, his flashlight off, navigating by lightning flash and memory. Nora followed close behind, her feet sinking into mud that sucked at her boots with every step. The creek bed was to her left. She could hear it rushing, swollen with rainwater, louder than she'd expected.

They found it fifty yards from the truck. The banks had overflowed, turning what was probably a gentle stream into a churning brown torrent. Grady stopped at the edge, assessing.

"We'll have to wade."

"How deep?"

"Knee-high, maybe. Hard to tell in this light."

It was thigh-high, and cold enough to make Nora gasp. The current pulled at her legs, trying to drag her downstream, and she had to plant each foot carefully before lifting the other. Grady went first, using a fallen branch as a walking stick, his free hand reaching back to help her when the footing got treacherous.

They made it across without going under, but by the time they climbed the far bank, Nora was shivering so hard her teeth were chattering. The rain was warmer than the creek, which didn't make it any more pleasant.

"Fence should be close," Grady said.

The creek ran south along what had been a property boundary line before the wildlife refuge absorbed it. Nora could feel the elevation drop as the trees thinned—the soil going from sandy to silty, the pine needles giving way to spartina at the margins. She knew this kind of ground.

The Cape Fear estuary pushed inland for miles in places, salt marsh threading into what looked like forest until you stepped wrong.

She stopped. Reached back and caught Grady's sleeve.

The ground ahead was dark. Not shadows—water. A sheet of it, maybe an inch deep, spreading through the tree roots where the creek had overflowed its banks. In daylight you'd see it. In this rain, at night, you'd step into it and find out what was underneath.

Thirty yards. The footing firmed. The trees pressed close again.

Grady came up beside her, breathing hard. He hadn't spoken. He'd watched her navigate and followed her line exactly, which told her he'd done some version of this before.

She didn't ask.

It was. They almost walked into it, the chain-link appearing out of the darkness like a gray ghost, the metal singing in the wind. Nora ran her hand along the links, feeling for the section Mary had described.

There. The chain-link was older here, the metal rough with rust, the links stretched and sagging. Someone had cut a hole at some point, probably kids looking for a place to party, or poachers after deer, and then patched it with wire that had since corroded. Nora pulled out the wire cutters she'd brought from the marina, the same ones she used for dock repairs, and went to work. The links parted with a series of soft pings that were lost in the wind.

Five minutes later, they had an opening big enough to crawl through.

“Stay low,” Grady whispered. “There could be cameras along the fence line, maybe dogs.”

They moved through the gap one at a time, the sharp edges of the cut chain-link catching at their clothes. Nora went first, flat on her belly in the mud, pushing through and then turning to hold the fence open for Grady. He came through fast, his shoulder catching once but tearing free, and then they were both inside the compound, crouched low in the undergrowth, listening.

Nothing. Just the storm, the wind in the pines, the rain hammering everything.

The house was a hundred yards ahead, a dark shape through the trees. No lights visible, no movement. Either everyone was asleep or they were waiting.

Nora pulled the .38 from her jacket pocket. The weight of it was steady in her hand, familiar. She’d carried it for years on the water, ever since a drunk tourist had pulled a knife on one of her dockworkers. She’d never fired it at anyone, but she’d practiced enough that she knew what it could do at close range.

They moved toward the house in a crouch, staying in the tree line as long as they could. The ground was soft, the pine needles slick underfoot, and every few steps Nora would pause and listen. But there was nothing. Just the storm and the river and the sound of her own breathing.

The compound was bigger than she’d expected. Not just the main house but outbuildings, storage sheds, staff quarters. A dock stretched out into the river, barely visible through the rain. The *Lady Justice* was tied there, rocking in the swells, her white hull gleaming wet in the occasional lightning flash.

Nora's boot came down on something that wasn't mud. She froze, looking down. A motion sensor, half-buried in the pine needles, its red light blinking steadily. Grady saw it at the same moment she did.

They waited. Ten seconds. Twenty. Thirty.

No alarms. No lights. No dogs.

"Disabled," Grady whispered. "Or broken."

"Or they know we're here."

They kept moving.

The main house loomed ahead. Two stories, wide porch, shuttered windows, dark.

They approached from the east side, where Mary had said the office would be. The windows on the second floor were dark, the shutters closed. Nora couldn't tell if anyone was inside. The porch was empty except for a stack of firewood covered with a tarp and two rocking chairs that swayed slightly in the wind.

Grady pointed to a door near the back of the house. Service entrance, probably. Less visible from the main rooms.

They crossed the open ground fast, boots splashing through puddles, and pressed themselves against the wall beside the door. Nora tried the handle. Locked.

They were in.

The interior was dark and warm, the air thick with the smell of old wood and gun oil and something else—tobacco, maybe, or the faint sweetness of bourbon that had soaked into everything over decades. They stood in a mudroom. Rubber boots lined up against the wall, rain slickers hanging from hooks, a bench piled with fishing gear.

Nora could hear voices somewhere deeper in the house. Low, conversational. She couldn't make out words, but the tone was relaxed, unhurried. Someone laughed. Someone else responded.

She stood still in the mudroom hallway and listened the way she listened for weather—not for what was there, but for what was wrong.

Two voices. Both male. One lower, doing most of the talking; one responding in shorter bursts. The rhythm of men who knew each other and weren't on alert. She could hear the fire—a deep draw and exhale, the pop of hardwood. Bourbon smell reaching even here, soaked into the plaster over decades.

Through the gap in the half-open door she could see firelight moving on the far wall. A shadow crossed it. Crossed back. Someone standing, shifting weight. A man who'd been up late and was waiting for something.

She counted. Two in the room she could confirm. The cleaner could be anywhere—upstairs, outside, running a perimeter in the rain. She hadn't seen him since the compound approach and his absence was worse than his presence. She knew where he was supposed to be. She had no idea where he actually was.

The window at the end of the mudroom was a quarter-inch ajar. Rain had gotten in. She could feel the air moving—coming from the north, shifting the cigarette smell toward her. If anyone in that room was paying attention to airflow, they'd know someone had opened the service door.

She nudged it fully shut.

The mantel above the fireplace had a clock on it. She could hear it now—a measured tick, steady under the conversation. An old mechanism, fully wound. It read eleven forty.

An hour before the storm peaked, if the weather service had it right. An hour of maximum cover. She needed to be out of this house in thirty minutes, ideally twenty.

She looked at Grady. He nodded toward the stairs visible through the next doorway. Second floor, east side. Cranston's office.

They moved through the mudroom into a hallway. Mounted animal heads watched them from the walls—deer, wild boar, a tarpon arched on a mahogany plaque. The floorboards were old pine, the kind that creaked if you stepped wrong, and Nora moved carefully, testing each plank before putting her weight down.

The voices were coming from a room to the left, down the hall. A door stood half-open, firelight flickering through the gap. Nora could see shadows moving on the wall, hear the clink of glass on glass.

The stairs were ahead. Narrow, steep, the treads worn smooth by a century of boots. They climbed slowly, one step at a time, keeping to the edges where the wood was less likely to give them away. Halfway up, a board groaned under Grady's weight, and they both froze, listening.

Nothing. The voices continued downstairs, uninterrupted.

The second floor was a hallway with doors on either side. The door at the end of the hall turned when she tried it.

Cranston's office.

"What are we looking for?" Grady whispered.

"Pilot's identity," Nora said. "A name. A photograph. Something that proves who runs this."

It was smaller than she'd expected, barely more than a storage room. A desk sat under the window, its surface buried in papers and file folders. Bookshelves lined one wall, stuffed with maritime charts and ledgers. A filing cabinet stood in the corner, its drawers partly open. And behind the desk, mounted into the wall at waist height, was a safe.

It was an old model, mechanical, the kind that required a combination. The kind that took time to crack if you didn't know the numbers.

Nora crossed to the desk and started going through the papers. Shipping manifests. Harbor records. Payroll documents. Names she recognized and names she didn't. Everything dated, cross-referenced, meticulously organized. This was years of operations, laid out in black and white.

"Nora." Grady was at the safe, his ear pressed to the door. "This is going to take time. More time than we have."

"Can you do it?"

"Maybe. If I had an hour and nobody disturbed me."

They didn't have an hour.

Nora scanned the office. There had to be something. A clue, a hint, somewhere Cranston would have written down the combination in case he forgot.

Her eyes landed on a photograph on the desk. A group shot, maybe a dozen people, standing on a dock with a trawler in the background. She recognized some of the faces—local fishermen, dock workers, people she'd seen around the harbor her whole life. And in the center, an older man in a hunting jacket, his hand on the shoulder of a younger man who looked familiar.

She leaned closer. The younger man was her father. Russell Banks, maybe forty years old in the photo, his face unlined, his hair still dark.

The older man was the one she'd seen downstairs. The one with the whiskey glass and the patient eyes and the decades of secrets behind them.

Pilot.

The photograph was dated on the back: 1992.

Eighteen years before the *Miss Carolina* sank.

They'd known each other that long. Her father and Pilot. Her father had been part of this organization for nearly two decades before he died.

Nora put the photograph in her pocket. "That's it. That's what we came for."

"The files—"

"Thirty seconds. Grab what you can." She started pulling papers from the desk—manifests, payroll documents, anything with names and dates—and shoved them into her jacket.

They should have left after twenty seconds.

"We need to go," she said. "Now."

"What about the safe?"

"We take what we can carry. If we can't get into the safe, we take everything else."

And then the door opened behind them.

A man stood in the doorway. Fifties, heavy build, a rifle in his hands. Not pointing it at them yet, but ready.

He looked at Nora, at Grady, at the papers scattered across the desk.

"You're making a mess," he said. His voice was flat, matter-of-fact. "The old man's not going to like that."

Nora raised the .38. Her hand was steady. "We're leaving."

The man with the rifle smiled. It wasn't a pleasant expression.

"No," he said. "You're not."

And then everything moved very fast.

* * *

The man with the rifle wasn't alone. Two more appeared behind him in the hallway, blocking the stairs. One had a shotgun, the other a pistol. They moved with the practiced efficiency of people who'd done this before.

"Put the gun down," the first man said. "Nice and slow."

Nora looked at Grady. His face was pale in the dim light from the hallway, his jaw tight. She could see him calculating odds, angles, distances. All of them bad.

She lowered the .38. Set it on the desk.

"Smart," the man said. "Hands behind your head. Both of you."

They did as they were told. The man with the shotgun came forward, kicked the .38 across the room, and patted them both down with one hand while keeping the shotgun trained on them with the other. He found a pocketknife, a folded map, a notebook, and Grady's backpack. Took them all.

"Downstairs," the first man said. "The old man wants to talk to you."

They were marched down the stairs, through the hallway, past the mounted animal heads and the darkened rooms. The voices Nora had heard earlier had gone quiet. Whatever conversation had been happening was over.

The room they were led into was large, paneled in dark wood, with a stone fireplace at one end and floor-to-ceiling windows looking out over the river. A fire burned in the hearth, throwing light across leather furniture and faded Persian rugs. The room smelled of woodsmoke and furniture polish and the kind of quiet that money buys.

The old man from the photograph was sitting in a chair by the fire, a glass of whiskey in his hand. He kept his gaze on the flames when they entered, his expression distant, thoughtful.

"Found them in Cranston's office," the man with the rifle said. "Going through the files."

"I see." The old man finally looked at them. His face was weathered, deeply lined, his eyes pale in the firelight. "Nora Banks. And Mr. Pruitt, I assume. Thomas's son."

Grady said nothing.

"I knew your father," the old man continued. "Good man. Terrible liar. That's what got him killed in the end—he couldn't lie to save his life. Literally." He took a sip of his whiskey. "But you're not here to talk about your father, are you?"

The old man swirled his whiskey. "Your cousin is in the boathouse. She came looking for you when you didn't come back." He let that land. "We'll decide what to do with her after the storm passes."

"You killed my father."

"No." The old man set his glass down. "I gave your father a choice. Work with me, or lose everything. He chose to work with me. For years, he chose that. And then, at the very end, when he was dying anyway, he decided to grow a conscience. He wanted to confess. To tell you everything. To clear his name before he went."

The old man stood up, walked to the window. The river was barely visible through the rain, just a dark movement beyond the glass.

"I couldn't let him do that. Not because I was afraid of being caught—I've spent over forty years building this operation, and I know how to survive investigations. But because he would have destroyed everyone else who'd ever worked for me. Every fisherman who took a little extra money to look the other way. Every dock worker who loaded the wrong cargo onto the right boat. Every harbor official who misfiled a permit. Your father's confession would have ruined hundreds of lives."

"So you had him killed."

"I had him silenced." The old man turned to face her. "There's a difference. He was dying anyway. The cancer was going to kill him in weeks. I just made sure he didn't take everyone else down with him."

Nora's hands were shaking. The man with the rifle behind her shifted slightly, ready if she moved.

"And now you're here," the old man said. "With your cousin and your reporter, trying to finish what Russell started. Trying to expose everything. And for what?

Justice? Closure? What exactly do you think you're going to accomplish?"

"The truth."

The old man laughed. It was a dry, humorless sound.

"The truth. Let me tell you about the truth, Nora Banks. The truth is that your father made a choice. He chose to work for me because he was drowning in debt and I offered him a way out. He chose to falsify harbor records, to look the other way when boats came in with the wrong cargo, to take money that he knew was dirty. He made that choice every day for twenty years. And at the end, when he tried to undo it, when he tried to confess, he wasn't being brave. He was being selfish. He wanted to feel better about himself before he died, and he didn't care who else got hurt in the process."

"That's not—"

"That's exactly what it was." The old man's voice was flat, final. "I'm not going to apologize for stopping him. I did what had to be done to protect everyone else in this organization. Including you."

"Me?"

"You think your father's confession would have ended with him? The FBI would have come after his family, his friends, everyone who might have known. They would have frozen his accounts, seized his property, questioned you and your mother until they found something to charge you with. That's what justice looks like, Nora. Not noble, not clean—just more people getting hurt.

He picked up his glass, finished the whiskey in one swallow.

"So here's what's going to happen. You're going to sit here until the storm passes. Then you're going to get in a boat with your cousin and your friend, and you're going to leave. You're going to go back to your life and forget you ever came here. And in exchange, I'm going to forget you broke into my house and tried to steal my files."

"And if we don't?"

"Then tomorrow morning, three bodies wash up on the riverbank. Tragic accident. Three people caught in the storm, swept away by the current. It happens every few years. Nobody will be surprised."

Nora met Grady's eyes. His face was expressionless, but she could see the calculations running behind his eyes. They were outgunned, outnumbered, in a house full of armed men in the middle of a storm. Walking away might be the only way to survive this.

But Mary. Mary was still out there, tied up in the boathouse.

"I need to know she's safe," Nora said. "Mary. I need to see her."

The old man considered this. Then he nodded to the man with the rifle.

"Take them to the boathouse. Let them see their friend. Then bring them back here. We'll decide what to do with them after they've had time to think."

* * *

The walk to the boathouse was a nightmare. The storm had intensified, the wind screaming through the trees, the rain coming down in sheets so thick Nora could barely see ten feet ahead. The man with the rifle walked behind them, a second man with a flashlight led the way, and they stumbled through the mud and the darkness toward the river.

The dock was old cypress planking, slick with rain and moss, stretching out over the marsh. Nora could feel it sway beneath her feet, could hear the pilings groan with each swell that pushed up from the river. The marsh grass bent flat in the wind on either side of the dock, and the water was high, lapping at the boards, close enough that she could feel the spray when a gust hit just right.

The man ahead of them was moving fast, the flashlight beam bouncing off the rain, sweeping back and forth across the dock. Nora followed, her hands still tied behind her back, Grady beside her doing the same. The man with the rifle was directly behind her—close enough that she could hear his breathing over the storm. If she stumbled he'd be on her before she could recover.

She put one foot in front of the other, the beam bouncing off the rain and the wet planking. The boards were slick underfoot, and with her hands tied behind her Nora had no way to catch herself if she slipped. She planted each foot flat and kept her weight centered, the same balance she'd learned walking icy dock boards at the marina in January.

The wind was stronger here, out of the shelter of the trees, coming straight off the river. It drove the rain sideways into her face and pushed against her chest. The black water of the marsh moved beneath them, the cordgrass bent flat in the gusts.

The boathouse was at the end of the dock. A rectangular structure of unpainted cypress planking, the wood gone silver with age, built out over the river on creosote pilings. A tin roof sloped toward the water, the rain drumming on it so loud that it drowned out everything else as they approached. The *Lady Justice* was tied up alongside the dock, rocking in the swells, her white hull gleaming wet in the flashlight's beam, her rigging slapping against the mast in an irregular rhythm.

The big man kicked the boathouse door open and shoved them inside.

Dark. Cold. The air smelled of diesel fuel and old rope and the brackish river water that sloshed visibly through the gaps in the floorboards. The floor was rough planking laid over the pilings, and through the gaps Nora could see the black water moving a foot below, rising and falling with each swell. The walls were unfinished cypress hung with equipment: crab pots and cast nets and coils of mooring line, orange life jackets stiff with mildew, a boat hook hanging from two nails. A wooden boat cradle sat empty in the center of the space, its timbers dark with oil.

They were shoved into the far corner and made to sit on the planking with their backs against the wall. The ropes that had held Mary were still tied to the wall brace. She was gone—moved somewhere deeper into the compound. The cypress boards were rough and splintered against Nora's shoulder blades, even through her wet jacket. The big man retied their wrists to a horizontal brace that ran along the base of the wall, checking each knot twice, then took up position by the door. He set the rifle across his knees, pulled his collar up against the cold, and settled in.

Even now, Grady was cataloging. Nora could see his eyes moving in the dim light, taking inventory: the guard's posture, settled in for a long shift; the bolt-action rifle across his knees, five rounds at most; the mooring lines running from the *Lady Justice* through the dock cleats just outside the door; the way the floorboards flexed with each push of tide beneath the boathouse. He was filing it. All of it.

For several minutes, neither of them spoke. The storm raged outside, the wind screaming through the gaps in the boathouse walls, the rain hammering the tin roof so loud it was hard to think. The *Lady Justice* strained against her mooring lines, her hull bumping the fenders with a dull, rhythmic thud, the cleats groaning against the dock each time a swell pushed her weight against them.

The cold settled in slowly. First the shivering, the involuntary shaking that Nora couldn't control. Then the deeper cold, the wet clothes pulling heat from her body, the wind finding every gap in the cypress planking. Her shoulders ached from the angle of her arms tied behind her. Her wrists were raw where the rope had rubbed the skin. The rough planking under her was hard and cold, every knot and splinter working through her jeans.

The guard shifted once, about an hour in. He uncrossed his legs, crossed them the other way, and pulled a phone from his jacket pocket. The screen's blue glow lit his face: broad nose, heavy brow, a scar or a crease running from his left ear to the corner of his mouth. He checked the screen, put the phone away, and went still again.

Time passed in the storm's rhythms. The wind would build to a howl, hold, then drop back to a moan. The rain came in bands, heavy and then light and then heavy again. The tide was rising. Nora could hear it in the water beneath the floorboards, the slap and gurgle growing louder, the gaps in the planking showing more water with each cycle. Through the boathouse wall she could hear the *Lady Justice*'s hull working against her lines, the fenders compressing and releasing, the rigging slapping.

Finally, Grady leaned close to Nora's ear. "Mary's not in the boathouse."

"I know."

"Pilot was lying. Or she's somewhere else in the compound."

"Either way she's not with us." Nora kept her eyes on the guard. "That's something."

"And us?"

Nora looked at the guard, at the door, at the sounds of the boat rocking in the storm. They had until morning, the old man had said. Until morning to make a decision that wasn't really a decision at all.

"We figure something out."

"Like what?"

"I don't know yet. But they made a mistake bringing us here."

"What mistake?"

"We're on the water." Nora shifted her weight, testing the ropes. They were tight, but not impossible. The big man had been more interested in speed than security. "I've spent my whole life on the water. I know these currents, these tides. If we can get to a boat, any boat, I can get us out of here."

"That's a big if. That guy doesn't look like he's going to fall asleep."

"Then we make him move. Create a distraction. Something."

Grady's voice was barely audible over the storm.

"What he said. About your father. About Russell choosing to cooperate."

"Don't."

"I'm not judging. My father made the same choice. Tommy Pruitt took their money, followed their orders, and he still ended up dead on that boat." Grady shifted beside her. "I spent two years hating him for that. Hating him for being weak. For getting himself killed chasing someone else's dirty money."

"And now?"

"Now I don't know. Maybe he was weak. Maybe he was trying to survive." Grady's voice was heavy. "I wasn't there when Laura died. She called, and I was on a deadline, and I said I'd call back in an hour. She died thirty minutes later. Stage four breast cancer, age thirty-eight. And I was chasing a story."

The words hung in the storm noise.

"So when the old man talks about choices, about what people do when they're backed into a corner, I don't know if I get to judge anyone anymore."

What would she have done, in her father's place? If someone had threatened her family, her livelihood, everything she'd built.

She didn't know.

"The old man," she said. "He's not Cranston. He's someone else. Someone bigger."

"Pilot."

"I think so. But I don't know who he is. I've lived in this county my whole life, and I don't recognize him."

"Maybe that's the point. Maybe he's been hiding in plain sight the whole time."

"There was a photograph," she said. "In the office. A group shot from some kind of anniversary party. The old man was in the center, but there was someone else, a man with a camera, standing off to the side. I know I've seen him before, but I can't remember where."

"What did he look like?"

"Older. Heavyset. Dark hair going gray. He had a beard, I think."

"That could be a lot of people."

"I know. But it's something. A thread." Nora flexed her wrists, feeling the rope bite into her skin. "We need to get out of here. We need to find Mary, get to the FBI, and figure out who that man is."

"One thing at a time. First we need to get past our friend over there."

The guard hadn't moved. He was staring straight ahead, the rifle across his knees, his face blank and bored. The phone came out again. The blue glow, the check, the phone put away.

"I have an idea," Nora said. "But you're not going to like it."

"I don't like anything about this situation. What's your idea?"

"We need him to come over here. Close enough that we can do something about it."

"And how do we do that?"

Nora took a breath. "I scream. Tell him I'm hurt, that something's wrong. When he comes to check, you hit him."

"With what? My face?"

"With your body. Your weight. Knock him down, and I'll do the rest."

"That's a terrible plan."

"You have a better one?"

Grady was silent.

"That's what I thought."

Outside, the storm hammered the tin roof. The tide was still rising, the water beneath the floorboards closer now, visible in the gaps whenever lightning flashed. They had until morning.

CHAPTER 7

The Storm

They waited.

The storm raged outside, wind screaming through the gaps in the boathouse walls, rain hammering the tin roof in waves that rose and fell like breathing. The *Lady Justice* groaned at her moorings, her fenders rubbing against the dock with each swell.

The guard hadn't moved. He sat by the door with the rifle across his knees, staring at nothing, patient as stone. They'd been there for—what? An hour? Two? Impossible to tell.

Nora tested the ropes again. The big man had tied them tight, but he'd been in a hurry, and the knots weren't perfect. She'd been working at them since they'd been left alone, twisting her wrists back and forth, feeling the rough hemp scrape against her skin. Slowly, millimeter by millimeter, the rope was loosening.

The boathouse was maybe thirty feet long and twenty wide, built on pilings over the water. Boats could pull in through a large opening at the river end. The structure was old, the wood weathered and gray, diesel and fish and rotting rope thick in the air. Fishing nets hung from the rafters. A workbench ran along one wall, cluttered with tools and engine parts. If she could get to that workbench, there might be something she could use—a knife, a screwdriver, anything.

But the guard was between her and the bench. And the guard had a rifle.

"You okay?" she whispered to Grady.

"Cold." His voice was thin. "But I'll manage."

"Can you move? If we have to run?"

"I can move. Don't ask me to do anything graceful."

"The cut—is it still bleeding?"

"Stopped, I think. Or slowed down." Grady shifted beside her, testing his own bonds. "Head hurts like hell, but I've had worse."

Nora looked at the guard again. He was maybe twenty feet away, sitting on an overturned crate, his back against the wall. The rifle was bolt-action. Old, probably a hunting rifle, the kind of thing you'd find in any rural home in Brunswick County. If he got off one shot, he'd have to work the bolt before he could fire again. That was maybe two seconds. Maybe three.

Two seconds wasn't much. But it might be enough.

"The plan," she said quietly. "You remember?"

"You scream. I tackle. We improvise from there."

"Can you do it? With your head the way it is?"

"I can do it." Grady shifted beside her, and she heard him wince. "Make sure your scream is convincing."

"It will be."

She gave the ropes one more twist. They were loose now—not loose enough to slip her hands through, but close. Another few minutes and she might be able to work free entirely.

But they didn't have minutes. They had until morning, and morning was getting closer with every passing hour.

They sat in silence for a while. The storm continued outside, wind and rain. Nora could feel the cold seeping through her wet clothes, into her bones.

"What's something you regret?" Grady asked.

The question surprised her. "What?"

Grady shifted against his ropes. "I'll go first. I already told you about Laura. The drive, the hospital."

"You did."

"What I didn't tell you—" He stopped. Started again. "After she died, the first thing I felt was relief." The word came out flat, stripped of everything. "Not grief. Relief. That the watching was over. That I could stop sitting in that room counting her breaths and go back to work." He exhaled. "I was packing my bag for Wilmington before the funeral flowers wilted. Told myself I was honoring her by finding the truth about my father. But that wasn't it. I couldn't sit still with what I'd felt."

"Grady—"

"The guilt came later. Months of it. Waking up at three in the morning, remembering her face, remembering that the first thing I'd felt when she stopped breathing was *free*." His voice was barely audible. "That's my regret. Not that I wasn't there. That when it was over, part of me was glad."

Nora didn't say anything. There was nothing to say that wouldn't make it smaller.

The guard shifted on his crate, the rifle settling across his lap. They both went still, watching. But he was adjusting his position, getting comfortable. After a moment, he went back to staring at nothing.

"Your turn," Grady said. "What do you regret?"

The rain drummed overhead.

"The last conversation I had with my father before he went into the hospital." The words came out slowly. "We fought. I told him I was tired of carrying his weight. Tired of cleaning up his messes my whole life. Told him I was done."

"What did he say?"

"Nothing. He looked at me with this expression—like I'd confirmed something he'd always suspected about himself." She swallowed. "Three days later, he collapsed. Never really woke up again. The last thing I said to him was that I was done with him."

"He would have understood."

"Would he?" Nora shook her head. "Doesn't matter. I said it. Can't unsay it." She turned to look at Grady. "I don't want absolution. I just want to stop hearing myself say it."

"That's not how regret works."

"I know."

They were quiet. The storm rattled the walls.

"What did you want?" Nora asked. "Before all this."

"Laura wanted three kids and a porch with rocking chairs." Grady's voice was careful, like he was handling something fragile. "I would have given her all of it."

"What about now?"

Nora looked at the guard, at the rifle, at the door beyond.

"Right now? I want to get out of this boathouse alive."

"Yeah," Grady said. "That's about the size of it."

The guard's chin dropped. His hand on the rifle went loose.

Nora watched his hands.

She'd done enough fuel-dock work in bad weather to know what tired looked like at two in the morning—the way a body stops arguing and starts making its own decisions. The guard's shoulders had rounded. His breathing was deep and regular. Cold air always won, eventually.

She gave it another five minutes.

Her thumb had cleared the rope. She held the progress.

"The letter," Nora said. Low. Not looking at him. "Your father's. You still have it?"

"Yeah."

"Good."

He was quiet a moment. "Why?"

She thought about the hospice room. Her father's eyes on the window while he talked. The things a man carries until they grow into him.

"Just wanted to know it was somewhere," she said.

He didn't answer. The river ran under the boathouse floor, dark and fast, taking whatever the storm had put into it.

The guard's head dropped. Stayed down three seconds. Four.

She worked her right wrist. Felt the second knot shift.

"Grady." She waited until he looked. Tilted her head toward the workbench along the wall. He followed her eyes. The claw hammer. The marine flare in its rack. The coil of wire.

His gaze came back.

One nod.

She measured the distance. Twelve feet to the workbench, eighteen to the door. The rifle was bolt-action, old, the kind that required working the action between shots.

Two seconds. Maybe three.

"On three," she said. "One. Two—"

The boathouse door banged open.

The guard was on his feet instantly, the rifle raised. But it wasn't an intruder—it was the cleaner, stepping in out of the rain, water streaming from his jacket, his face tight with something that might have been anger or might have been concern.

"Change of plans," he said. "We're moving them now."

"Now? In this storm?"

"Boss's orders. The woman—the one who got away—she made it to town. Called the police." The cleaner wiped rain from his face. "We've got maybe an hour before this place is crawling with cops. Everything has to be cleaned up before then."

Nora's mind raced. Mary had made it. She'd called the police. Help was coming—but not fast enough. If they got on that boat, they were dead. The river in this storm was a death sentence even without someone trying to kill them.

Beside her, she heard Grady's breathing change—steadier, more controlled. She knew what he was doing: running the numbers. Distance to Southport, response time for a rural department in a storm, how many minutes since Mary escaped the truck. The numbers weren't good.

The cleaner cut the ropes binding them to the chairs, then stepped back, the knife still in his hand. "Stand up. Slowly."

Nora stood. Her legs were stiff from sitting, her wrists raw where the ropes had been. Beside her, Grady rose more slowly, one hand touching the cut above his eye.

"Move." The cleaner gestured toward the door. "The boat's waiting."

They walked out into the storm.

The rain hit Nora like a fist, cold and hard, driving the breath from her lungs. The wind was worse than before—a sustained howl that made it hard to stand upright, that turned every loose object into a projectile. She could barely see the dock in front of her, barely see the *Lady Justice*.

The cleaner pushed her forward. "Keep moving."

The dock was slick with rain, the boards groaning under their feet. Nora counted steps—ten to the boat, maybe fifteen. The guard was behind them with the rifle. The cleaner was to her left, close enough to touch, the knife still in his hand.

Ten steps. She had ten steps to figure out how to survive this.

She glanced at Grady. He gave her a barely perceptible nod.

Nora stumbled. It wasn't hard to fake—the dock was slick, the wind was screaming, and she was exhausted. She went down hard on one knee, crying out as her hands hit the wet boards.

"Get up." The cleaner reached for her arm.

She grabbed his wrist and pulled.

He wasn't expecting it. He stumbled forward, off-balance, and Nora twisted under him, using his momentum to throw him past her. He hit the dock hard, the knife skittering away into the darkness.

Behind her, Grady moved. She heard the impact—body on body, a grunt, a curse. The rifle went off, the shot deafening even over the storm, and Grady cried out—hit, she thought, the bullet must have caught him somewhere. But he kept fighting, kept struggling, the sound of men grappling in the rain.

Nora scrambled to her feet. The cleaner was already rising, reaching for something at his belt—a gun, she realized, a pistol in a holster she hadn't seen. She kicked him in the face before he could draw it.

He went down again, blood streaming from his nose. Nora grabbed the pistol from his belt, turned, and saw Grady and the guard struggling at the edge of the dock. The guard was bigger, stronger, but Grady had gotten inside his reach, was holding onto him, keeping him from bringing the rifle to bear.

"Nora!" Grady's voice was ragged. "Go!"

"Not without you!"

She raised the pistol. The two men were too close together—she couldn't get a clean shot without risking

Grady. She ran toward them instead, looking for an opening—

The guard threw Grady off. He stumbled backward, hit the railing, and went over the side.

The splash was lost in the roar of the storm.

Nora fired. The shot caught the guard in the shoulder and spun him around. He dropped the rifle and grabbed for the wound, his face contorted with pain.

She didn't wait to see what happened next. She ran to the railing and looked over.

The water was black and churning, waves crashing against the pilings, foam white in the darkness. She couldn't see Grady. She couldn't see anything.

"GRADY!"

No answer. The storm, the wind, the rain hammering down.

Behind her, she heard the cleaner getting to his feet. Heard him shout something to the guard. She had seconds—maybe less.

She jumped.

The water was cold. Colder than the creek had been, colder than anything she'd ever felt. It closed over her head and dragged her down, the current spinning her, disorienting her, pulling her away from the dock.

She fought to the surface, gasping, treading water. The *Lady Justice* was above her, her white hull looming against the darkness, her propellers maybe ten feet away. If the engines started now, if the current pulled her into those blades—

She kicked hard, putting distance between herself and the boat.

The dock was—there, maybe thirty feet away, with figures moving on it, flashlights sweeping the water. She could hear shouting, but the words were lost in the storm. The cleaner was back on his feet, pointing, gesturing toward the river.

"GRADY!"

No answer. The rain and the wind and the waves crashing against the pilings.

A wave hit her in the face and she went under again. When she came up, she was further from the dock, the current carrying her downriver. She could see the boathouse now, could see the lights of the main house on the bluff above. The river was taking her south, away from the compound, away from the men who wanted her dead.

But Grady was still in the water. If he was still alive.

Something bumped against her in the darkness.

She grabbed it—a body, limp and heavy. Grady. His eyes were closed, his face slack, blood from the cut on his head mixing with the river water. She got an arm around his chest and kicked, fighting the current, trying to keep his head above water. He wasn't moving, wasn't helping. Unconscious or dead, she couldn't tell.

The shore. She had to get to shore.

She swam. The current was against her, the wind was against her, her clothes were dragging her down. The pistol she'd taken from the cleaner was gone—lost in the fall, probably at the bottom of the river now. She was unarmed, injured, exhausted, and trying to save a man who might already be dead.

But she'd been swimming in these waters since she was a child. She knew the current weakened near the banks, where the water eddied behind fallen trees and marsh grass. She knew there was a sandbar fifty yards downstream, a place where the river had deposited silt for decades, where the water was shallow enough to stand. She knew that if she could hold on, keep moving, the river would do the rest.

Her feet touched bottom.

The sandbar was maybe twenty feet across, a strip of mud and shells that barely broke the surface. She dragged Grady onto it and collapsed beside him, coughing, shaking, her lungs burning from the cold and the effort. The rain was still coming down, the wind still howling, but they were out of the water. They were alive.

"Grady." She rolled him onto his back and pressed her ear to his chest. Heartbeat—faint, but there. He was breathing, shallow and ragged, his chest rising and falling in stuttered rhythm. "Grady, wake up."

He didn't respond.

She tilted his head back, checked his airway, pressed on his chest like her father had taught her years ago. One, two, three—breathe. One, two, three—breathe. She'd done this on a drowning tourist once, years back, had pumped his chest until the paramedics arrived. He'd lived. Grady would live too.

He coughed. Water came out of his mouth, and he gasped, his eyes flying open.

"Easy. Easy." Nora held him down as he tried to sit up.

"The guard—"

"I shot him. He's down." Nora looked back toward the dock. The flashlights were still moving, still searching the water. They hadn't seen her—the storm had hidden her, the darkness had swallowed them both. But they would figure it out eventually. They would come looking.

She had to move.

She grabbed Grady under the arms and started dragging him toward the shore.

The marsh was a nightmare.

Every step sank into mud that sucked at her boots and threatened to pull her down. The cordgrass was sharp, cutting her hands and face as she pushed through it. And Grady was heavy—heavier than she'd expected, a dead weight she had to drag one agonizing foot at a time.

But she kept moving. Through the marsh, toward the tree line, away from the dock and the house and the men who wanted them dead. The storm covered her, hid her, drowned out the sounds of her passage.

She reached the trees and stopped, leaning Grady against a pine trunk, trying to catch her breath. Her hands were shaking—from cold, from exhaustion, from adrenaline that had nowhere left to go.

But she couldn't rest. Not yet.

"Grady." She slapped his face, gently at first, then harder. "Grady, wake up. I need you to wake up."

His eyes fluttered. Opened. Focused on her face.

"Nora?"

"Yeah. It's me." She almost laughed with relief. "How do you feel?"

"Like I went swimming in a hurricane." He tried to sit up and groaned. "What happened?"

"You went over the side. I pulled you out." Nora helped him into a sitting position. "Can you walk?"

"Maybe. Where are we?"

"In the woods, south of the compound. I don't know exactly." She looked around, trying to get her bearings. The trees were dense here, blocking what little light the storm allowed. She could hear the river to her left, which meant north was that way. Maybe. "We need to keep moving. They'll be searching for us."

"The boat—"

"Forget the boat. Mary made it. She called the police." Nora stood and offered Grady her hand. "We have to keep moving until help gets here."

Grady took her hand and pulled himself up. He swayed for a moment, then steadied, one hand against the tree trunk.

"How long?"

"The cleaner said an hour. Maybe less now."

They started walking.

The woods went on and on.

Nora led the way, pushing through underbrush that clawed at her clothes, stepping over roots that threatened to trip her in the darkness. Grady followed close behind, his breathing labored, his footsteps uneven. Every few minutes she would stop and listen, straining to hear pursuit over the roar of the storm.

Nothing. The rain and wind covered their tracks, made flashlights useless, turned the forest into a maze where anyone could get lost.

But they couldn't walk forever. Grady was weakening—she could hear it in his breathing, see it in the way he stumbled. His wound was still bleeding; she'd seen the dark stain spreading across his shirt when she'd dragged him from the water. He needed rest, needed medical attention. He needed to stop moving.

"There." Nora pointed ahead. Through the trees, a shape—a structure of some kind, angular and dark against the storm-black sky. "A building."

"What kind of building?"

"I don't know. Let's find out."

It was a cabin. Old, weathered, probably a hunting shack abandoned years ago. The windows were boarded over, the porch sagging, the roof missing shingles in a dozen places. But the walls were standing and the door was closed, and right now that was enough.

Nora pushed the door open and stepped inside.

The cabin smelled of rot and animal musk. Something had been living here—raccoons, probably, or possums. But it was dry, or at least drier than outside, and there was a fireplace against one wall with a stack of old wood beside it.

"Get inside," she said. "I'll check it out."

She moved through the cabin quickly, checking corners, looking for threats. Nothing. One room with a fireplace, a broken table, a mattress so stained and moldy she wouldn't have touched it on a bet. But there was a door in the back—a closet, maybe, or a bathroom.

She opened it.

Not a closet. A storage room. And inside—

Nora stopped.

There were boxes stacked against the walls. Dozens of them, labeled with dates and names. Some of the labels were faded, barely legible; others were fresh, the ink still dark. The boxes went back decades—dates from the

1980s, the 1990s, all the way up to the present. And in the corner, sitting on a wooden chair with her hands tied behind her back, was Mary Galloway.

Her face was bruised, one eye swollen shut, her good arm hanging at an odd angle that suggested it had been dislocated again. Her clothes were torn and muddy. But she was breathing. Alive.

"Mary."

Her cousin's eyes opened. It took a moment for them to focus.

"Nora?" Her voice was a croak, barely audible over the rain drumming on the roof. "How did you—"

"Later." Nora was already working on the ropes. The knots were tight—professional, the kind tied by someone who'd done this many times before. "Can you walk?"

"I don't know. They—" Mary winced as Nora pulled at the knots. "They caught me at the truck. I tried to run, but there were too many of them. Four, maybe five. I got maybe a hundred yards into the woods before they tackled me." Her voice was bitter. "So much for the head start."

"You called the police. Before they caught you?"

"I tried. I don't know if it went through. The storm was messing with the signal."

"The cleaner said you got through. Said help was coming."

"Then maybe something went right." Mary coughed. "First time tonight."

"They wanted to know if I had other backups." Mary's laugh was bitter. "I told them no. I lied."

"You have other backups?"

"Three. Hidden in places they'll never find." The ropes came loose, and Mary pulled her arms forward, grimacing as blood flowed back into her hands. "One in a safety deposit box in Wilmington under a fake name. One on a server in Iceland. And one buried in a coffee can behind my grandmother's grave in the Galloway family plot."

"Jesus, Mary."

"I've had eight months to plan for this. I knew they'd come for me eventually. I knew they'd want the files." Mary flexed her fingers, wincing. "I made sure there was always another copy. Always another way to bring them down."

"Nora, the files they're moving—they're here. In this cabin. I saw them bring the boxes in."

Nora looked at the boxes stacked against the walls. Dates going back decades. Names she didn't recognize—and a few she did. Cranston. Banks. Galloway.

"This is it," she said. "This is everything."

"The backup location. They were going to burn Delacroix, but they needed somewhere to keep the records. Somewhere nobody would look." She gestured at the cabin. "An abandoned hunting shack on the edge of the wildlife refuge. Perfect."

Nora heard footsteps behind her. Grady, standing in the doorway, his face pale but alert.

"We found them," he said.

"We found more than that." Nora gestured at Mary. "Help me get her up."

They got Mary on her feet. Her legs buckled immediately, and Grady caught her before she hit the floor. She hung there for a moment, eyes squeezed shut, the blood rushing back into legs that had gone dead hours ago. Then she locked her knees and stood on her own.

"What about the boxes?" Grady asked.

"We can't carry them. Not in this storm, not in our condition." Nora looked at the stacks of evidence—thirty years of crimes, all of it right here, waiting. "But we can make sure they don't disappear."

"What are you doing?"

"Leaving a message." Nora walked to the closest box and pulled it open. Inside were folders, documents, photographs. She rifled through them, looking for something specific, looking for names she recognized.

One folder caught her eye. The label read "Pruitt, T.—2010" in neat handwriting. She pulled it out and opened it.

Inside were photographs. Thomas Pruitt at work on the docks. Thomas Pruitt at a bar, talking to a man whose face was blurred. Thomas Pruitt getting into a car outside his house, the license plate visible. Surveillance photographs, taken over what looked like months.

And a document. A single sheet of paper, typed, with a signature at the bottom.

I, Thomas Pruitt, acknowledge receipt of $25,000 for services rendered in connection with the scheduled maintenance of the vessel "Miss Carolina." *I understand that this payment is final and that no further discussion of this matter is expected or permitted.*

The signature was shaky, the letters uneven. The signature of a man who knew he was signing something that would haunt him forever.

"Grady." Nora's hands were shaking. "Come here."

He came. He looked at the paper. His face went pale, then red, then still.

"That's my father's signature."

"I know."

"They paid him. Twenty-five thousand dollars." Grady's voice was barely a whisper. "To help them kill three people."

"He didn't know anyone would die. Nobody was supposed to be on that boat." Nora put a hand on his arm. "Your father made a mistake. He trusted the wrong people. But he wasn't a murderer."

"No. He was just a coward. A coward who took their money and kept his mouth shut and died because of it."

"He died because they killed him. Because he was a loose end they needed to tie up." Nora put the folder down and pulled open another box. "Don't let them make you hate him. That's what they want. That's how they win."

She found what she was looking for in the third box. A folder labeled "*Miss Carolina*—Insurance Documentation."

She opened it. Inside were photographs of the boat. Invoices for parts that had never been installed. Statements from witnesses who had been paid to lie. And at the bottom, a single sheet of paper with a list of names.

The crew of the *Miss Carolina*. Next to each name was an amount—money they'd been paid, she assumed. And next to two of the names was a single word: "Handled."

Thomas Pruitt. Handled. Russell Banks. Handled.

"Handled" meant whatever it took. Her father and Grady's father—one dead in the water, one bought into silence and left to rot with it.

Nora folded the whole folder and shoved it inside her jacket. Then she looked at the rest of the boxes—at the years of evidence, the decades of crimes, the proof of everything Pilot had done.

She looked at what they couldn't carry. Two dozen boxes, stacked floor to ceiling. There was no way to take them. There was no way to call Torres and hold this room—Pilot's men were somewhere on this property, and they had minutes, not hours.

But she wasn't leaving them intact.

"We need something to carry these." Nora looked around the cabin. A canvas duffel hung on a nail by the door, old and stiff with mildew but intact. She pulled it down.

"Fill it," Nora said. "Fast. Harbor records first, then the Cranston correspondence. Whatever's dated earliest."

They worked without talking. Grady pulled folders, Nora checked labels, Mary directed them to the boxes she recognized from eight months of research. The bag filled in ninety seconds—as much as it would hold, maybe a third of what was there.

Then Nora heard it. An engine on the gravel road. Low and distant, but getting less distant.

She worked faster. Grady heard it too—she could tell by the way his hands stopped being careful. Mary went still, listening, then pointed at a box in the corner. "That one. The manifests."

Grady grabbed it, pulled the top third of the folders, stuffed them in. The zipper wouldn't close all the way. He forced it.

The engine sound shifted. A door somewhere in the tree line. A radio crackle, short and sharp.

"That's enough." Nora looked at what remained. Box after box of names she recognized—harbor workers, county commissioners, dock hands. People who had made one bad choice fifteen years ago and had been paying for it every month since. Names Pilot had been using to keep this town quiet. If they walked out and left these boxes, he walked back in and reclaimed every piece of leverage he'd built. The blackmail didn't end. It just changed hands.

She wasn't going to let him have it.

"There's kerosene in the corner. They were using it for the lanterns."

Nora found kerosene—two one-gallon cans, nearly full. She started pouring it over the boxes, working methodically, making sure every stack was soaked. The smell was sharp and chemical, cutting through the mustiness of the cabin.

When the cans were empty, she stepped back.

"Get outside. Both of you."

Grady helped Mary to the door. Nora followed, stopping at the threshold. She looked back at the cabin—at thirty years of evidence, at the proof of everything Pilot had built and everyone he'd destroyed.

Burning this wouldn't absolve her father. Nothing could do that. But the people whose names were in those boxes hadn't chosen to be there. They'd been put there. And she wasn't leaving Pilot the key to their doors.

She struck a match and threw it.

The kerosene caught with a whoosh, flames racing across the floor, climbing the walls, consuming the boxes and everything inside them. Within seconds, the cabin was an inferno, fire roaring toward the ceiling, smoke pouring out the windows and door.

Nora backed away, watching it burn.

"We need to move," Grady said. "They'll see the fire."

"Let them." Nora turned away from the flames. "By the time they get here, there won't be anything left."

They ran.

The cabin roared behind them, flames tearing through the kerosene-soaked interior, smoke boiling up black and thick into the thinning rain. Nora didn't look back but she could feel the heat on her neck for the first hundred yards, and she knew from the light it threw against the wet tree trunks that they'd see it from the main compound. Good. Let them come. There'd be nothing left worth saving.

The storm was weakening now—the rain coming in bursts rather than sheets, the wind dying to gusts that came and went. Dawn was coming; Nora could feel it, even if she couldn't see it yet.

They moved as fast as they could, which wasn't fast enough. Mary was limping badly, her injured arm clutched against her chest. Grady was fading, his face gray, his breathing labored. And Nora's legs were going numb, her body burning through its last reserves.

But they were alive. All three of them, alive and moving.

"The road," Mary gasped. "It should be close. Quarter mile, maybe less."

"Which road?"

"The county highway. The one that runs past the wildlife refuge." Mary stopped, leaning against a tree, her chest heaving. "If we can get there, we can flag down a car. Get to town. Find the police."

"Can you make it?"

"Do I have a choice?"

They kept moving.

The road appeared through the trees—a strip of wet asphalt, empty and dark, gleaming in the first gray light of dawn. Nora stopped at the tree line, scanning for headlights, for movement, for any sign they'd been followed.

Nothing. The road and the rain and the pale sky. The storm had finally broken, the clouds thinning, the wind dying to occasional gusts that stirred the treetops but didn't bend them. To the east, the sun was rising behind the clouds, turning the sky from black to gray to a pale, washed-out blue.

"We made it," Mary whispered. "We actually made it."

"Not yet." Nora stepped out onto the pavement. "We need a car. We need to move before they get to this road."

A car was coming. She could hear the engine before she saw the headlights—a low rumble, getting closer, moving fast despite the wet roads. She stepped into the center of the lane and waved her arms, making herself visible, making sure they'd stop.

The headlights appeared around a curve. The car was a sedan, dark-colored, moving fast, too fast for the conditions. For a moment Nora thought it wasn't going to stop—thought it would plow right through her, leave her bleeding on the asphalt. But the brakes squealed, the car fishtailed, and it came to a halt maybe twenty feet away, the engine idling, the headlights blinding.

Nora shielded her eyes, trying to see past the glare.

The driver's door opened.

"Easy." A man stepped out, his hands raised, his face hidden in the headlights. "I'm not armed. Take it easy."

Nora didn't have a weapon anymore—the pistol was at the bottom of the river. But she didn't let her hands drop, didn't let her stance relax.

"Who are you?"

"My name is Bennett. Chief Bennett. Southport Police." He stepped forward, and Nora could see him now—middle-aged, heavyset, with a broad face and tired eyes. He was wearing a rumpled uniform that looked like he'd thrown it on in a hurry, the shirt untucked, the badge crooked. "We got a call about a disturbance at the Delacroix property. Multiple shots fired, possible kidnapping. Are you the one who called?"

"That was my cousin." Nora nodded toward Mary, who was leaning against Grady, barely able to stand. "Mary Galloway. She needs a hospital. We all do."

"We've been shot at, beaten, and thrown in a river. We need medical attention and we need it now."

Bennett took another step forward. His eyes moved from Nora to Mary to Grady, taking in their condition—the blood, the bruises, the mud and river water that caked their clothes. His expression was neutral, professional, the look of a cop assessing a situation.

"All right. Let's get you to the hospital." He reached for his radio. "I'll call for backup, get an ambulance out here—"

"No."

Bennett stopped, his hand on the radio.

"No backup. No ambulance. We don't know who we can trust." Nora met his eyes. "We'll go with you. Just you. To the hospital, and then to the FBI field office in Wilmington."

"The FBI? Ma'am, this is a local matter—"

"This is a federal matter. Racketeering, wire fraud, murder. We have evidence that implicates half the county government, including the sheriff's department." Nora didn't blink. "We're not going anywhere near the sheriff's department until we've talked to the feds."

Bennett's face was unreadable.

"All right. We'll do it your way. Get in the car. I'll drive you to the hospital, and then we'll talk about next steps."

Nora hesitated. Something wasn't right. The way Bennett was standing, the way his eyes kept flicking toward the tree line. The fact that he was alone—no partner, no backup, on a call about multiple shots fired and possible kidnapping.

"How did you know where to find us?"

"Like I said, we've got units searching the whole area. I was heading toward Delacroix when I saw you on the road."

"From which direction?"

"What?"

"Which direction were you coming from? The fire's to the north. If you were heading to Delacroix, you would have seen the smoke. Would have known something was wrong."

Bennett's smile flickered.

"Why don't you put the gun down, Ms. Banks? You're safe now."

"I'm not holding a gun."

Bennett's expression changed. Something cold moved behind his eyes.

He drew.

Nora was already moving. She dove to the left, hit the pavement, rolled. The shot went over her head—she heard it crack past, felt the heat of it near her ear. She came up in a crouch, looking for cover, looking for anything—

Grady tackled Bennett from behind.

They went down in a tangle of limbs, the gun going off again, the shot wild, disappearing into the trees. Nora scrambled toward them, saw Bennett trying to bring the gun around, saw Grady's hands on his wrist, struggling for control.

She grabbed a rock from the shoulder of the road—fist-sized, heavy with rain. She brought it down on Bennett's head.

He went limp.

Grady rolled off him, gasping, one hand pressed to his side. The wound was bleeding again—Nora could see the blood spreading across his shirt, darker now, more of it.

"We need to go," Mary said. She was standing by the car, the driver's door still open, the engine still running. "Before he wakes up. Before more of them come."

Nora grabbed Bennett's pistol and checked it. A .38 revolver. Standard issue. Full cylinder minus two rounds.

"Get in the car."

They got in. Nora behind the wheel, Mary in the passenger seat, Grady in the back with his hand pressed to his wound. The car was still warm, the heater running, the radio crackling with static.

She floored it.

The tires spun on the wet asphalt, then caught. The car shot forward, leaving Chief Bennett unconscious on the road behind them.

"Where are we going?" Mary asked.

"Wilmington. The FBI field office."

The road unwound ahead of them, empty and wet, the dawn light flat and gray on the asphalt. Nobody spoke. The wipers beat back and forth, clearing rain that was already thinning to mist.

CHAPTER 8

The Reckoning

Grady was dying.

Nora could see it in the gray pallor of his face, in the shallow rhythm of his breathing. His hand had stopped pressing against the wound and lay there, limp and blood-soaked, on the seat beside him. The bullet had caught him in the side during the dock fight. The fabric of his shirt was torn. The dark stain had spread until it covered half his torso.

The road unwound ahead of them, wet asphalt gleaming in the early light. They'd been driving for maybe fifteen minutes, and every minute felt like an hour. The stolen police car still smelled of Bennett's cigarettes and aftershave, a sickly combination that made Nora's stomach turn.

"Stay with me," she said. "Grady. Stay with me."

"Trying." His voice was barely a whisper. "Hard to keep my eyes open."

"Then talk to me. Tell me something. Something good about your father."

Mary had turned sideways in the passenger seat to watch Grady in the back, her injured arm cradled to her chest, her face tight with the effort of it. In the rearview mirror, Grady's face was gray against the window, his breath fogging the glass in shallow circles. The sun was rising behind them, painting the sky in shades of pink and gold.

"He taught me to fish," Grady said finally. "Out on the sound, before dawn. He'd wake me up at four in the morning, and I'd complain, and he'd say—" He coughed. "He'd say the fish don't care if you're tired."

"Keep talking."

"We'd sit there in the boat, in the dark, not talking much. Listening to the water. Watching the stars fade." Grady's eyes were closing. "He was just a man." His hand found hers, weak but insistent. "Don't let me die in this car, Nora."

Nora pressed the accelerator harder. The speedometer climbed: seventy, eighty, ninety. The road was empty, the storm having cleared the early morning traffic, and she took the curves faster than she should. The car's tires squealed on the wet pavement, but she didn't slow down. She counted the circles Grady's breath made on the glass. When the circles stopped, she would know.

"Carl's place," Mary said from the passenger seat. "It's closer than the hospital. He can stabilize him."

"Carl's a vet."

"Carl's a combat medic who happened to end up treating animals. He saved my life." Mary leaned toward the back seat. "He can save Grady's."

The road ahead was empty: Wilmington maybe twenty minutes away, the hospital another ten past that. Carl's place was five minutes, maybe less. In the back seat, Grady's breathing had gone shallow enough that she could no longer hear it over the engine.

"Where?"

"Take the next right. Gravel drive, cinder-block house. You'll see the sign for the clinic."

The road was a two-lane blacktop off Route 133, no center line, ditches on both sides filling with storm runoff. The houses were set back behind stands of loblolly pine, each one on a few acres, each one invisible from the next. Carl's was a single-story cinder-block ranch with a metal roof and an addition built onto the back that was bigger than the house itself, the clinic. A gravel drive curved through a yard of wiregrass and sand, past a wooden sign that read REEVES VETERINARY in hand-painted letters that were peeling at the edges. Two kennels flanked the clinic entrance, empty now, their chain-link gates standing open. A flatbed truck sat beside the house with a crate of fencing supplies in the bed.

Mary reached for the charging cradle on the dash and came away with a cell phone—a department-issued brick, heavy and generic. She typed quickly with her good hand.

"Calling ahead," she said. "He needs to be ready."

Nora heard the phone ring through the speaker, then Carl's voice, rough and immediate.

"Who is this?"

"It's Mary. We're two minutes out. Gunshot wound, massive blood loss. Get your surgical suite ready."

The line went dead. Mary lowered the phone.

Carl was waiting on the porch when they pulled up.

He was a big man, broad-shouldered and gray-haired, his face deeply creased, the skin around his eyes sun-damaged and drawn tight across the cheekbones. He was wearing scrubs and rubber boots, and he came down the steps before the car had fully stopped.

"Inside," he said. "Now."

They got Grady out of the car, half-carrying him, half-dragging him. He was barely conscious now, his feet stumbling on the gravel, his head lolling forward. Carl led them through the house, past a front room with a recliner and a television and stacks of veterinary journals on every flat surface, past a kitchen that smelled of coffee and the sharp sweetness of betadine, to the back addition. The surgical suite was a converted garage: poured concrete floor with a drain in the center, overhead fluorescent panels that buzzed when Carl hit the switch, stainless-steel counters along two walls lined with instruments in autoclave bags. A large-animal examination table dominated the room, its surface padded with a rubber mat stained from years of use. The air smelled of isopropyl alcohol and iodine and, underneath it, the faint copper tang of old blood.

"On the table."

They lifted Grady onto the steel table. Carl was already cutting away his shirt, exposing the wound: a ragged hole in his side, still seeping blood, the flesh around it angry and swollen.

"Bullet's still in there," Carl said, probing the wound with gloved fingers. "Small caliber, probably a .22. Cracked at least two ribs on entry. Didn't hit anything vital—missed the kidney by maybe an inch—but he's lost a lot of blood."

He looked up at Nora, his expression grim. "I can get the bullet out and stop the bleeding. I can pump him full of fluids to keep his blood pressure up. But he needs a real hospital for a transfusion. Without it, he's got maybe six hours before his body starts shutting down."

"Will he live?" Nora asked.

Carl was already pulling instruments from drawers, his hands moving with practiced efficiency. "If you get him to a hospital in time. If infection doesn't set in. If he doesn't go into shock before then." He hung a bag of saline from the IV pole. "A lot of ifs."

"Do what you can."

"I always do." Carl gestured toward the door. "Wait outside. This is going to take a while."

Nora didn't want to leave. She wanted to stay, to hold Grady's hand, to do something besides stand in a doorway and watch. But Carl was right. She'd only be in the way.

"Mary. Come with me."

They went outside.

The porch was a concrete slab with a corrugated tin overhang, two plastic chairs and a coffee can full of cigarette butts on the railing. From here Nora could see the gravel drive, the flatbed, the tree line of loblolly pines that screened the property from the road. A rooster crowed somewhere behind the clinic. The storm had left the yard scattered with pine needles and small branches, and the air was heavy with the smell of wet earth and resin.

The dawn was breaking fully now, the sky turning from gray to pink to pale blue. Nora sat on the edge of the concrete and tried to breathe. Through the wall behind her she could hear Carl moving: the clink of instruments on the steel tray, a cabinet opening and closing, the hiss of something pressurized. Once, she heard Grady moan, a sound that came through the cinder block muffled and distant, and her hands went tight on her knees.

Mary sat down beside her, arm held tight against her ribs.

"Carl's good," Mary said. "He saved my life when I came to him with a dislocated shoulder and a fever of a hundred and four."

"I know," she said.

They sat. Instruments. Movement. A machine humming. Once, water running. Once, surgical scissors snapping. A mockingbird in the pines. The sun climbed. The gravel steamed.

Mary got up and walked to the edge of the porch, then walked back and sat down again. Nora didn't move. She kept her hands flat on her knees and watched the steam rise from the gravel and listened for sounds from behind the wall. At some point a yellow cat appeared from beneath the flatbed, crossed the yard in no particular hurry, and disappeared around the side of the clinic.

"The FBI," Nora said finally. "We need to get there. We need to—"

"Nora." Mary's voice was careful. Deliberate. "There's something I need to tell you."

Nora turned to look at her.

"I found something else," Mary said. "In the files. Something I didn't tell you before."

"What?"

Mary pulled a photograph from her jacket pocket. It was old, the colors faded, the edges worn soft. Three men standing on a dock, a trawler visible behind them. Nora recognized the dock—it was the commercial pier in Southport, the same one she walked past every day going to work. But the boats were different, older, their paint unfaded. The photograph was from another decade.

The man on the left: Thomas Pruitt. Grady's father.

The man in the middle was her father. Russell Banks, younger. Unlined. Smiling.

The man on the right: older, broad-shouldered, one hand on Russell's shoulder. She'd seen him two nights ago at Delacroix.

Pilot.

"There's more," Mary said quietly. "On the back."

Nora turned the photograph over. Written in faded ink, in handwriting she didn't recognize: *Russell, Thomas, and the old man. Good catch, 1992.*

"Eighteen years before the *Miss Carolina* sank," Mary said. "They knew each other. Your father, Grady's father, and Pilot. They were working together." She paused. "There's something else. I found Russell's birth certificate in the files. Pilot's full name is on it. He's your grandfather, Nora. Russell's father."

Nora stared at the photograph. The dock. The boat. The three men. The old man's hand was on Russell's shoulder. She'd looked at that hand two nights ago and not known what she was seeing.

"The files I found," Mary continued, "they go back to the eighties. Import manifests, harbor records, payroll documents. Your father's name is all through them. Not as a victim. As a participant."

"No."

"I'm sorry, Nora. But he knew. He knew what Pilot was doing, and he helped him do it. For years. Long before the *Miss Carolina.*"

The photograph was shaking in Nora's hand. She put it down on the concrete beside her and pressed both palms flat against the rough surface to stop them from trembling.

"The *Miss Carolina* wasn't the beginning," Mary said. "It was the end. The thing that finally made him want out."

Her father's hands. Scarred and callused, the knuckles swollen from decades on the water. The patience in them when he was teaching her to tie knots, his voice saying Try again without frustration, without judgment. The morphine drip. His eyes finding hers: *I need to tell you something*.

"Why didn't you tell me before?"

"Because I wasn't sure you'd still help if you knew." Mary met her eyes. "I needed you to stop Pilot. I couldn't risk you walking away."

"I wouldn't have—"

"You would have hesitated. And hesitation gets people killed." Mary's voice was flat. "Pilot still killed him."

The door to the clinic opened. Carl stepped out onto the porch, pulling off his surgical gloves. Blood streaked his scrubs from chest to knees. He looked exhausted.

"He's stable," he said. "For now. I got the bullet out, stopped the bleeding, put in some internal sutures where the ribs fractured. He's sedated, on IV fluids and antibiotics."

"How long do we have?" Nora asked.

Carl checked his watch. "Six hours. Maybe eight if he's lucky and strong. After that, his body won't have enough red blood cells to carry oxygen. He'll go into organ failure." He met her eyes. "You need to get him to Wilmington Hospital before that happens. I can't do a transfusion here."

Nora and Mary exchanged glances.

Six hours.

Enough time to finish this. Barely.

"He's sleeping. Sedated." Carl sat down on the porch edge, his knees cracking. He pulled a pack of cigarettes from his shirt pocket, shook one out, and lit it. "Whatever you're planning to do next, you've got about five hours before you need to get him to a hospital. After that, the math stops working."

"Five hours," Nora repeated.

"Give or take." Carl exhaled smoke. "You want my advice? Get him to Wilmington now. Whatever else you think you need to do, it can wait."

"It can't." Nora stood up. "Mary and I are going to the FBI. We have evidence. Testimony. Enough to bring down the organization that's been running this county for thirty years."

Carl studied her through the smoke. His expression didn't change.

"And you think they'll let you?"

"They don't have a choice."

"Everyone has a choice." Carl tapped ash into the coffee can. "The question is whether they'll make the one you're hoping for."

Nora thought about that. About the FBI field office in Wilmington. About walking through those doors with everything she knew and trusting that the people inside would do the right thing. About the photograph in Mary's pocket, her father's face from 1992, his hand on a boat rail, Pilot's hand on his shoulder.

"We're going," she said.

Carl shrugged. Took another drag.

"Then go. I'll watch him. But you're on a clock now. Don't forget that."

Nora glanced through the window into the clinic. She could see Grady on the table, his chest rising and falling, the IV line running from his arm to the bag of saline hanging above him. He looked small on that table. Fragile. Like something that could break.

"Five hours," she said.

"Five hours." Carl stood up, ground the cigarette out against the porch railing. "After that, he's dying whether you're here or not."

* * *

The yellow cat was still crossing the yard when the black SUV turned into the drive.

Nora saw it through the clinic window as she and Mary moved toward the car. The vehicle was coming fast on the gravel, no headlights, kicking up a rooster tail of wet stone. Her hand went to the .38 at her waistband before she'd finished processing what she was looking at.

"Carl."

He was still on the porch. He saw it too. He dropped the cigarette.

The SUV stopped hard in the gravel and three men got out before the dust settled. They moved like they'd practiced it: the first through the yard gate with a shotgun already at his shoulder, the second circling wide toward the clinic entrance, the third heading straight for Nora.

She had the .38 up but the shotgun was already pointed at her face from maybe eight feet away. Close enough to see the man's finger indexed on the trigger guard. Close enough to understand the math.

"Put it down," he said.

She didn't. Not yet. "Who sent you?"

He didn't answer.

Carl stepped off the porch, hands up, moving between Nora and the man with the shotgun. "He can't be moved. Whatever you want, he can't be moved yet—you'll kill him."

The second man was already inside the clinic. Nora heard the crash of equipment, instruments off a tray. Then Grady's voice, hoarse and confused, trying to fight.

"Don't." She took a step toward the clinic door. The shotgun barrel tracked her. "He has a bullet wound. He'll tear the sutures."

The third man came out of the clinic with Grady. One man under his arms, the other at his legs, hauling him like cargo. Grady's face was sheet-white, the IV still in his arm, the line dangling and dripping. He was trying to get purchase with his feet and finding nothing. His eyes found Nora across the yard.

Carl stepped forward again. "I'm telling you, if you move him now—"

The man with the shotgun shot Carl in the chest.

The sound was enormous in the still morning. Carl went straight down, no stumble, no grab at the wound. The coffee can fell off the railing and landed beside him in the gravel, cigarette butts scattering across the wet stone.

Mary screamed. Nora's finger was on the trigger but the shotgun was still up and she was eight feet away and if she fired she was dead and Grady was dead and it would change nothing.

The men loaded Grady into the SUV. He got one hand free and grabbed the door frame and they pulled him loose and put him in and shut the door.

The man with the shotgun kept the barrel on Nora until the SUV's engine turned over. Then he took a step back. Just one.

"Message," he said. His voice was flat, professional. "Delacroix. One hour. Come alone or he dies."

He got in the passenger seat. The SUV backed out of the drive.

One of the other men was already in Bennett's stolen police car. The engine caught. It pulled out behind the SUV and they were gone, both of them, dust still hanging in the air above the empty gravel where Carl had been standing.

Nora stood in the yard with the .38 in her hand and Carl at her feet and the yellow cat watching from beneath the flatbed, and the morning birds going on like nothing had happened.

Mary was on her knees beside Carl, one hand pressed to his chest, but his eyes were open and fixed and there was nothing there. The blood spread slow and dark through the gravel.

"We have to go." Nora's voice came out flat, the emotion driven down somewhere deep by the weight of the next thing and the thing after that. She put a hand on Mary's shoulder. "We can't help him."

Mary looked up at her. Her face had gone somewhere past grief into a kind of terrible clarity.

"Then we finish it," she said.

They got in Carl's flatbed and drove north.

* * *

The FBI field office in Wilmington was a low brick building off Market Street, wedged between a bail bondsman and a pawn shop, its windows tinted dark and its parking lot half-empty. A single American flag hung from a pole by the entrance, limp in the still air. No signs. No identifying markers except a small brass plaque by the door.

Nora and Mary went inside.

The receptionist looked up from behind bulletproof glass. Her eyes widened slightly at their appearance—

soaked through, mud-caked, Mary's arm in a makeshift sling—but she picked up the phone without comment.

"Can I help you?"

"We need to speak to someone about an ongoing investigation," Nora said.

"Do you have an appointment?"

"No. But we have information about a case. A federal case."

"What case?"

"The Pilot investigation."

The receptionist's hand stopped moving toward the phone. Her gaze moved from Nora to Mary and back.

She picked up the phone. Spoke quietly into it, her voice too low to hear through the glass. Hung up. Pressed a button. The door beside the reception window buzzed.

"Someone will be right with you."

They waited in a room with beige walls and government-issue chairs and a water cooler in the corner that hummed and clicked. A clock on the wall. A poster about reporting suspicious activity. Nora counted the seconds. Mary sat with her eyes closed, her arm held close to her body.

The door opened. A woman stepped through—mid-thirties, dark hair pulled back, suit that looked expensive but worn, the kind of professional competence that came from years of making people talk who didn't want to. Her gaze swept over Nora and Mary with the expression of someone assessing a crime scene.

"I'm Special Agent Torres," she said. "You mentioned Pilot."

"We have evidence," Nora said. "Documents. Testimony. Enough to prosecute. And we have a hostage situation. Grady Pruitt—he's been investigating his father's murder for two years, he's been shot, and they took him less than an hour ago.

They gave us a deadline."

Torres didn't react. Didn't smile, didn't frown, didn't show surprise or skepticism or anything else.

"Come with me."

They followed her through a hallway of numbered doors, past offices where people sat at desks staring at computer screens, past a break room where someone was microwaving something that smelled like burned popcorn. Torres led them to an interview room: a table, four chairs, a recording device on a tripod in the corner. No windows. The air conditioning was loud enough to make Nora's ears ring.

"Sit," Torres said.

They sat. Torres sat across from them and folded her hands on the table.

"Start from the beginning," she said. "Tell me everything."

So Nora did.

She told Torres about her father's deathbed confession. About Mary's investigation. About the *Miss Carolina* and the three people who died when the boat was deliberately sunk for insurance money. About the letters Mary had found, the manifests, the payroll records stretching back decades. About Pilot and his organization, about the docks and the boats and the money moving through the harbor. About Grady's father, Thomas Pruitt, and the letter he'd written to his wife before he died. About Chief Bennett and the web of people who'd been paid to look the other way.

She told Torres about Delacroix. About the cabin full of files they'd burned because there was no other way to strip Pilot of the leverage he'd used for thirty years to keep people quiet.

She told her everything.

Mary added details. Dates. Names. Account numbers. The things she'd memorized from the files before they went up in smoke. The photographs Grady had taken, the USB drive she'd hidden. The trail of evidence that stretched from 1985 to the present day.

When they finished, Nora set the bag on the table and placed Mary's USB drive beside it. Torres looked at both.

"Eight months of documented research on the drive," Nora said. "Harbor records, Cranston correspondence, shipping manifests going back to 1987 in the bag. We couldn't carry everything, so we burned the rest."

Torres unzipped the bag and looked inside without touching anything. She picked up the drive. "How much is here?"

"Enough."

Torres sat back in her chair. She looked at the bag, then at Nora.

"Your grandfather," she said. It wasn't a question.

"Yes."

Torres was already standing.

"I need to make some calls. This is bigger than I thought."

She turned to Nora. “Stay here. Don’t talk to anyone. Don’t leave the building.” Then, quietly: “And don’t trust anyone you don’t already know.”

“What does that mean?”

Torres set her pen down. When she looked up, something had shifted in her expression—not quite warning, not quite confession.

“We’ve had three warrants go cold in the last two years,” she said. “Evidence rooms accessed. Witness interviews leaked before we could act on them.”

“Someone tipped them.”

“Until I know who it is, I can’t trust my own chain of command. Which means I don’t go through it. I go around it—directly to a federal judge I trust outside this district. These files give me standing to do that without tipping anyone.”

“How careful?” Nora said. “Grady has a gunshot wound and maybe five hours before organ failure. How much careful can you afford?”

Torres stood. She hesitated, then opened a file drawer and pulled out a thin folder. She set it on the table in front of Nora. The tab read: CAPE FEAR MARITIME - SEALED BY ORDER USM NC-ED.

“This is from 2019. Federal marshals service, Eastern District. They were tracking Cape Fear Maritime Holdings through interstate commerce violations. Smuggling, mostly. Small stuff. The investigation was six months old when it got shut down.” Torres tapped the folder. “Sealed by order of a federal judge in Raleigh. Outside our jurisdiction, outside our case. But I’ve been watching those shell companies for three years, and every time we get close, someone higher up makes a phone call."

She pulled the folder back. "Whatever you're dealing with, it's bigger than Brunswick County. This goes to Raleigh. Maybe higher."

She turned and walked out of the room.

Nora and Mary sat in silence. The recording device's red light was still on.

"Whatever happens next," Mary said, "the truth is on the record."

"It's not over. Not until he's in handcuffs."

Mary leaned back in her chair and closed her eyes. She looked like she hadn't slept in days, and she probably hadn't. Nora watched the red light on the recording device and listened to the air conditioning and the muffled sounds of the building around them, people moving behind walls, a phone ringing somewhere far away.

She opened the door.

Torres was standing in the hallway, her phone in her hand, her face the color of the walls.

"What is it?" Nora asked.

"I know who made the call." Torres's voice was flat. "One of my own people. He accessed the intake log twelve minutes after you sat down."

The linoleum floor had a pattern—small gray diamonds on white. Nora looked at it.

"Your intake log." Nora's voice was flat. "Who else has access to it?"

"It's internal. Restricted."

"But whoever accessed it—they know we came in. That we're talking." She took a step toward the door. "And they work for him."

Torres said nothing.

"Pilot set a deadline. Come alone or Grady dies." Nora held her gaze. "He knows I didn't. He knows exactly where I am and what I'm doing. What do you think that does to his calculus on keeping Grady alive?"

Torres's jaw tightened.

"The deadline was leverage," Nora said. "It's gone. Grady isn't leverage anymore. He's a liability with a bullet hole in him and a federal warrant closing in." She stepped past Torres. "How long does it take to isolate your leak?"

Torres didn't answer.

"Then I'm going."

"Ms. Banks." Torres stepped in front of her. "You walk into Delacroix alone, you die. They will kill you both."

"Maybe. But if I wait for you to clean your own house, Grady dies for certain." Nora stepped around her. "How long do hostages last at Delacroix? You know the history of that property. You know what happens to people they stop needing."

Torres's hand didn't come up to stop her.

"I need one hour." Her voice came quiet and fast. "One hour to isolate the leak and move with a tactical team I trust. Proper authorization. Clean chain of custody." She paused. "If you go in there now, anything you find is inadmissible. Anything you do is illegal. And I cannot protect you."

"I'm not asking you to."

"Ms. Banks—"

"They don't negotiate," Nora said. "That's not what that place is. You know what they do up that river. People go in and don't come out and nobody asks questions because half the questions go straight back to them." She held Torres's gaze. "You want to spend your hour clearing paperwork while Grady bleeds out on their floor?"

Torres stood very still.

"You're not leaving this building," she said.

"Are you arresting me?"

"I should."

"But you won't." Nora walked toward the door. "Because you know I'm right."

Torres didn't move to stop her. She stood in the hallway with her phone in her hand and her face unreadable, something Nora couldn't read and didn't trust.

Then she pulled a business card from her jacket pocket. Set it on the table just inside the door.

"There's a number on the back," she said quietly. "Direct line. When you find him—if you find him—call it immediately. I'll have a team ready to move the moment I hear from you."

Nora took the card.

Torres reached into her jacket again. Car keys. She set them beside the card without looking at Nora.

"Parking garage. Spot forty-seven." Her voice had gone flat and professional again, the careful voice of someone making sure her words were precise. "Blue sedan. It's not in the system yet."

"You're giving me a car."

"I'm giving you one hour." Torres's eyes came up. Hard. "The rental is clean—no GPS, no agency markings, no way to track it. After that hour, I'm bringing a team to Delacroix whether you're back or not. And when this is over, if you are still alive, we are going to have a very long conversation about obstruction of justice."

"I'll look forward to it."

"I didn't give you that." The words landed careful and deliberate. "I didn't authorize this. Are we clear?"

Nora understood.

She turned toward Mary.

"Stay here," she said. "Tell them everything else you know. Every backup location, every piece of evidence, every name you haven't given them yet."

"Nora—"

"If I don't come back, you're the only one who can finish this." Nora gripped her cousin's hand. "Promise me."

Mary's eyes were wet. But her voice was steady.

"I promise."

Nora walked out of the FBI field office into the afternoon sun. The parking lot was half-empty, the asphalt radiating the day's stored heat. The American flag on the pole by the entrance hung limp in the still air. She didn't look at the security cameras. She didn't look back. Carl's flatbed was where they'd left it. She reached under the seat and found the .38. Four rounds. She put it in her jacket pocket.

The parking garage was two blocks down. Spot forty-seven. The blue sedan sat anonymous and plain under the fluorescent lights, no agency plates, no markings of any kind. She got in.

She pressed the accelerator and kept driving south.

CHAPTER 9

Blood

The road to Delacroix was empty.

Nora drove through the afternoon heat, the windows down, the salt air filling the car. The storm had scrubbed the world clean, left everything sharp-edged and bright. The marshes glittered in the sunlight, the cordgrass swaying in a breeze that carried the scent of mud and brine and the faint chemical tang of the paper mill upriver.

The .38 was in the center console where she'd left it. Torres's card was in her pocket. One hour, Torres had said. One hour before she sent a team.

Nora checked the clock on the dashboard. Forty-three minutes left.

The road narrowed past the wildlife refuge, the live oaks closing overhead until their branches wove together and the light came through in coins on the blacktop. Spanish moss hung from every limb, gray-green and still in the windless afternoon. The Cape Fear River, flat and brown and wide, moved south toward the ocean with the slow patience of something that had been doing this work for ten thousand years. A great blue heron stood in the shallows near the far bank, motionless, watching.

She'd only ever been here at night, in the storm. In daylight the road was just a road. Cracked asphalt, drainage ditches choked with pennywort, a faded yellow sign warning of a curve ahead. A box turtle was crossing the blacktop ahead of her, unhurried, ancient-looking. She steered around it. Ordinary. That was worse. The ordinary was where the worst things lived.

Hands on the wheel. Mouth dry. She swallowed and tasted copper and old coffee.

The road curved along the edge of the wildlife refuge, the trees pressing close. She passed the turnoff where they'd parked last night and kept going. The main entrance to Delacroix was a quarter mile further, marked by a rusted iron gate and a sign weathered to illegibility.

She turned onto the service road.

The gate was open. Yesterday it had been locked, guarded, the spike strip deployed across the gravel. Now the chain hung loose, the guard booth empty. A paper coffee cup sat on the booth's ledge, lid still on, a wisp of steam no longer rising from it. Whoever had been here had left recently and without hurrying.

They were expecting her.

Nora slowed the car to a crawl, scanning the tree line. Nothing. The compound was maybe a quarter mile ahead, hidden by a curve in the road. Gravel popped under the tires. A Carolina wren called from somewhere in the understory, two sharp notes and then silence. The air smelled of warming pine needles and the river.

She drove through the gate.

The gravel drive wound through a corridor of live oaks, the trunks massive, their bark rough and dark, some of them four feet across at the base. They must have been here before the house, before the road, before anyone thought to build anything on this bend of the river. The moss hung so thick from the lower branches it brushed the roof of the car.

The house appeared around the final bend. It looked different in daylight. Smaller. More ordinary. An old hunting lodge with a wraparound porch and peeling white paint, the kind of place wealthy men from Wilmington had built in the 1940s for duck season and bourbon and getting away from their wives. The tin roof had rusted in patches to the color of dried blood. Wisteria had colonized the east side of the porch, the vines as thick as her wrist, the last brown seedpods still clinging from autumn. The dock stretched out into the river where the *Lady Justice* was still moored. The boat sat low in the water, its white hull streaked with tannin stains from the river.

Three vehicles in the drive. The black SUV. A pickup truck. Bennett's dark sedan, mud-streaked from the service road.

Nora parked behind the pickup and got out. The .38 was in her hand.

The front door of the house opened.

The cleaner was in the wicker chair near the railing, a newspaper folded on the armrest beside him. He stood when she pulled up. No urgency. No alarm. He was wearing leather shoes, Nora noticed. Polished. Not a man who planned to run through the marsh.

"Ms. Banks." He didn't seem surprised. "He's been waiting for you."

"Where's Grady?"

"Alive. For now." The cleaner descended the steps, his hands visible at his sides. "The boss wants to talk. After that, depends on how the conversation goes."

"And if I shoot you right now?"

"Then the men inside kill your friend. And you." The cleaner stopped at the bottom of the steps. "But you're not going to do that. You came here for answers." He gestured toward the house. "End of the hall. Don't keep him waiting."

He didn't ask for the gun. She noticed that.

Nora walked past him and into the house. The screen door banged shut behind her. The hallway was cool after the heat outside, and her skin prickled with the sudden change.

The interior was dim, the curtains drawn, the lamps casting pools of yellow light that didn't reach the corners. Mounted animal heads lined the hallway: a ten-point buck, a wild boar with yellowed tusks, a tarpon arched on a mahogany plaque, its silver scales gone dull. Leather furniture in the rooms she passed, and the fragrance of lemon oil and the faint sourness of a house that had been closed up too long. Somewhere a grandfather clock was ticking, the sound heavy and measured. She walked down the hallway to a set of double doors, heavy oak with brass handles gone dark with decades of hands.

She could hear voices behind the doors. Low. Conversational.

She pushed them open.

The room beyond was a study. Larger than the office upstairs, with floor-to-ceiling windows that looked out over the river. The Cape Fear filled the glass, brown and enormous, the far bank a dark line of cypress trees. Bookshelves lined the remaining walls, and not for show. The shelves held maritime atlases, tide charts, bound ledgers with years stamped on their spines in gold. A brass ship's clock ticked above the mantel, its face yellowed, its mechanism audible in the silence of the room. A fire was burning in the hearth despite the warmth of the day. The heat pressing against her. Mahogany desk, massive. Decanter, glass, bare leather blotter.

No photographs. No diplomas. Nothing personal except the books and the fire.

Two men.

The second man sat behind the massive desk, a glass of whiskey in his hand. The old man from the night before. Pilot.

Her grandfather.

But it was what lay beyond the desk that stopped her breath.

A hospital bed had been set up near the windows—the kind with rails and wheels, out of place in the hunting lodge's study. Grady was in it, restrained at the wrists and ankles with medical cuffs attached to the bed rails. An IV line ran from his arm to a bag of clear fluid on a metal stand. His surgical wound was freshly bandaged with professional dressings, not Carl's field work. He was pale, sedated, but his chest rose and fell with steady rhythm.

They'd kept him alive. Not out of mercy—out of strategy.

Pilot had turned Grady into bait, and he'd invested in keeping that bait fresh.

Grady's eyes were half-open, unfocused. When Nora moved, his gaze tracked toward her slowly, drugged but aware. His lips moved, forming her name without sound.

She could see it now. In the daylight, knowing, she could see what she'd missed in the dark. The jaw. The set of the eyes. Pilot's head tilted slightly left when he was listening—the same tilt her father had. His hands on the whiskey glass were weathered, the knuckles swollen, the nails trimmed short and clean. Hands that had done physical work once and hadn't in a long time. He wore the same hunting jacket as last night, a canvas field coat that had been expensive thirty years ago, and he sat behind the desk like he'd grown out of it. Not leaning. Upright. Settled.

He watched her come into the room. He didn't stand. He didn't blink. He watched her standing perfectly still, measuring everything.

"Nora." He said her name slowly. "I hoped you'd come."

"Let him go."

"In time. First, we talk." He gestured to a chair across from the desk. "Please. Sit."

"I'll stand."

"As you wish." Pilot took a sip of his whiskey. "You've caused me more trouble in three days than anyone has in thirty years."

"I'm not here for your approval."

"No. You're here for him." He nodded toward Grady. "And for answers." He set down his glass, then adjusted it—a quarter inch to the right, aligning it precisely with the corner of the leather blotter. "I can give you both. The question is whether you're willing to listen."

"I already know everything I need to know. You're my grandfather. You built this organization. You killed my father."

"I didn't kill Russell. I had him killed. There's a difference."

Nora's left hand opened and closed at her side. On the mantel, the ship's clock ticked. Outside, a mullet jumped in the river, the splash carrying faintly through the glass.

"Not to me."

"No. I suppose not." Pilot stood and walked to the window. The river light caught his face. He looked like something the river had deposited. Weathered, mineral, old beyond counting. "You want to know how it started."

"I want to know why."

He turned back to her. "My mother cleaned houses in Wilmington. Six days a week, twelve hours a day. Scrubbed toilets for people who wouldn't let her use them. She died at sixty-one. Her heart quit." He said it flatly, without self-pity. "My father worked the docks when there was work. Fell off a loading crane drunk when I was fourteen. No pension. No insurance. I quit school that year."

"So you had it hard. That doesn't—"

"I'm not asking for sympathy. I'm telling you why." He walked back to the desk. His hand trailed along its surface, the polished mahogany, a slow possessive stroke. He poured himself another measure of whiskey from a cut-glass decanter. Didn't offer her one. "I didn't know your father existed until he was almost grown. His mother. I'd known her one summer, when I was nobody. She never told me about the boy. Married a fisherman named Banks, raised him as his own."

Nora's throat tightened. "When did you find out?"

"Russell was nineteen. Needed money for the Navy. His mother came to me. She'd heard I'd done well. Wanted to know if I'd help." Pilot picked up his whiskey but didn't drink. "I told her I'd pay for everything. Training, equipment. But he could never know where it came from."

"So you bought him."

"I helped him. I watched from a distance. Watched him become a man, come home, marry your mother." His voice went rougher underneath. The veneer of the transactional man thinning, something older and rawer showing through. "I was at your christening. Stood in the back of the church. Didn't talk to anyone."

He was at the window again, his back to her, and for a moment Nora could see the shape of his skull through the thin white hair. The vertebrae at his neck. He was old. He was her blood. She tightened her grip on the .38.

"You could have told him the truth."

"Told him what? That his real father was a criminal?" Pilot shook his head. "I gave him a better story. But when he was thirty, the fishing business failed. He owed money to the wrong people. I stepped in through intermediaries. Made the debt disappear." He set down the glass. "Your father was smart. Too smart. He figured out someone was pulling strings. Came to me wanting answers."

"And you told him."

"Everything. Who I was. What I'd built. He didn't take it well. But he agreed to work with me, the legitimate side. Managing properties. The marina. A way for us to be in each other's lives."

Outside, a cormorant landed on one of the dock pilings and spread its wings to dry, black and angular against the river. Nora watched it for a half second. The ordinary world, continuing.

"Until the *Miss Carolina*."

Something in Pilot's face cracked, then sealed over. A fissure opening and closing in stone. He put one hand flat on the desk and pressed down, steadying himself.

"That was never supposed to happen." His voice was quieter now. "Russell's only job was the harbor records. But he went back that night. Said he'd forgotten something on his boat. He was there when it went wrong."

Nora's grip tightened on the .38. *Russell Banks has been briefed and understands his role*. Pilot was rewriting history. The evidence said otherwise.

"When three people were killed."

A silence. A boat passed downstream, its engine a low drone that faded and was gone.

Then: "Yes."

The word sat between them. Pilot didn't look away. Nora didn't either.

The whole south wall was glass. Through it the Cape Fear moved in late afternoon light, the surface copper and black.

In the hospital bed near the window, Grady's breathing was slow and ragged through what might have been a broken nose. A drop of blood fell from his chin onto the white sheet. Nora could hear it hit the fabric.

Three people killed. The river that carried them still moving past this room.

"And you trapped him."

"I gave him a choice. Stay silent, and I would take care of him, take care of you. Or talk." He spread his hands. "He chose silence. For fifteen years. Not because I threatened him. Because he loved you. He didn't want you to know what he'd done."

"What you made him."

Pilot's jaw worked. He picked up the whiskey glass again, put it down without drinking.

"He was going to destroy everything, Nora. When he started talking, he wasn't threatening me. He was threatening every job, every business, everything that depends on this organization."

"So you had him killed."

Pilot walked to the fire. He stood with his back to her, one hand on the mantel, his knuckles white where he gripped the wood. The ship's clock above him read 3:47. She'd been in this room for less than twenty minutes. It felt like hours.

"I gave him a chance to stop. I sent people to reason with him. He said no. He said he was tired of lying. He said he wanted you to know the truth." Pilot's hand trembled against the mantel. He pulled it away. "I made a decision. The hardest decision of my life."

Nora stared at him. This old man. This monster.

"You want me to feel sorry for you."

"I want you to understand."

"I understand. You killed your son because he was going to tell the truth. That's all there is to understand."

Pilot looked at the fire. The coals had collapsed on one side, orange and black, the heat pushing against Nora's shins from across the room.

"You know the Varnamtown fleet," he said. His voice had changed. Not defensive. Not pleading. Quiet. "Fourteen boats, 1994. The docks were rotting. The county wouldn't pay for repairs. State said it wasn't their jurisdiction. Federal said apply for a grant and wait three years." He picked up the poker and pushed the collapsed log back into place. Sparks climbed the flue. "I paid for the docks. Cash. Took six weeks. Those fourteen boats kept fishing. Forty-some families kept eating."

Nora said nothing.

"The processing plant on River Road. Eighty-two jobs. The owner was going to sell to a developer from Charlotte—condos, a marina for sailboats nobody here can afford. I bought the note. Kept the plant open." He set the poker back in its stand. "The school roof in Bolivia. The volunteer fire station in Dosher. The clinic that treats watermen who can't afford insurance." He turned from the fire. "I watched Carteret die. Dare. Towns that used to fish, used to build boats. Now they sell T-shirts and rent kayaks to tourists."

The river moved past the windows. The same river that had carried the *Miss Carolina* down to the bar. The same water.

"Russell understood that," Pilot said. "At the end, before the rest of it—he understood. He didn't like it. But he saw what would happen if it all came apart." He looked at Nora, and the transactional mask was gone. He just looked old. “Every family on that waterfront. Every kid who works the docks in summer. Every old man running crab pots because it’s all he knows. You tear this down, they don’t get justice. They get a recession.”

The fire had burned low. The room was warmer than it had been.

She knew the Varnamtown fleet. She’d processed three of those boats’ registration renewals every year since she’d taken the harbormaster job. She knew which captains had sons who worked the docks in summer, which ones had daughters in community college on what was probably somebody’s dirty money filtered through a legitimate paycheck.

Her father had known too. And he’d stayed.

The .38 was heavy in her hand. She hadn’t lowered it. She noticed that her arm had stopped shaking.

“That’s not my problem.”

“It will be. When you’re the one who did it.” He said it without accusation. A man stating what he’d concluded a long time ago. “You’ll carry that the same way I carry Russell. Not because you were wrong. Because being right cost more than you thought it would.”

The fire popped. He picked up his glass, drank, set it down. The ice had melted. Nora could see the diluted amber, the ring of water the glass left on the mahogany. He looked at the ring for a moment, then moved the glass two inches to the left, centering it on the blotter. Straightened the pen beside it. Then he sat down.

“I have a proposition.” His voice was different now. Transactional. The roughness gone. “I’ll let Grady go.

Right now. No conditions. You walk out of here together and drive away." He picked up his glass. "I know where you've been this morning. I know what you gave them. Documents without testimony are paper—I've buried paper before. I'll disappear. I have resources, places where no one will find me. You'll never see me again."

"In exchange for what?"

"Your silence. You don't testify. You don't share what you know. You let the investigation die like all the others have."

"And the organization continues."

"Under new leadership. The transition would be smooth. The county wouldn't notice the difference." Pilot's eyes were calm. "Everyone wins. The jobs stay. The businesses survive. And you don't spend the rest of your life looking over your shoulder."

Outside the glass, the river had changed. The light had gone from copper to pewter—the tide turning, the current shifting direction, the water pulling back toward the sea. A branch that had been drifting upstream was sliding the other way.

The clock on the mantel read 3:52. Torres's hour was running out. Nora could feel the minutes in the room like something with weight.

Across the room, Grady shifted in the hospital bed. He shook his head. Almost imperceptibly.

Don't do it.

"Here's the problem with your offer," Nora said. "The circle's too wide. You can't buy my silence and Mary's and Grady's. There are too many people who know."

"You'd be surprised how little evidence matters when the right people are motivated to make it disappear."

"Maybe. But they also have me. And Mary. And whatever Grady can tell them about his father's murder." Nora shook her head. "You can't kill everyone who knows."

Something went out of Pilot's face. Not emotion. Structure. The architecture of control that had held his features in place since she'd entered the room shifted, and for a fraction of a second the face beneath was someone she didn't recognize. Then it was gone. He straightened in the chair. His hands went flat on the desk.

"Then we have a problem." Pilot glanced toward the door. His shoulders had changed, the stillness hardening, his whole body going glassy and taut. "I have six men in this house, all armed, all loyal. And your friend here is one bullet away from joining your father."

Nora raised the .38. The grip was slick with sweat. She tightened her hand around it.

Pilot didn't flinch.

"You know what I see when I look at you?"

Nora said nothing. She already knew.

"Then shoot me." He stepped closer. Close enough that the barrel of the .38 was inches from his chest. She could smell him now: whiskey, woodsmoke, the cedar of old closets, and underneath all of it the sour-sweet smell of an old man's skin. "Go ahead. You've earned it."

The room was very quiet. Fire crackling. The river moved outside the windows. From the hospital bed came the slow, labored pull of air through broken ribs. And underneath it all, the tick of the ship's clock, counting off the seconds she had left before Torres sent the team.

Nora looked at the man in front of her. Her grandfather. The man who had built an empire and destroyed a family and believed, with absolute certainty, that he was right. The jawline was her father's. The eyes were her own.

She felt the weight of the .38, the polymer grip warm in her palm, the trigger under her index finger. She could pull it. One pound of pressure. Less than it took to open a jar. The old man's chest was right there, rising and falling, and she could end thirty years of it with one contraction of her hand.

She moved her finger to the guard. Then she let the barrel drop, the muzzle tracking down his chest to the floor, her arm lowering until the gun hung at her side.

For a long moment they stood there. Grandfather and granddaughter, three feet apart, the gun pointing at the floorboards between them. The clock ticked. The light through the windows had shifted, the sun lower, the shadows of the cypress trees stretching across the river toward the dock. The fire had burned down to coals, the room darker than it had been when she'd entered, the corners receding into shadow.

The study door burst open.

Dutch Petersen filled the doorway, a Remington 700 bolt-action in both hands, the barrel up. His face was red and sheeted with sweat, his eyes darting between Pilot and Nora and the windows behind them. He was breathing hard, his chest heaving under a denim shirt dark with perspiration. Behind him, somewhere deeper in the house, Nora could hear boots on hardwood, men moving fast.

"Sir, we've got a problem. Vehicles coming up the road. Feds. Black SUVs, at least three."

Nora looked at Dutch. The heavyset frame, the graying hair, the face she'd known all her life. Looking for the stress points. Everything cracked somewhere.

"You," she said. "You were working for him. The whole time."

The fish house. Dutch on the loading dock, legs over the water, cigarette trembling between his fingers. Three tries to light it. Red-rimmed eyes. *I want to do one right thing before I die.* Her hand went slack on the .38 for half a second.

"I was following orders," he said. He wouldn't meet her eyes. "Same as everyone."

"You got my father killed."

Dutch's face twisted. "I did what had to be done—"

"We don't have time for this," Pilot said, his voice sharp. "Dutch, get the men to the boats. We're leaving."

"What about them?"

Pilot looked at Nora. At Grady. At the gun in Nora's hand.

"Kill them both."

Dutch's hands shook on the rifle—the same tremor from the fish house, the same tremor from fifteen years of guilt. He raised it anyway.

Nora fired first.

The .38 roared in the enclosed room, the sound enormous, a concussive pressure that hit her chest and ears simultaneously. The shot caught Dutch in the shoulder, spinning him around, the rifle clattering to the hardwood floor. He went down hard, screaming, and one of the bookshelves behind him sprayed splinters where the bullet exited and kept going. The nearest window cracked from the concussion—a single fracture line running from corner to corner, the river still visible through the break. Cordite and gun smoke filled the study, acrid, layering over the woodsmoke and whiskey. Nora's ears were ringing, a high whine that flattened every other sound to something distant and underwater.

Pilot was moving. Reaching into his desk drawer—

Nora turned and fired again. The bullet hit the desk, spraying splinters. Pilot ducked, and by the time he came up, Nora was across the room, the gun pressed to his temple. She could feel the thin skin over the bone, the faint pulse underneath. The old man's breathing was fast and shallow against her forearm. She noticed the veins in his hands, the liver spots, the white stubble he'd missed shaving along his jaw.

"Don't move."

Pilot froze. His hand was still in the drawer, inches from a small revolver.

"Take your hand out. Slowly."

He did. The hand came out empty, trembling. He placed it flat on the desk beside the other one, palms down, fingers spread.

Doors slamming outside. Voices shouting. Through the ringing in her ears, Nora could hear boots on gravel, the bark of commands, the heavy diesel idle of armored vehicles.

"You're making a mistake. The organization will survive—"

"Get on the floor. Hands behind your head."

He didn't move.

"Now."

Pilot looked at her. Then, slowly, he lowered himself to his knees. His hands went behind his head. The hunting jacket rode up, showing the white shirt beneath, untucked, and for the first time he looked like what he was. An old man on his knees on a hardwood floor.

"Everything your father died to protect," he said. "You're throwing it away."

"My father didn't die to protect you. He died because you killed him." Nora stepped back, keeping the gun trained on him.

The doors flew open.

Torres was first through, weapon drawn, followed by a team of agents in tactical gear. She stopped in the doorway for a half second, reading the room—Pilot on his knees, Dutch on the floor bleeding, Nora with the .38 pointed at the floorboards.

"You're late," Nora said.

"You're alive." Torres's eyes moved to Pilot, to Dutch, back to Nora. "We'll discuss your definition of one hour later."

The team swept the room in seconds, two agents on Dutch where he lay bleeding on the floor, two more training their weapons on Pilot, one cutting toward the windows to clear the corners. The room that had held a private reckoning was suddenly full of boots and Kevlar and shouted call signs.

"Clear!" someone shouted from the far side of the room. Dutch was moaning on the floor, pressing his good hand against the wound in his shoulder, blood pooling on the hardwood beneath him.

"Nora." Torres lowered her gun. "You okay?"

"I'm fine. He needs a hospital." She nodded toward Grady.

"Medevac's landing in five minutes." Torres looked to two agents. "Get him outside."

They released Grady's restraints and lifted him from the hospital bed, carrying him toward the door. The medical cuffs had left marks on his wrists and ankles, the skin red and irritated. He looked back at Nora as they carried him through the study, his drugged eyes finding her across the room. His hand reached out, found hers for a moment, squeezed. His grip was weak. His fingers were cold. But they held on for as long as they could before the distance pulled them apart.

"Thank you," he managed. "For coming back."

"I wasn't going to leave you."

They carried him out. She heard their boots on the porch, then on the gravel, then the sound of an ambulance door opening.

Torres walked to where Pilot was kneeling and pulled out handcuffs.

"You have the right to remain silent. Anything you say can and will be used against you in a court of law. You have the right to an attorney. If you cannot afford an attorney, one will be provided for you."

Pilot said nothing. Two agents hauled him to his feet and led him toward the door. He passed within a foot of

Nora. He didn't look at her. She could hear his breathing, the shuffle of his shoes on the hardwood, and then he was through the study doors and gone and the room smelled of gun smoke and old whiskey and the fire that had burned itself out in the grate.

The room was quiet for the first time since she'd entered it. The clock on the mantel had stopped—she didn't know when. The river was still there through the cracked window, unchanged—the same current that had been running past the glass when Pilot admitted to murder, when he made his offer, when Dutch came through the door.

Through the window, Nora could see more vehicles arriving: ambulances, more FBI, a forensics team in blue windbreakers unloading equipment cases from a van. Yellow tape was already going up around the porch columns. And there, being led to an SUV in handcuffs, the cleaner. His forgettable face finally fixed in the harsh light of consequences.

Torres appeared beside her.

"You did a good thing here," she said. "A hard thing."

Nora walked out of the study, down the hallway past the mounted tarpon and the yellowed tusks and the ten-point buck that watched her with glass eyes, and through the front door into the afternoon sun. The light was blinding after the dim study, and she stood blinking on the porch while her eyes adjusted. Agents moved around her, carrying evidence bags and laptop cases, escorting prisoners. The ambulance with Grady inside pulled down the gravel drive, its lights on, no siren. The live oaks swallowed it up. Then it was gone.

She stood on the porch alone. The wicker chair where the cleaner had been sitting was empty, the newspaper still folded on the armrest. The salt air was warm. An osprey circled above the dock, riding a thermal, and the river moved slowly past the pilings, as it always had.

CHAPTER 10

The Tide

Six weeks later, the sun came up over the water.

The morning was cool for late November, the air carrying the first real edge of winter, a sharpness that cut through the usual salt and mud. The boats rocked gently in their slips, their rigging chiming in the breeze, and across the harbor, the Oak Island lighthouse stood silhouetted against a sky turning from gray to pink to gold. The light was different now than it had been in August, lower and thinner, coming at an angle that stretched the shadows of the pilings halfway across the basin. The water had changed color too, gone from the warm brown-green of summer to something colder, almost pewter in the early light, the current visible in long smooth lines running seaward.

She'd been coming here every morning since she'd returned to work. Not because she had to, her shift didn't start until eight and it was barely past six, but because she needed it. The quiet. The water.

The dock was wet with overnight dew, the wood dark, the metal cleats cold to the touch. Frost had settled on the windshields of the boats nearest the breakwater, a thin white film that would burn off by eight. November on the coast didn't bring the hard freezes of the Piedmont, but it brought this: a sharpness in the predawn air, a skim of ice on the freshwater puddles in the parking lot, the breath visible for the first time since March. The harbor felt different in this season. Quieter. Smaller. The summer boats were gone, hauled out or covered, and what remained was the working fleet, a dozen trawlers and crabbers and gill-netters that would be here in every month of the year.

A brown pelican glided past, low over the surface, its reflection rippling beneath it. In the marsh beyond the breakwater, an egret called, that harsh prehistoric sound that had been the soundtrack of her childhood. The smell of pluff mud and diesel fuel mixed together in a combination that should have been unpleasant but instead felt like home.

Down the dock, Jimmy Sellers was loading ice into the hold of his trawler, the crushed ice rattling into the fiberglass hull like gravel. His son was on the foredeck coiling line, fifteen years old, still half-asleep, his movements automatic. The boy had his father's shoulders and his mother's face, and he worked without being told what to do next. At the fuel dock, the pump was already running, the diesel smell sharpening the cold air, and Nora could hear the meter clicking from where she stood. Two slips down, a crabber she didn't recognize was checking his pots, stacking the wire traps on the stern and replacing the bait cups with fresh mullet. He'd arrived last week from Calabash, looking for a seasonal slip. She'd given him one. Beyond the fuel dock, someone was running an outboard in neutral, the two-stroke engine sputtering and catching and settling into a steady idle that carried across the water.

A shrimp boat was heading out past the breakwater, its nets raised, its outriggers spread like wings against the brightening sky, its engine rumbling across the harbor. The *Mary Louise*, captained by Danny Reeves, Carl's nephew. Danny raised a hand from the wheelhouse. Nora raised hers back.

She heard footsteps on the dock behind her and didn't turn around.

"You're here early."

Grady's voice. He walked up beside her, moving carefully. Six weeks had healed the surface damage, the split lip closed, the bruising around his eye faded to a faint yellow-green that was visible only in certain light. But the ribs were slower. He lowered himself against the piling next to her in stages, one hand braced on the wood, his weight settling carefully, his breath catching once before he got settled. He had a paper cup of coffee from the coffee shop on Howe Street, and he held it in both hands against the cold. His jacket was too light for the weather. He'd come down from D.C. with a suitcase full of summer clothes and hadn't replaced them yet, or hadn't thought to. He looked thinner than he had six weeks ago, the bones of his face more prominent, but the color was back in his skin and his eyes were clear.

"Couldn't sleep," she said.

"Me neither." He stood beside her, close enough that their shoulders almost touched. His coffee steamed in the cold air.

They watched the sun rise. The light caught the water and turned it gold, then orange, then a pale shimmering white. Neither of them spoke.

The harbormaster's office was the same as it had always been, cramped, cluttered, smelling faintly of coffee and marine varnish. The same filing cabinets, the same charts above the desk, the same radio crackling with weather reports and the occasional Coast Guard advisory.

Nora hung her jacket on the hook behind the door, started the coffee maker, the old Mr. Coffee that had been in this office since before she was hired, and sat at her desk. The morning's paperwork was waiting in the wire tray where she'd left it Friday. Slip renewals, fuel deliveries, inspection schedules. She worked through the stack one form at a time, signing where she needed to sign, noting discrepancies, filing the completed pages in the cabinet behind her. Through the office window she could see the dock, the boats, the water, and beyond it the flat gray line of Bald Head Island against the sky. A cormorant sat on the nearest piling, its wings spread to dry in the thin November sun.

Her phone buzzed. A text from Mary.

Landed in Raleigh. Interview went well. Will call tonight.

Mary had been offered a position with the state attorney general's office, their public corruption unit. She'd spent three weeks in Wilmington after the arrests, working with Torres and the federal prosecutors to build the case, living out of a hotel room near the courthouse and eating takeout at the conference table where the evidence files covered every surface. She'd called Nora twice a week, sometimes more. The calls were short, professional, but once, at the end of one of them, Mary had said *I'm glad you came to my door that night* and hung up before Nora could respond. Now she was in Raleigh, interviewing. Figuring out what came next. They all were.

On the radio behind her, the local news cycled through its noon update. Bennett's name came up, his attorney filing another motion, another delay. Cranston's plea deal was mentioned in passing, old news by now. Nora turned the volume down. She'd hear about it when it mattered.

Torres had called three times since the arrests. The first call, two days after, had been brief—they had Pilot in federal custody, Cranston was cooperating in exchange for a sentencing recommendation, Bennett had been picked up at his sister's house in Lumberton. The second call was a week later, longer, walking Nora through what the financial records showed. The third had been last week.

"Dutch Petersen," Torres had said, and Nora had felt her hand tighten on the phone. "He's going to make it. Surgery went well. He was coherent enough to give a statement from the hospital bed."

"What kind of statement?"

"The useful kind." A pause. "He's been feeding Cranston information for eleven years. Small things, mostly. Rumors about who was asking questions. Names of people who came around the marina. He says he didn't know about the *Miss Carolina* until after it happened."

"Do you believe him?"

Torres had taken a moment. "I believe he believes it. Whether it's true is something the prosecutors are going to work out."

Nora had thought about that for a long time afterward. Dutch on the fish house dock, three tries to light his cigarette, red-rimmed eyes. I want to do one right thing before I die. Maybe he had. In the end, under oath, from a hospital bed with a bullet wound in his shoulder—maybe that was the one right thing.

Or maybe he was just afraid.

She didn't know. She was learning to be all right with not knowing.

At noon, she walked down to the waterfront park for lunch.

The park ran along the river for two blocks south of the marina, a strip of grass and live oaks and iron benches that faced the water. In summer, the benches were full of tourists eating ice cream from the shop on Moore Street. Now, in late November, the park was almost empty. The live oaks had held their leaves, dark green and leathery even now, but the sweetgums along the path had gone bare, their branches black and intricate against the sky. Fallen leaves collected in the gutters and along the base of the seawall, wet and brown, smelling of tannin. The light was flat and silver. A pair of laughing gulls worked the shoreline, picking through the wrack. Across the channel, the old fish house on the point was closed for the season, its dock empty, its tin roof catching the weak sun.

Nora found an empty bench that faced the channel and sat down, unwrapping the sandwich she'd brought from home. Ham and cheese on wheat, the same lunch she'd been eating since high school. The bread was from the bakery on Lord Street. The cheese was sharp cheddar, the kind her father used to buy in blocks from the IGA and slice with a pocket knife.

A woman approached, hesitant. She was young, early twenties, dark-haired. She held her purse strap in both hands, her knuckles tight, but her chin was up and her eyes were steady.

"Excuse me. Are you Nora Banks?"

"I am."

"My name is Sarah Rodriguez. My grandmother was Elena Rodriguez. She was on the *Miss Carolina* when it went down."

Nora set down her sandwich.

"Please," she said. "Sit down."

Sarah sat lightly, on the edge of the bench. "I've been wanting to talk to you. Ever since the news came out about what really happened." She twisted the strap of her purse between her fingers. "My family is planning a memorial. For the people who died. My grandmother, and Iris Galloway, and—" She hesitated. "And Thomas Pruitt. We know he was part of it, but he still died. He still left a family behind."

"Thomas Pruitt."

"We talked to his son, to Grady. He agreed his father should be included. Not celebrated, but remembered. Acknowledged."

Nora's hand went still on the bench beside her. Grady had never mentioned this. That he'd been asked, that he'd said yes. That he'd chosen to let his father's name stand alongside the women his father had helped kill.

Sarah squared her shoulders. "We're doing the memorial next month, on the anniversary. At the Methodist church in Southport, with a reception after. The whole town is invited. We want it to be a beginning. A way to move forward without forgetting."

"That sounds right."

"We'd like you to speak. If you're willing. To tell the truth about what happened. Not the official version, but the real story."

"I'd be honored," she said.

Sarah's face broke into a smile, sudden and wide, and for a moment she looked like a different person entirely.

"Thank you." She pulled a card from her pocket. "My number's on there. Call me and we'll work out the details."

Sarah walked away down the paved path, her steps lighter than they'd been when she arrived. Nora watched her go, watched her pass the laughing gulls and the bare sweetgums and turn the corner toward Howe Street.

She picked up her sandwich and put it down again. Grady had said yes. He'd agreed to let his father's name stand next to the names of the women his father helped kill. She didn't know when he'd made that decision, or what it had cost him, or whether he'd tell her about it if she asked. She knew him well enough now to know he might not.

A container ship was moving up the channel toward Wilmington, enormous and slow, its hull rust-streaked, its wake rolling toward the seawall in long gentle swells that slapped against the stone and settled. She watched it pass. She finished her sandwich. She sat for a while longer, the bench cold under her legs, the wind off the river pressing against her face, and listened to the gulls arguing over something in the shallows. A jogger passed behind her on the path. The clock on her phone said one-fifteen. She'd been sitting here for over an hour.

She gathered her lunch bag and walked back to the office.

* * *

Sunday came.

Nora drove to her mother's house with Grady in the passenger seat and a bottle of wine. The road from the marina to her mother's neighborhood wound through the older part of Southport, past the Baptist church and the bait shop with its hand-painted sign and the cemetery where six generations of fishing families were buried under live oaks so old their roots had lifted the oldest headstones off-true. Her mother's house was a yellow clapboard bungalow on a street of similar houses, each with a screened porch and a square of yard and hydrangeas along the front that had gone bare weeks ago, just gray sticks in mulch. A wreath of dried magnolia leaves hung on the front door. The porch light was on, though it was still afternoon. Nora's father had installed that light, and her mother turned it on when she was expecting company, which meant always on Sundays.

"Relax," Grady said. "It's dinner."

"It's dinner with my mother, who knows everything now and has opinions about everything."

"I can handle opinions."

"You say that now."

Her mother met them at the door with a hug for Nora and a handshake for Grady that quickly turned into a hug as well. She was wearing the apron she'd worn every Sunday for twenty years, cotton with a faded floral print, and she smelled of bread flour and Jergens hand lotion. She was smaller than Nora remembered, or Nora noticed it more now. The six weeks since the truth had come out had put new lines around her mouth, deepened the ones around her eyes. Her hair was grayer at the temples. But her grip was strong when she took Grady's hand, and her voice was steady when she said *come in, come in, everything's almost ready*. The house smelled like pot roast and fresh bread, and the table was set with the good china, the white plates with the blue rim that came out for holidays and company. A bowl of rolls sat under a cloth napkin. The silver was polished. Three place settings, three cloth napkins folded into triangles, three water glasses already filled.

They sat down and her mother said grace, the same grace she'd said every Sunday since Nora was a child, and then there was the passing of dishes and the filling of plates and the quiet that falls over a table when people are hungry and the food is good. The pot roast was tender, falling apart on the fork, and the bread was still warm from the oven.

Her mother turned to Grady. "How are the ribs?"

"Getting there. Doctor says another month before I can do anything useful."

"And what will you do? When you're useful again?"

Grady set down his fork. "There's a weekly paper in Southport that needs an editor. I talked to the owner last Tuesday."

Nora looked at him. He hadn't told her this.

He'd been in Southport for six weeks, staying in a rented room above the hardware store on Moore Street, and she'd assumed he was recovering. Waiting to go back to D.C. Waiting for something.

He hadn't said anything about staying.

She looked at him across the table. His ribs were slow to heal and he moved carefully and he'd been reading the State Port Pilot every morning at the coffee shop on Howe Street, which she'd noticed and hadn't said anything about. She'd thought he was killing time.

"A newspaper man," her mother said. She studied him across the table, looking for what was behind what was visible. "Russell read the paper every morning. Cover to cover. Even the classifieds."

"Yes ma'am."

Her mother held his eyes for a moment. Then she passed him the rolls.

After the plates were cleared, Nora sat at the table while Grady stood at the kitchen sink with his sleeves rolled to the elbow. She could see the welts on his wrists where the dock line had been, still pink, still raised against the skin. He washed each dish slowly, carefully, turning the plates under the water, stacking them in the rack with a deliberateness that had more to do with sore ribs than technique. Her mother stood beside him with a dish towel, drying each plate as he set it down. Steam rose from the sink. The kitchen window was dark, and the overhead light made the room feel close and warm. Nora could hear the clink of dishes and the running water and the occasional murmur of her mother saying *that one goes in the cabinet above the stove* or *careful, the handle's loose on that pot*.

Her mother dried her hands on the dish towel and came back to the table. She took Nora's arm.

"Come with me," she said. "There's something I need to give you. I should have done it weeks ago."

They walked down the hallway together, past the school photos in their frames, past the thermostat her father had installed crooked and her mother had never fixed, past the bathroom door that still stuck if you didn't lift the handle. The living room was at the back of the house, small, with a braided rug and a reading chair and bookshelves her father had built from pine boards and L-brackets. A lamp with a green shade sat on the end table, casting the room in soft light. Her mother went to the third shelf from the top, moved aside a framed photograph of Nora's fifth-grade class, and reached behind the row of paperbacks to where a shoebox was wedged against the wall.

She pulled it out. A Nike box, old, the cardboard soft at the corners and darkened with attic dust, the lid held on with a single rubber band that had gone brittle and cracked when she pulled it off. The box was heavier than it looked.

"After you told me the truth about your father, I started going through his things. The boxes in the attic, the old files in the garage." Her mother's hands were trembling slightly. She held the box in front of her, and Nora could see the effort in her face, the tightness around her eyes. Her lips were pressed into a line that was holding something back. "I found these. Hidden behind the Christmas decorations."

She handed the box to Nora. Their hands touched on the cardboard. Her mother's fingers were cold.

Nora lifted the lid. Inside were envelopes, dozens of them, each one addressed to her in her father's careful handwriting. The paper was yellowed with age, the ink faded to a pale blue, but the words were still legible.

To my daughter Nora, on her first birthday.

To Nora, age 5.

To Nora, when she's old enough to understand.

"He wrote them over the years," her mother said. "Starting when you were born, continuing until right before he died. He never sent them. I don't think he ever intended to. But he wrote them." Her voice caught. "I didn't read them. They're not for me. But I thought you should have them."

Nora stared at her father's handwriting. Decades of it. A whole life of things he couldn't say out loud, stacked in envelopes behind the Christmas decorations.

"Thank you," she said.

Her mother's hand found her shoulder. Squeezed once. Then let go.

"Now. Who wants dessert?"

After dinner, Nora sat on the back porch with the shoebox in her lap.

Grady had offered to stay, but she'd asked for time alone.

The night was cool, the stars bright overhead. Orion, visible above the tree line, low in the east, tilted on his side like he always was in November. A dog barked somewhere down the street. A car passed, its headlights sweeping across the fence. The porch boards were cold through her jeans. She pulled her jacket tighter and set the box on her knees.

There were thirty-one envelopes. She'd counted them when her mother went to cut the pie. Thirty-one, spanning from her first birthday to two weeks before her father died. Some were thick, several pages folded inside. Some were thin, a single sheet. All of them sealed. The envelopes at the bottom of the box were more yellowed than the ones on top, the ink darker, the handwriting steadier. She held the earliest one up to the porch light and could see the shadow of the paper inside, covered on both sides.

She set the earliest one down.

She reached into the middle of the stack instead and pulled one at random. The envelope was addressed in her father's handwriting, the letters more controlled than the ones at the top of the pile, the ink a deeper blue. To Nora, age 14.

She opened it.

My dear Nora,

You argued with me this morning about the boat. You said I was being overprotective. You said every other girl your age was allowed to take a skiff out past the breakwater alone, which I happen to know is not true, but I also know that's not really the point.

The point is that you were right. You know those waters better than most adults I've worked with. You read the current the way some people read faces. I watched you dock the Whaler last week without touching the pilings once, which is more than I can say for myself at twice your age.

I said no anyway. You slammed your bedroom door. Your mother told me I was being unreasonable.

Here is what I couldn't tell you: I said no because I'm afraid. Not of the water. Of losing you. There are things I've done that I can't undo, and I live with the possibility, every day, that they will find their way back to you. That something I chose will cost you something you didn't.

I don't know how to explain this without explaining everything. And I can't explain everything. Not yet. Maybe not ever.

What I can tell you is that the door-slamming and the arguing and the way you look at me sometimes like you're measuring whether I'm worth the trouble—I hope you keep doing all of it. I hope you never stop pushing. The world will try to make you smaller. Don't let it.

I'll probably say yes about the skiff next week. Don't tell your mother I said that.

Your father, Russell

Nora sat with the letter in her lap for a long time. The dog down the street had stopped barking. The stars had shifted. She could feel the cold of the porch boards through her jeans but she didn't move.

There are things I've done that I can't undo.

He'd known. All those years, he'd known it was coming for her eventually. And he'd written it down because he couldn't say it, and hidden it because he couldn't send it, and stayed silent because he thought silence would protect her.

She folded the letter carefully along its original creases and put it back in the envelope.

She opened the last letter, the most recent, dated two weeks before her father died. His handwriting was shaky, the letters uneven, the pen pressing harder in places where his hand must have been trembling. But she could read them.

My dear Nora,

I'm running out of time. The doctors say weeks.

I'm going to try to tell you in person. I owe you that. But if I can't, if I don't have the courage, I hope you'll find these someday.

I love you more than I've ever loved anything. You are the best thing I ever did. And I'm sorry for leaving you with this.

Your father, Russell

Nora closed the letter. She put it back in the envelope, put the envelope back in the box, and closed the lid. The rubber band was broken, so she held the lid shut with her palm.

She sat in the dark, holding the box on her lap. The stars moved. The dog stopped barking. A freight train sounded its horn somewhere north of town, two longs and a short, and the sound carried across the flat coastal plain and faded into the marsh.

Then she went inside.

* * *

The next morning, Nora was back at the marina before dawn.

The water was calm, the sky clear. She stood on the dock with her coffee and watched the light change, darkness to gray, gray to gold. The fishermen were already moving, checking nets, warming engines. The harbor smelled of diesel and salt and the cold edge of coming winter. December was three days away. The tourists were gone. The charter boats sat idle in their slips, their covers lashed down, waiting for spring. What remained were the boats that would be here in January, in February, in the worst of it. The crabbers and trawlers and gill-netters crewed by people who fished these waters in every season because it was what they did.

Jimmy Sellers passed her on the dock, a thermos under one arm, his son trailing behind him still half-asleep.

"Morning, Nora."

"Morning, Jimmy. Looks calm out there."

"Radio says small craft advisory by afternoon. We'll be back by noon." He kept walking. His son waved without looking up.

Down at the fuel dock, the crabber from Calabash was topping off his tanks. He raised a hand. Nora raised one back. She'd need to process his slip renewal before the end of the week. Beyond the breakwater, a pelican dove and came up empty and dove again, patient, tireless, working the same water it had worked yesterday and would work tomorrow.

At her mother's dinner table the night before, between the pot roast and the dessert, her mother had asked the question Nora had been waiting for. *Is there any news about your grandfather?* Nora had told her what Torres had said in their last call: federal custody, awaiting trial, no bail. Her mother had nodded once and passed the pie.

Nora walked toward the harbormaster's office, the dock boards solid under her boots, the cleats and coiled lines and fenders in their places. She passed the slip where the *Carolina Dawn* sat, its booking calendar full through February, and the empty slip where the *Sea Breeze* would return in the spring. A pair of mallards paddled between the pilings, unhurried, leaving V-shaped wakes in the still water. She reached the office door and fit the key in the lock. The door swung open and she could smell the coffee and marine varnish and hear the radio crackling with the morning forecast.

Behind her, the tide was turning, the water rising against the pilings, steady and patient, as it always had. She thought about what the tide took—her father, the old certainties, the version of this place she'd grown up believing in. She thought about what it left. The dock under her boots. The key in her hand. The work ahead.

Torres had called last week with an update. Bennett was cooperating. Cranston had taken his plea. The organization's financial records were being traced through three states. Most of the accounts had been frozen.

Most.

There was one anomaly Torres had mentioned in passing, a detail she'd found in Mary's files. A shell company account that had been emptied two days before the arrests. The transfers went through Grand Cayman, then disappeared into a network Torres's team was still unraveling. The signature on the authorization wasn't Pilot's or Cranston's. No one they'd identified.

"Probably nothing," Torres had said. "Pilot's people covering their tracks."

Probably.

Nora unlocked the office door and went inside.

THE END

Author's Note

The waters of the Cape Fear feel different—darker, more restless, carrying something the Georgia coast doesn't quite hold. Where Saint Simons Island, the setting of my first novel, offers sanctuary, the Carolina coast offers reckoning.

Southport is a real place, and readers familiar with Brunswick County will recognize many of the landmarks, waterways, and rhythms of tidal life depicted in these pages. The marina, the marshes, the working docks—these are drawn from observation and affection. But this is a work of fiction, and I have taken liberties with geography, institutions, and history where the story required it.

What the Tide Took began as a question: What happens when the secrets a family keeps to survive become the things that destroy them? The answer led me to Nora Banks and the waters she's spent her whole life navigating—the ones on the charts, and the ones that don't appear on any map.

I hope you felt the salt air and the weight of the current. And I hope, like Nora, you found something worth surfacing for.

With gratitude,
Blake Gunnels

Other Coastal Stories

While the Nora Banks series explores the modern coast of North Carolina, Blake Gunnels also writes historical fiction set along the Southern Georgia coast.

WHAT THE TIDE KEPT – Free Short Story

Meet Nora Banks at fifteen—before the marina, before the job, before she knew what silence cost. A prequel set on the Cape Fear River.

THE CHRISTMAS KEEPER – Free short story set on Saint Simons Island, Georgia. On Christmas Eve 1876, lighthouse keeper Jonas Miller finds a stranger face-down in the marsh—feverish, hollow, wearing a cavalry coat worn to nothing. A man who has been running a long time. What the Miller family does next is the whole story.

GET ONE OR BOTH FREE STORIES HERE:

BY THE LIGHT OF THE BLUFF – Winner of the 2025 International Firebird Book Award for Southern Fiction

A widow arrives on the Georgia coast in 1873 with her two children and a violent past. A lighthouse is rising on the eastern bluff. And the man building it is about to become the one thing she didn't plan for.

Available now at www.blakegunnels.com

About the Author

Blake Gunnels is a designer, coastal explorer, and writer whose work is shaped by a lifetime of returning to the shores of Saint Simons Island, Georgia. His memories of the island span decades of family traditions—early morning kayak trips with his son along quiet marsh creeks, fishing off the village pier, biking beneath ancient oaks, exploring Fort Frederica with his daughter, sharing meals at beloved local restaurants, wandering the village shops, and searching for the Tree Spirits hidden in the island's live oaks. These moments became the fabric of seasons spent together, all under one roof, filled with stories, laughter, and the enduring rituals of coastal life.

It is from this love of place that the BluffLight series was born—stories rooted in lighthouse history, maritime life, and the quiet grace found along the Georgia coast. His debut novel, *By the Light of the Bluff*, won the 2025 International Firebird Book Award for Southern Fiction.

By profession, Blake is a practicing landscape architect specializing in the renovation of apartment and condominium communities, resorts, and commercial properties. His design work—restoring worn places and helping them thrive again—mirrors the themes of renewal and redemption that run through his fiction.

What the Tide Took marks a departure from the historical fiction of his Saint Simons novel into the darker waters of contemporary coastal thriller.

When he isn't writing or designing, Blake can be found hiking pine-lined trails, boating through tidal estuaries, traveling to new landscapes, or chasing waterfalls with his long-time girlfriend, Tammy. Together, they seek out hidden corners of nature, search for the perfect margarita, and savor the quiet beauty of the world—whether spotting a winter manatee grazing in the shallows or standing together in the hush of a cold December sunrise.

A Note to the Reader

Thank you for diving into the dark waters of *What the Tide Took*. I hope Nora's journey through secrets, reckoning, and hard-won truth stayed with you past the final page.

Stories like this one find their readers through word of mouth. If you have a moment, please consider leaving a short review—it makes a real difference.

Your words help readers find stories worth reading. Thank you for being part of this one.

Connect With The Author

Website: blakegunnels.com
Email: blake@blufflight.com
Facebook: facebook.com/BlakeGunnelsAuthor

Until we meet again—*let your course be true.*

www.ingramcontent.com/pod-product-compliance
Lightning Source LLC
LaVergne TN
LVHW100518110826
845146LV00002B/693

* 9 7 9 8 9 9 8 9 5 7 8 6 4 *